poison roses

BOYS OF BELLEROSE
BOOK 1

TATE JAMES

JAYMIN EVE

Tate James

Jaymin Eve

For anyone who has loved and lost...

...then got the opportunity to fuck his new best friend and make his life hell.

Whoops, is that not how it goes?

follow us

For book discussions, giveaways, and general shit talking from Tate or Jaymin, please check out their reader groups on Facebook:

Tate James – The Fox Hole

Jaymin Eve – The Nerd Herd

For as long as I could remember, I was the girl who lived on top of the hill, in the bright blue house with the white fence and a shared pool in the backyard. That was where I first met Jace... and Angelo.

When I was four years old, Jace's family moved into the house next door, and our parents were instant friends. Jace had a mop of blond hair and the sweetest smile I'd ever seen. Up until the moment he tried to drown me.

This is really where my story started. The part I like to think of as *The Before*.

When my life was sunshine and laughter, rather than storms and heartbreak.

When I loved the boy next door and he loved me.

When *his* best friend was *my* fiercest protector, even in our darkest days.

Before I made the impossible decision that popped our perfect bubble of happiness and shattered our dreams of a future *together*. My doomed choice spiraled us all down different roads.

That's how I ended up on this one. This crappy road.

The After.

BILLIE

Tears tracked down my cheeks as I clutched the straps of my torn duffel bag. Panic and despair twisted my insides up in such a tight knot I could hardly breathe. How had it come to this?

"Please," I begged, "just one more week and I swear I'll have the money. I just need a couple more shifts and—"

The weathered old woman shook her head, her mind fully made up. "Nah, I've heard all that shit before, girl. You had your warning; you didn't pay. Now you gotta go. I've got other pathetic waifs who *can* pay already waiting for this room."

She was done listening to me beg and plead as she

shoved me out into the street and slammed the front door behind me.

Fuck.

Now what?

I had nowhere to go. Fucking *nowhere*. Mrs. Glass had been right to kick me out on my ass because I was full of shit. Even if she'd let me stay, I had no work lined up to earn that rent money. Now I also had nowhere to sleep tonight. The one small mercy was that she'd kicked me out in daylight, so I had a few hours to find somewhere safe to, hopefully, avoid being raped or murdered when night fell.

"Hey." A throaty female voice jarred me out of my melancholy thoughts. "You okay?"

I glanced over to see the speaker. It was a twenty-something chick who I vaguely recognized from Mrs. Glass's building—she lived on the floor above me. Or... had. I no longer lived there.

Sniffing back tears, I nodded. "Yeah. I will be." I always was. This wouldn't be my first night sleeping in an alleyway or, probably, my last.

The woman arched a brow in disbelief. Cigarette perched between her long, brown fingers, she took a drag before responding. "Old bitch kicked you out, huh?"

I nodded, not trusting my voice. The panic and fear of the unknown was sitting in my throat like a golf ball.

"You got work?" the woman pushed, her dark eyes running over me from head to toe in an appraising sort of way.

I frowned. "No. But I'll figure something out, thanks." My words were clipped and tight, but I wasn't desperate enough to become a hooker. Not yet, anyway. Another week might see me change my stance on that. Technically, I had money. I had plenty of money. I just refused to use it. There was no way my parents—working class, middle income parents—could have left me millions in my inheritance without foul play involved. I was *sure* if I ever accessed that account, whoever killed them would come for me.

She rolled her eyes. "Relax, petal. I'm not soliciting you, but I might be able to help out. You got any waitressing experience?"

Oh. "Y-yes," I quickly replied, nodding. "Sorry, I thought... Yes, I've waitressed loads. Do you know someone hiring?"

Her smile was understanding as she tossed her long braids back over her shoulder. "Hiring? No. But you might be able to pick up some cash shifts while half the floor team are off with the flu." She finished her cigarette and dropped it to the dirty pavement, grinding the toe of her shoe on it.

Now that I paid more attention, I realized she was dressed in a short black skirt, stockings, and a white blouse. The huge, purple faux-fur coat she wore on top was what had given me the wrong impression.

"My shift starts in twenty minutes, though," she continued, rising to her feet, "so you better think quick. And get changed. You got something more restaurant-friendly in that big old bag?"

I nodded again, feeling like a bobblehead. "Yes, absolutely."

"Great!" My new friend grinned, then stuck her hand out for me to shake. "I'm Liz, by the way."

Offering a smile, I took her hand. "Billie." Liz indicated for me to walk with her, and I hoisted my heavy bag over my shoulder. "Uh, I shouldn't really look a gift horse in the mouth, but why are you helping me, Liz?"

She shot me a sidelong look. "Did you just call me a horse?" My eyes widened in horror, but she quickly laughed. "I'm teasing, Billie; chill. And technically, I'm not helping you, *you're* helping *me*. We were so fucking short-staffed last night it was a joke. Then *we* got blamed for the bad reviews from customers because the service sucked."

I winced, able to sympathize. Customers were brutal and didn't care why there weren't enough servers on shift, only that their drinks took too long. "I get it," I murmured. "Well, I'm grateful, anyway."

Liz's smile was warm, and she offered a one-shouldered shrug. "Don't thank me yet; I still need to convince my boss. But given the blasting I heard him get from the owner over the phone last night? Shouldn't be a hard sell. Come on, it's this way."

She had a quick pace, and I hurried to keep up with her long legs as she led the way through the streets of Siena. As we hurried, she chatted a little about how the other servers had caught a stomach flu from a party they'd all been at. Liz didn't get it, because she'd been stuck on the closing shift.

"That was lucky," I commented, and she gave a throaty laugh.

"Was it? Now I have to pick up the slack for them. Then again, it worked out lucky for you." She led me down an alleyway and past some dumpsters to a heavy door with chipped paint. "Here we are. Just... steer clear of the chefs. They're assholes."

I laughed. "Isn't that a job requirement?"

She snickered, then pulled open the door. It led us directly into the back of the kitchen where all the ice machines, trash cans, and spare stock were kept, and

Liz directed me to a tiny staff restroom where I could get changed.

"I'll go let Gary know you're here to save our asses tonight," she told me as I squeezed inside. "Then I'll give you the tour."

I'd been so caught up in my crappy day, in the emotional rollercoaster of being evicted and then saved by Liz's job offer, I hadn't even asked what sort of restaurant she worked in. But as I changed into my black skirt and white blouse, the mouthwatering smells of rich tomato and melted cheese rolled under my nose.

"Oh shit," I whispered, sniffing again. Maybe I was mistaken? But it definitely smelled like Italian food. "No, I can't be that unlucky. Surely."

Siena, Illinois, had such a dense Italian population there was an Italian restaurant on every street corner. I must have seriously screwed up in a past life if my "saving grace" had brought me full circle to a Ricci family restaurant.

"Hey! You look great," Liz told me with a wide smile as I emerged. She stood with a stressed-looking middle-aged man in a bow tie. "This is Gary."

I gave the manager a tight smile and offered my hand. "Hi, thank you for—"

"You know how to waitress?" Gary snapped, not interested in my hand or my pleasantries. "You know what? I don't even care. Just do what you're told, and I'll give you cash at the end of the night. Tips are all yours."

My brows rose, and Liz just nodded encouragingly.

"Told you we were desperate." She laughed as Gary stomped away into the kitchen. "Come on, I'll show you around before we open."

The second we stepped out into the dining room, I knew my desperate hope from before was long gone.

"Giovanni's?" I said in a high, squeaky voice. "This is a Ricci restaurant?"

Liz turned back around to give me a puzzled frown. "Yeah. Didn't I tell you that already?"

I shook my head frantically. "No. No, you definitely didn't. I'm so sorry; I can't—"

"Bullshit," she snapped, propping her hands on her slim hips. "You literally have nowhere to go, Billie. What does it even matter who owns the restaurant? Gary's going to pay cash, and you can crash on my floor until you speak to Mrs. Glass tomorrow."

She was right. Of course she was right. The Ricci family owned thirty restaurants in Siena and countless other businesses. The odds of one of them *actually* coming into this exact venue on the one night I worked was so improbable...

So I put on my brave face and let Liz carry on with

her tour—all the while repeating to myself that it would be fine. It was *just* a job.

It didn't take long to see why Liz had been so quick to offer me a job. There were only two other servers working that night, and with how many customers they catered to, there should have been at least seven on the floor. On the upside, though, as the night progressed the workload kept me so busy I could barely give the Ricci family even a second thought.

Hell, I actually enjoyed myself. That was something I hadn't experienced in a *long* time.

"Billie!" Gary barked as I polished glasses at the end of the night. "You saved our asses, girl. Do you need a more permanent position?"

My brows shot up in surprise. "Um, yes! Yeah, I do." Fuck the Ricci family; they wouldn't even recognize me if they saw me working here, anyway. And the tips were *good*. Better than anything I'd had in years.

Gary gave a curt nod. "I'll get the paperwork done tomorrow."

Liz gave me a wide smile, then called me over to the kitchen where the chef had put out some staff meals for us. She needed to stay for a late booking, but I was technically finished for the night. Gary had counted out my pay, and I'd almost wept.

The food was just an added bonus on an already

great night. It'd been a *long* time since I'd eaten authentic Italian, so I almost had a mouth orgasm when I tasted the spinach and ricotta cannelloni that the chef had given us.

"Good, huh?" Liz laughed as I inhaled my food. From the dining room, the sound of men's voices traveled out to us, and she sighed. "Looks like my late booking is here. Finish up, then head back to the house; I'm room twenty-eight." She handed me her key, and I gave her a startled look.

"Um..."

"Just don't steal my shit, alright," she told me with a laugh, and I was going to guess she didn't have much there *to* steal. Otherwise, why trust a total stranger?

I quickly polished off my food, then washed my plate and ducked into the staff toilet to pee. While I was in there, I peeled off my white blouse, folding it to put away in my bag, just in case I didn't have time to wash it before my next shift. I was wearing a tank top underneath, anyway, and it wasn't *freezing* outside. It'd do.

Before I even finished packing my bag, a loud bang came from the front of the restaurant, quickly followed by another, and I stiffened with fear. Were those gunshots? A second later the sound of male voices traveled through to where I hid, and no one sounded worried. Surely, if someone had fired a gun, there would be a fraction more panic going on in the restaurant.

I breathed a sigh of relief. It was probably a car backfiring in the street, and my paranoia was making too much of it. But then as I left the toilet, I heard a familiar voice. The sort of voice that made me freeze in panic.

Fuck. *Fuck.*

It'd been six years since I heard that voice, but I was in *no way* ready for a reunion with the man it belonged to. So I did the cowardly thing and ducked back into the toilet to hide.

Not a moment too soon, either. Shouts from the dining room came closer, accompanied by the sound of breaking glass and scuffling feet. Curiosity had always been a curse for me, and I peered through a crack in the door as a heavyset man was pushed through the storeroom. His hands were up and he was babbling pleas, but I couldn't understand a word of it. The rush of my own pulse in my ears was too loud as I laid eyes on Angelo Ricci.

His handsome face was so achingly familiar, but the boy I'd known was long gone. In his place was a hard-edged man with haunted eyes and a gun in his hand. Fuck. Angelo was aiming a gun at this guy.

"Get him out into the alley," he snapped to the guy beside him, and they shoved the begging man outside. Angelo followed, and so did two other guys with guns. Holy crap, why did they all have guns?

Fear coursed through me like electric shocks, and a cold sweat formed all over my body, but I couldn't move. I had to stay hidden and pray that none of them needed to pee. Oh god. What if they found me? Would they kill me? I'd seen too much already, I was sure.

That certainty got worse as the raised voices in the alleyway got more intense. This time there was no mistaking the sound of a gunshot.

"Fuck," I breathed. I needed to get the hell out, but how? Angelo and his guys were in the alleyway, presumably having just shot a guy. I didn't want to be next.

Panic urging me forward, I abandoned my duffel bag and slipped out of the toilet stall. The back door was still ajar, and I couldn't stop myself from peeking out. Angelo was like a fucking magnet for me.

It was dark outside, but there was no mistaking the body on the ground at Angelo's feet.

Holy shit. *Holy shit!*

I must have made a sound because his gaze snapped up, locking eyes with me like we had some kind of sick magical connection. I saw the second he recognized me, his brown eyes widening under the dim outdoor lights and his lips parting in shock, but I wasn't sticking around for a reunion.

Nope, I was *gone.* I took off running to the front of the restaurant, terror flooding through my veins as I smacked my hip on the corner of a table, then tripped over something.

"Billie!" his gut-wrenchingly familiar voice shouted after me, and I scrambled to hide behind the bar. What the hell had happened here? Where was Liz? And Gary? And...

"Find her, and kill her," another man snarled, his voice harsh and guttural. Familiar, too, but I couldn't place it as easily as Angelo's. "Then come back here and clean up this mess. We can't let this fuckup get back to Giovanni."

Footsteps sounded, and the door opened and closed with people, *hopefully,* leaving the restaurant. I wasn't stupid enough to think I was alone, though. Not when Angelo had *seen* me.

I tucked into a tiny ball behind the bar, shaking with fear. Tears poured from my eyes, but I was too scared to make even a single noise. Then I realized what I'd tripped over before scurrying behind the bar.

Liz's beautiful brown eyes stared at me from where

she lay crumpled on the floor. Lifeless. A pool of blood surrounded her, and a small scream escaped my throat.

I tried to choke it back, but it was too late. A strong hand seized the back of my neck, grabbing a handful of my hair as I was hauled from my hiding place.

"Got you," an unfamiliar, greasy man leered, brandishing his gun in my face.

This was it. This was how I died. Just like Liz...

Thinking of her made me glance down, and it was even worse from this vantage point. Blood coated her entire blouse, soaking the white fabric in crimson. I'd never been good with blood, but for the first time I was relieved when my ears started ringing and my vision went dark. Angelo could shoot me if he wanted. I'd never know.

Someone grunted a curse as my body went limp and I fell into a dead faint.

BILLIE

Someone was stroking my hair when consciousness returned to me slowly. It wasn't in a creepy or threatening way, it was... soothing. Gentle. Their fingers combing softly through my dirty, dark blonde hair with reverence.

"Bella," a husky male voice murmured, "I can't believe you still faint at the sight of blood."

Angelo. Holy shit, it was *Angelo*.

"What the fuck were you doing here tonight, Bella? After all this time..." He released a long sigh. "Shit, what a mess."

He didn't yet know I was awake. I hadn't opened my eyes and he seemed to be talking more to himself than expecting an answer, so I played possum. It wasn't easy, though, when the boy I used to love was sitting close enough to kiss, his fingers stroking the side of my face.

Where was I? I was lying down, somewhere comfy, but the last thing I remembered was the guy who'd pulled me from my hiding place. The one who was going to kill me.

A door opened, and the air shifted like Angelo had moved away. I didn't dare open my eyes, though.

"Sir, we caught up with the rat," a man said. "What do you want done?"

Angelo gave a grunt. "I'll deal with him."

"What about her?" the man asked. I was going to assume he was talking about me... unless he meant Liz. Fuck, she was dead. There had been *so* much blood. Had Angelo killed her himself? He'd killed the guy in the alleyway, I was sure of it.

"I'll deal with her, too," my childhood love said in a hard-edged voice. "She's not going anywhere."

The door closed a moment later, and a loud click echoed through the room. Angelo was gone, and he'd locked me in.

Cautiously, I cracked my eyelids open to check if I was alone. When I didn't see anyone, I sat up. A light wave of dizziness made me sway, but it was gone in a second and I could look around. We were in an office, and I'd been lying on a small leather couch, the faint scent of Italian food lingering in the air. We were still in the restaurant. Why? Why hadn't he just shot me while I was unconscious?

Someone screamed, and I no longer cared for the why of it all, I just knew I needed to get the *fuck* out of the restaurant. The way Angelo had said he would *deal with* me gave me shivers of pure terror, and I wasn't sticking around to find out what that meant. The screams from outside the office said enough.

I'd already heard the door lock, so my only option was the window. It was tiny, but squeezing through a small window could hardly be worse than whatever was happening to cause those screams out in the restaurant. Fuck hanging around to see what they'd do to me for spying on them; I was going to do what I did best.

Fucking *run*.

The window was painted shut. Of course it was.

"Okay, come on, Billie," I muttered aloud, "come on, think. Think. You can get out of this."

Determined, I hunted the desk drawers until I came up with a blunt letter opener. Perfect! Or as good as it would likely get. Besides, I just needed to free up the painted part that was sticking the window shut.

Apparently, I was due for a small dose of luck because it only took a couple of minutes to chip the paint away with the letter opener, then the window was open. I needed to drag the chair over to reach high enough to squeeze out, but even so, it was a struggle. My hips got stuck when I was halfway out, and panic made me frantically wiggle my way free.

Of course that then sent me crashing headfirst to the concrete, and I just barely got my hands out in time to save my face taking my full weight.

For a few moments, I lay there in the dirty alley, trembling with shock and fear. Then the back door to the restaurant banged open and I dove behind the closest dumpster to hide.

Two men stepped out, but they didn't see me. They weren't even looking for me, they'd just come out for a cigarette, but it left me trapped there because they were between me and the street. The other end of the alley ended in a locked gate.

Minutes ticked by, and sweat dripped down my spine. How long would it take before Angelo went back to the office to "deal with" me? The second he opened the door he would know I'd gone out the window; it was wide open.

I needed to get as far away from Giovanni's as possible. Fast.

Finally, the two guys finished their smoke and headed back inside the restaurant. I barely waited for the door to click shut before bolting out of my hiding spot.

My shoes slapped the pavement as I ran, my breathing coming in jagged gasps as I tried to put as much distance between me and my impending death at the hands of my ex-love. But I had no fucking idea where I was going. I had no home. No friends. No family... and I'd just lost what few possessions I had left.

The police weren't an option. Angelo's family held too much power in this city.

A shout came from somewhere behind me, sending a sharp spike of fear through me, and I ran faster. Fuck stopping to look. Fuck risking getting caught *again*. I'd had my whole dose of dumb-bitch clichés for one night, thank you. So I just... ran. Aimlessly.

After a while, though, I realized that I was completely and utterly lost. I'd ended up in an area of Siena that I wasn't familiar with, and my feet ached. It had to be past midnight—without my phone I was only guessing—and I could hear the thumping bass of a nightclub somewhere nearby. But I was also convinced someone was following me.

When I paused to catch my breath, leaning against

a traffic light and trying to work out *where the fuck* I was, I caught sight of my pursuer. Or I confirmed there *was* someone following me and he was getting closer with every second I stood there paralyzed with fear.

One of Angelo's goons? Or a random creep? Or just my paranoia? I wasn't hanging around to find out. When the traffic light changed, I took off running again.

This time, the dude sped up, and I could officially cross paranoia off my list.

I ducked around the next corner, heading in the direction of chatter and music. Surely, he wouldn't attack or shoot me where there were witnesses. Enough witnesses that he couldn't kill them all, at least.

Relief washed over me when I saw the crowds of people gathered outside a nightclub, and hope flared inside my chest. This looked like a place I could blend in and lose my tail. I had no money, no ID, so I couldn't go inside, but surely, I could hide between a couple of big dudes?

A deep shiver ran through me, and I hurried forward, brushing past a group of girls, who gave me the stink eye. Fucking hell, I wasn't cutting in line, I was trying to stay alive.

I paused near a larger group of people, both men and women, talking and smoking cigarettes on the far side of the nightclub entrance. At least no one would make a scene and kick me out of line if I just... lurked. Especially the way I leaned against the wall behind one of the burly bouncers.

Feeling sufficiently hidden, I glanced back the way I'd come. A darkly suited man with an undercut and short ponytail was looking around, a deep scowl on his face and a phone to his ear. As he twisted around, searching, I spotted a gun on his hip. Shit, I was so screwed.

The group I was hiding within had just finished their cigarettes too.

Filled with panic and hardly daring to breathe, I slipped further past them, ducking behind the biggest guys and probably looking like a total crazy person, until I could dart into the next alleyway. So long as my pursuer didn't see me run in here, I could hide until he gave up and left. In theory. But there wasn't really a lot of time to debate any other options, so I just went for it.

Inside the alleyway, I spotted a line of dumpsters loaded with trash bags, some taller than me, so I raced over to them. A sound behind me made me flinch and—stupidly—look in the direction I'd come. There was no one there; my stalker hadn't found me yet. But I wasn't looking where I was going anymore and ran straight into a wall.

The impact knocked me back onto my ass, which I had no issue with because it meant I could scurry behind the dumpsters and hide better. I could safely say I seriously regretted never taking more than one women's self-defense class.

"Uh, are you okay?" someone asked, and I gave a yelp of fright.

Holy shit. I hadn't run into a wall, I'd run into a *person* and hadn't even noticed. I tucked tighter into a ball and blinked up at the human wall. It was a guy, but there was a light behind him, casting his features all in shadow.

But, you know, he wasn't trying to shoot me, so that had to be a good thing.

"Y-yeah. Sorry. I didn't see you there." My voice shook almost as badly as my body now was. "Sorry."

I had no idea what to do now. Or how to get rid of him quickly. This guy could draw attention to me if my stalker looked inside the alleyway. Crap, was that light on me, too? It'd been a terrible idea to head into a dead-fucking-end. What was I thinking?

"Here, let me help you up," the guy offered, tossing his cigarette to the ground and stomping it out. Then he extended a hand.

I needed to stay hidden. Badly. But if I just cowered here in a ball, he was likely to call the club's security or something. Or worse, a mental institution. So I rolled the dice and took his hand.

His palm was warm, his fingers strong as they wrapped around my hand, his wrist flexing as he pulled me up from the ground. I found my feet and immediately positioned myself in a sheltered position behind the tall dumpsters. Sure, this guy could probably be seen, but that shouldn't be a problem. Right?

"Are you okay?" he asked again, swiping a hand through his hair. It was shaved on the sides, heavily gelled in the middle. Like he'd been rocking one of those douchey fauxhawks. But shit, now that I could see him better, my eyes widened at how *hot* he was. Piercing green eyes, olive skin, and a damn ring in the side of his lip that drew way too much of my attention. Just my luck, running into a total ten while escaping a fucking *murderer*.

He was still waiting for my response, and I was staring at him like I was starstruck. Cringing, I ducked my eyes away and wrapped my arms around myself.

"Um, yeah. I'm sorry I ran into you. I wasn't looking where I was going." I wet my lips and couldn't resist a quick peek around the dumpster. Half of me expected to see ponytail dickhead standing there with his gun in hand, but the alley was empty.

The guy I'd run into touched my elbow, and I nearly leapt out of my skin. My pulse galloped, and I sucked in a sharp breath of fright before catching myself.

Instead of looking freaked out, he just scowled and ran his gaze over me. "You're running from someone," he observed. It was a statement, not a question. "Are you hurt?"

I shook my head, too shaken to even try and lie. "No, I'm fine," I replied in a whisper. "I just need to hide for a minute."

He frowned deeper, staring down at me. Then he gave a short nod. "You're freezing; come inside." He tipped his head to the fire escape door slightly further down the alleyway. A beer bottle was wedged in the door, holding it from latching, and music trickled from inside.

I shook my head. "N-no, I'm fine. Thanks."

The guy's brows shot up in surprise. I guess with that face he didn't hear *no* very often from girls. I bet he had a body to match, too. This was *so incredibly* not the time to be flirting with a cute guy in an alleyway; maybe I'd hit my head when I fainted.

"You're not fine," he disagreed. "You're cold, terrified, and covered in blood."

"I'm what?" I peered down at myself, then let out a small scream. There was blood all over the side of my arm and now that I was paying attention I realized my tank top was wet. Wet and sticky. I had no idea if any of the blood was mine after the fall from the window, but I knew for sure some was Liz's. Frantic, I went into panic mode, tearing the stained fabric off my body in revulsion, leaving myself just in a black bra, as I tried *really* hard not to pass out again. Scrubbing the fabric down my arm, the shaking in my body grew stronger.

"Oh my god," I gasped over and over. "Oh my god. Oh my—" Bile rose up in my throat. "I'm going to be sick." I leaned over, bracing my hands on my knees as my stomach lurched. Nothing came up, though. Thank *fuck*.

"Here." My new friend shrugged off his leather jacket, then pulled his t-shirt off. Before I could voice a protest, he'd tugged the shirt over my head, and I pushed my arms through the sleeves on autopilot. The fabric was still warm from his body, and smelled of smoke and cologne.

Through the fog in my panicked mind, I finally realized what I'd done. "What? No, I can't take your t-shirt!" I protested, straightening up and pushing my hair out of my face. Oh shit, he really did have a body to match his face—slim but well-built, with washboard abs, and *covered* in tattoos. Was that a piercing in his nipple? That and the lip had me wondering where else he might be pierced.

Billie, no!

His grin was pure confidence as he put his jacket back on and left it open. "Sure you can. You can't go walking around in just a bra and skirt, no matter how hot you look. You'd freeze."

My lips parted, but I had no comeback. My brain wasn't functioning as fast as it should be.

"Besides, the leather jacket over bare chest is totally rock and roll, no one will question me." He flashed another disarming smile and backed up a couple of steps. His fingers wrapped around the door handle of the fire exit, and he tugged it open. "You coming or what?"

I bit the side of my lip, confused as fuck. *No* should be my response. Surely, I'd already been hiding long enough that Angelo's thug had gone. But even if he had... where was I going? I had nothing. My bag—with my clothes and all my money—was back in the restaurant.

So I found myself nodding. If nothing else, maybe I could steal someone's jacket to keep me warm on the streets tonight.

The cute guy held the door open wider for me to

pass by, then gently touched a hand to my lower back as he followed me inside.

"Come on, I'll get you a drink," he said in my ear as the music got louder. "You look like you need it."

If that wasn't the truest statement I'd ever heard.

Angelo was a murderer... and now he wanted *me* dead.

I really did need a drink.

RHETT

The club was loud, packed, sweaty. I'd been suffocating under the attention earlier, hence why I'd slipped out the fire escape for a cigarette. I'd just needed a fucking second *alone*. Now, though, I was glad for the crush of patrons that gave me an excuse to reach down and link my fingers through hers.

I was oddly pleased with how loud everything was, meaning I needed to lean down so close my lips brushed her ear as I directed her to the VIP area.

She looked *so hot* in my t-shirt I could barely keep my thoughts straight. Fuck, I didn't even know her name. But better yet... she didn't seem to know *mine*.

I needed to get a fucking grip, though. She'd been running from someone, probably an abusive boyfriend. She'd been totally fucking terrified out there in the alleyway, shivering and small, looking up at me like a kicked puppy. The last thing she needed was for me to hump her fucking leg right now.

There was no point staying in the main part of the dance floor; I'd be mobbed in seconds, and I sensed that would send the skittish chick running for the hills. For some reason that bothered me. Reasons I wouldn't be examining tonight.

Making my way toward the VIP section, I kept her close, and it didn't escape my attention that she kept obsessively checking our surroundings. Violence against women was a trigger for me, and I half hoped that whatever fuckbag was after her showed his damn face tonight.

I could use a little release.

"Wait."

Her soft voice managed to reach me, even over the pounding bass. She tugged my hand , and I paused and turned toward her, waiting for her to speak.

"I can't be here," she said, shaking her head. Her eyes were boring into mine unflinchingly, and I wished it wasn't so dark in here. I wanted to know their true color, since they weren't all green, or all brown. There were unusual flecks that I could just make out, which appeared to match the natural golden highlights in her hair.

"Why can't you be here?" I pushed, wanting her story.

"I'm putting you in danger. I need to escape... I need to hide."

She looked pale, and fragile in my shirt as it engulfed her. Fucking caveman part of my brain really liked seeing her in my clothing.

"Just stay for a drink," I told her. Fuck knew why I couldn't let her leave, but I never ignored my instincts. Not anymore. And tonight, they'd decided that we had to help this chick. "Stay, and I will make sure you're safe. Let me help you."

She was torn, her expression falling, but as she let out another deep breath, I knew that, for now, she was staying. Who knew how many more times tonight I'd have to talk her off a ledge, but for once, when dealing with someone else's demons, mine stayed quiet.

Toying with the hoop in the side of my lower lip, I changed tact and detoured us back to the enormous main bar. Around the far side, away from the dance floor, it wasn't so crowded. It was also out of sight of the VIP area, which meant I could keep her all to myself for a while.

My band was my family, but she certainly wouldn't be the first beautiful girl I'd lost to one of them. Sue me for taking my opportunity as it presented itself.

Eyes were on me from all directions, but I ignored them all. My focus was locked on the golden-haired girl clutching my fingers so tight it hurt. She was giving me whiplash, the way she shifted between wanting to flee and *maybe* trusting me. Understandable, though, if she was fleeing an abusive partner. I hated men who beat on women. Cowards, every last fucking one of them.

"Let's sit over there," I suggested, nudging her in the direction of a velvet sofa that had just been vacated. Empty glasses still littered the table, but a waitress arrived to clear them as we sat down.

I ordered a beer, then turned to ask the pretty girl what she wanted to drink. Her cheeks were flushed pink, though, and her fingers twisted in the hem of my shirt as she meekly asked for a water.

Frowning, I held up a hand to pause the waitress.

"Just water? No offense, but you seem like you could go for something stronger after..." I gestured to my shirt. Meaning, *after all that blood*. "Or do you not drink? Totally cool, if you don't."

She grimaced, seeming to shrink smaller in her seat. "No, I drink. But... I have no money..."

I bit my lip, toying with my piercing before I said

something dumb and scared her off. She was so guarded, and if she was anything like the other women I'd known like her...

"Make that two beers please," I told the waitress. "Please bring them sealed."

The girl beside me gave a small sound but made no comment on my somewhat unusual request. But shit. She seemed like the type who'd be cautious of being drugged. The least I could do was put her mind at ease for just one drink.

"I hope you drink beer," I murmured, running a hand over the back of my neck and suddenly second-guessing myself.

Her smile was lopsided and small, but fuck, it was beautiful. "Beer is just fine. Thank you."

I forced myself to sit back on the sofa, draping my arm along the back of it in an attempt to look cool and casual. I hadn't been this nervous talking to a girl in *years*.

"What's your name?" I asked, watching her carefully. Her fingers still toyed with the hem of my t-shirt, but it was more of a fidget than a nervous gesture.

Her tongue swept over her perfect lips, and she tossed me another lopsided smile. "Probably best I don't tell you. Plausible deniability and all that."

A dull note struck through me at that brush off. "But then what will I call you?"

She shrugged. "Anything. Nothing. It doesn't matter. By morning I'll probably just be a statistic."

What the fuck did she mean by that? She thinks she'll be dead? Oh. Hell no.

Our waitress returned with our beers, and my nameless companion watched like a hawk as the bottles were opened in front of us.

"Anything-Nothing is a terrible name," I teased when the waitress was gone—not without tossing me some flirtatious looks. "I have to call you *something*. You don't seem like the kind of girl for *darling, babe,* or *princess.*"

She laughed, coughing on a huge swallow of beer. "Please don't ever call me *princess.*" Taking another gulp, she seemed to be thinking. "Call me Thorn, then. It's pretty accurate to my prickly personality, anyway."

Surprise saw my brows hitch. "Thorn?" I tested it out, holding her golden-green gaze. "I like it."

Her lopsided grin turned brighter, and my breath caught. "So, what do I call *you* then?" she asked, her gaze leaving mine and running down my bare chest. My jacket was open, my ink on display. Was I imagining a touch of heat in her eyes when her gaze returned to my face?

I took a sip of my beer to distract myself.

"What do you call me?" I repeated in a somewhat husky voice. Shit, I even *sounded* horny.

Anything you fucking want, Thorn.

Clearing my throat, my gaze scanned around us, noting the attention we were already holding. Our time was limited. Either my security would find us or the press would. So I'd damn well better make the minutes count.

"Rhett," I told her honestly, watching for even the slightest flicker of recognition in her eyes.

She tipped her head to the side. "Rhett," she murmured, her voice turning my name into something sinfully sexy. "That's so... old Hollywood glam. Not what I expected from a guy like you."

I chuckled, relaxing more into the sofa and letting my fingertips brush her golden hair. "Oh yeah? What did you expect my name to be? Probably something totally douchey like Zeplin or Razor, huh?"

She gave a soft laugh, shrugging. "If the shoe fits, *Zep.*"

Giving a dramatic groan, I indicated to the waitress to bring us another round. Thorn had nearly finished hers already, but it was comforting to see she'd stopped twisting her fingers in the hem of my shirt. Like maybe she was relaxing?

"So… want to tell me what happened to you tonight?" I asked gently after a beat of silence.

She shook her head. Fair enough.

"Are you sure it wasn't your blood?" I asked instead, worried she might have a wound hidden from me right now.

Her nod was tight. "I'm fairly sure," she whispered. This time when her amber eyes met mine, they were haunted by shadows. "It was my friend's. S-she…" her chin wobbled, and I reacted on instinct.

Closing the gap between us, I wrapped my arms around her thin frame, pulling her into me like I could somehow shelter her from the demons already inside her head. "Hey," I whispered, my lips against her hair. "I'm sorry; I shouldn't have pried. You don't have to tell me."

Her shoulders trembled, but she pulled away a moment later. "I shouldn't be here," she told me, shaking her head. "If he finds me—"

"He *won't*," I growled. I didn't even know who *he* was, but goddamn if I wasn't already committed to saving this girl from *him*. "Where would you go if you weren't here? Where were you running to when I found you?" She'd said she had no money. No possessions. It was *cold* out there tonight too.

My hands were still on her back, and she didn't

seem bothered by it. But the way her cute nose wrinkled confirmed what I already suspected. She had no clue where to go or what to do. If I let her walk away now, she would be right. By morning, she'd be a Jane Doe in the morgue, the victim of either crime or the cold.

"Here's what we're going to do," I told her, struggling to keep my voice calm and reassuring. "You're going to come back to my hotel with me. Not… like *that.*" *Unless you want to, in which case I won't say no.* "Just to sleep. Shower. Warm up. Eat. Then in the morning, if you want to tell me more about who you're running from, maybe I can help."

She drew a long breath, her brow marked with a crease of worry. "And if I don't want to tell you?"

I gave a small shrug. "I won't make you. But at least I can have a clear conscience for not leaving you out there on the street tonight. Deal?"

My lungs flat fucking refused to work while I waited for her answer. It was probably foolish of me to push this so hard. She could be making the whole thing up to get close to me and sponge off my fame. It wouldn't be the craziest shit we'd seen. But… her genuine fear was unmistakable. This girl was shit scared of *someone,* and I needed to help her. Need, not want.

Finally, though, she gave a small nod. "Okay. Deal." Then she blushed. "Thank you, Rhett."

Christ, that was like an arrow through my heart. "No thanks needed, Thorn. Come on, I just need to let my friends know I'm leaving. Otherwise, they'll send a fucking search party out after me."

Ignoring the fresh drinks that had just been delivered, I offered my hand to Thorn, weaving our fingers together as I pulled her to her feet. I liked the way her hand felt in mine. Like we just fit together perfectly.

"If you're here with friends, I don't want to—" she started to protest as I led the way back to the VIP area.

I spun around in midstride, giving her my full attention. "Trust me. You're doing me a *massive* favor giving me an excuse to bail out. I definitely need to be the one thanking *you*."

Her answering smile was sly, almost flirtatious. I loved it. "Well then, in that case I feel better about accepting your help, Rhett."

Every step we took closer to the VIP area felt like a mistake. She had no idea who I was, but there would be no hiding it once she'd met my friends. None.

My stomach sank as a painfully familiar song started playing through the club, and the patrons went *wild.* Thorn, though, just looked annoyed when I glanced back at her. How curious.

"Not a Bellerose fan?" I asked, stroking her wrist with my thumb as we continued across the club.

She shook her head. "Definitely not. But hey, I won't think less of you if you're a fan. You had to have at least *one* personality flaw."

Oh my fucking—

Thorn was a joker. Cute as hell. Personality flaw, my tight ass.

"Come on, funny girl, let's tell my dickhead friends I'm alive and get out of here before the music gets worse."

"If that's possible," she muttered, just loud enough for me to hear. Ouch.

The security guards at the base of the VIP steps moved aside to allow us entrance without a word. My own personal security would be upstairs, and no doubt they'd have a few choice words about me taking off alone again. But by now, I'd made it more than clear that they worked for me, and when I needed to breathe, I was gone.

The mysterious girl at my side pushed in closer, and I swear to fuck my heart did some stupid sort of flip in my chest. Yeah, alone time was appealing, but she... she was more appealing.

When we stepped onto the top level, with its swanky velvet couches and crystal chandeliers, I felt her steps slow again. "Uh, Rhett? Who are you?" she asked when I turned back. "I mean, clearly, you're richer than this grunge image suggests, but even rich doesn't usually get you access to"—she waved her hand—"all of this."

Amusement tugged at my center. "Rich gets you everything, sweetheart. Trust me."

She narrowed her eyes, and for the first time, there was less *lost waif* about her appearance. "Not me," she shot back before blinking like she couldn't believe she'd sassed me.

Fair call, though. Two steps into VIP and I was already acting like an entitled asshole again. It was embarrassing how quickly that'd happened. Thank fuck she'd stuck a pin in my ego before I could mess things up.

"Rhett!" My name rang out before I could change my mind about introducing Thorn to my friends, and I fought down the annoyance. My best friend had some fucking timing on him, that was for sure.

I didn't turn from her though, keeping all of my focus right where I wanted it to be: on the enigma that had stumbled into my alley. "Ignore him," I said, before blinking at how deathly pale she suddenly was. "Wait, are you okay? You look..." *Scared.*

Part of me wondered if she'd recognized the distinct, raspy tones of our lead singer. Jace's voice was pretty unmistakable. Another part was kind of pissed that I'd been dumb enough to ruin everything by bringing her up here. If she recognized Jace my anonymity was blown, but it was going to happen sooner or later. Best to deal with the fallout now, before she saw the paparazzi camped in front of our hotel later.

Thorn tried to pull away from me. Violently. But our hands were still joined, and I wasn't ready to let her go... not now, and probably not even tomorrow, despite my casual offer of *one night.*

"Ignore him," I said quickly. "He acts like he's the boss of us all when we're out, but he's really just a control freak."

Her lips trembled, and she was so pale now I wondered if she was about to pass out as she stopped fighting me. Maybe she was faking her dislike of the music and was secretly a *huge* fan? The fucking "Jace effect" was seriously annoying. I'd seen girls faint at his feet plenty of times, but I *really* didn't pick Thorn to be one of them.

"I give zero shits about your groupie of the night,

Rhett," Jace growled, sounding like he was right behind me now. "I was just coming over to let you know your expensive-ass tequila is at the table. Oh, and the bruiser twins are about to kick your ass for wandering off on your own again—"

His words cut off with a sharp inhale as he moved close enough to see the chick I was all but sheltering against my chest. It was such a dramatic pause, followed by a definite shift in his mood to dark and angry. Strong enough that I could feel the vibes. What the fuck?

Tearing my gaze from Thorn, I debated punching Jace in the hopes he would fuck off before he scared her away. She'd already been terrified enough for one night —the last thing she needed was another aggressive and angry male in her face.

It was too late though. Her attention was locked on him; only she wasn't staring awestruck at Jace or flipping out at being in the presence of fame. She wasn't fluttering her lashes and throwing herself at him.

She was terrified.

"What the *fuck* are you doing here?" Jace suddenly snarled, and I didn't even wait to analyze why I was shifting her behind me so I could face off against my best friend of years when I'd known her all of thirty minutes.

"You better back the hell away, Jace," I warned, ready to take him down if necessary. Jace might be three inches taller than my six feet one, but I'd grown up fighting for my life. We'd be a close match, but I had extra incentive tonight. Protective energy fueled me like no other.

"Do you have any idea who the fuck you're protecting?" he spat. His fury grew as his bright blue eyes darkened.

"I'm sure you're about to tell me," I snapped, "but I'm *still* warning you to back the hell up." I was already readying myself for this fight.

Thorn's small hands slipped under the back of my jacket, her fingers against my skin sending a shiver down my spine. I froze, in case lashing out at Jace somehow hurt her.

"I'll go," she said, soft but resolute. "I didn't know… if I'd even suspected…" Her sigh was heavy, and her touch almost apologetic. "I'll go."

"No!" I protested, reaching back to grip her hand tightly. "I'm not sending you back out there just because Jace is being—"

"That's *her,* Rhett!" my best friend roared. "That's *Billie.*"

My eyes locked with Jace as shock and denial rippled through me. I desperately wanted to believe he was joking, but I knew deep down... Jace wouldn't lie. Not about this. Not about *her*.

Thorn gave a pained noise at my back, trying to tug her hand free once more.

Billie.

Thorn was *Billie Bellerose.*

The Billie Bellerose.

The girl next door who had almost completely destroyed Jace. She was the reason our band was called Bellerose. My best friend's former muse and perpetual destruction.

Fuck. Fucking fuck.

four

BILLIE

Eight years, two months, sixteen days, and change. That's how long it had been since I stared into blue eyes that used to darken in desire for me. Now it was fury.

"She needs to fucking leave!"

It hadn't escaped my attention that since his first *What the fuck are you doing here,* Jace had done his best not to address me directly. His gaze didn't turn to me again, and I wondered how his hatred still sliced through my chest almost as hard as it had the last time we were together.

I never want to fucking see you again, Billie Bellerose. You're throwing away the best fucking thing in your life, and now you'll see my face everywhere. I'll be haunting you, Rose, but thank fuck I'll never have to see your deceitful face ever again.

He'd turned and walked away after those guttural words and, true to his promise, did not look back. Not once. Not when my house burned down and my parents both died. Not even when I spent a month in intensive care. And I didn't blame him for it.

Jace had gone on to become the biggest rock star in the world, spitefully name his band after me, and create album after album of songs that told *our* story. All to ensure I never forgot what I'd lost.

As if I ever could. But what this big bastard didn't know was... I'd done it all for him.

And I was done with being punished for it.

The last eight years had been torture, and it was time that I stepped out of the shadows and stood on my own two feet. After all, it was probably my last night alive. I might as well get some of my pain out before taking a bullet to the brain, courtesy of *his* ex-best friend. When I sidled around Rhett, he tried to move with me, but when I put my hand on his arm to halt his movement, he stilled. For a rock star, he was surprisingly gentle. A knight in shining armor.

The exact person I would have chosen to run into when I was terrified and in need of shelter.

But he couldn't protect me against this, and I didn't want him to fight with his friend over me.

This was my fucking fight, and it was long overdue. The irony of running into Jace the same night I was fleeing Angelo wasn't lost on me, either. Whoever was controlling my fate thought they were really fucking funny.

"Fuck you, Jace." The words spilled from me in a low, husky rush. Not as tough as I'd wanted them to be, but my voice was steady, and that was about all I could ask for.

It was his turn to still, but unlike Rhett, Jace was a cobra preparing to strike.

In near slow motion, he turned away from his bandmate and locked his gaze on mine. The air all but sizzled as we stared each other down. Well, *up* for me since he was even fucking taller than the last time I'd seen him. Bastard was six and half feet of ripped rock star god. I was five and a half feet of homeless waif. We were not the same, but I'd never let him know that.

"What did you say to me?" he murmured, outraged, and I felt the tingles of that low tone run down my spine. Jace, with his tanned skin and dark blond hair that was short on the sides with longer, streaked-platinum strands on top, had the voice of a fucking angel.

He was absolutely devastating up close.

It never surprised me that he was continually voted the most desirable man in the world. There was a magnetism about Jace that could not be replicated. He'd been born with it, and now, at twenty-six, he was beyond the beautiful boy I'd fallen in love with.

Still beautiful, of course, but harder... stronger... his muscled arms standing out in the torn tank he was wearing over black jeans and boots. I'd never feared my safety in his presence, but tonight, as he leaned in over me in an intimidating manner, my chest grew tight.

This was not the Jace I'd known and loved.

"Cat got your fucking tongue, Billie?" he sneered, full lips thinning. "You were in the middle of trying to grow a damn backbone, remember?"

Shit. I'd gotten distracted by his looks—unfortunately, not for the first time—but his not-so-kind reminder of my weaknesses sent another shot of anger through me.

"After all of these years," I snapped out ,"you *seriously* still think—" I cut myself off there because he didn't need to know that story. Not when he'd just act like I was making shit up to appease his anger. I wasn't even sure I could speak the words out loud to explain my choices that fateful day. The day of my sixteenth birthday when I'd so deliberately broken his heart.

Whatever else he thought of me, I *was* guilty of that.

"Sorry," Jace leaned in looking anything but sorry. "I think I missed some of your bullshit. Did you trail off for a reason? Lies getting all muddled in your head?"

Rhett, inserting himself between me and Jace again, must have had enough, and I blinked as I was once more staring at the back of his jacket. "Just leave her alone," he said softly. "She's had a rough fucking night, and she doesn't need one more aggressive guy in her face."

Jace's laugh was dark and raspy. "You poor, deluded fuck. She stared at you with those syrupy golden-green eyes and smiled her signature half smile, huh? You saw perky tits and a perfect ass, and she had you snared. It's her MO, brother. She's a manipulative, cheating bitch, and she saw you coming from a mile away. Not like Rhett is that common a name these days, right? Everyone knows *Bellerose*."

It was my turn to snort laughter now, as exhaustion pressed in on me. I was homeless, jobless, and very near lifeless. And this arrogant fuck thought I cared that they were rock stars. He thought I'd somehow *planned* to confront him tonight? He was deluded.

Jesus. If I could have chosen *literally* any other fucker to run into tonight, I would have. Hell, I'd even take the damn gun-wielding goon back out on the street at this point.

Rhett must have felt me laughing against his back, since I was fairly sure it was too loud to hear the soft, sad sound. He turned then and met my gaze as I stared up at him. "Hey, you okay, Thorn?" he asked me.

He was still using my nickname, and I didn't have time to wonder why I liked that.

"I didn't know who you were," I told him, fairly sure he wasn't going to believe me. "If I had..." *I'd have run just as fast as I had from Angelo's guys.*

"I know," he said without even a beat of hesitation, and I blinked at the sincerity in his words. "I believe you, Thorn."

A rumbling growl of anger escaped from Jace. "You're a fucking moron, Rhett, and I don't have time for this shit. A bottle of Macallan single malt is at the table with my name on it. Just get rid of her as soon as you blow your load. I don't want to see her again. Ever."

He stormed out, and I forced myself—nails gripping into my palms—to not follow his path with my gaze. Instead, I remained as I was, staring up at the most unlikely guardian angel. "You sure you believe me?"

The slowest smile tilted up his lips but didn't quite reach the piercing green of his eyes. "I've been in this business for a long time. I know groupies. I know those who pretend not to know who we are. You had no clue who I was when I told you my name."

My throat was tight all of a sudden. Not often was I trusted or given the benefit of the doubt. My own fault, really, since I put myself into shady situations to survive. But it was a head-spin of a change. "I know how famous Bellerose is," I said slowly, "but for my own sanity, I made sure that if the band, or its members, were ever mentioned, I changed the channel... closed the book... turned the radio off." Another sad laugh escaped. "I even contemplated changing my name, but I never had the money or time to waste on it, so I just told people my last name was Belle."

Rhett's expression softened again, and part of me wondered how the hell someone so kind could be a rich and famous rock star. It made no sense, but he was the guardian angel I needed tonight. "What instrument do you play in Bellerose?" I asked.

There was no way he was a drummer. Drummers were always assholes.

Drummers and lead singers.

"Lead guitar."

His eyes never left my face, possibly because he was trying to catch me in a lie, or maybe it was something else. "I should have guessed that," I told him. "Your fingers have the same calluses that Jace's always did." And Angelo's, back when *he'd* been in Jace's band. "I didn't notice at first, running for my life and all that, but... now I feel stupid."

"You wouldn't have stayed if you knew..." Confusion and worry touched his brow, and I knew I'd let this go on too long already.

Sucking in a deep breath, I forced myself to take a step back as a new song blasted through the space, much louder than the previous. Thankfully, they were giving the Bellerose hits a break.

"I should go now," I told him. "I need to figure out my next move, and I don't need to be dealing with Jace as well as Angelo."

The skin around his eyes tightened. "Angelo Ricci?"

Of course the current best friend of Jace would be aware of the former best friend. Fuck, Jace and I'd grown up with Angelo. I barely had a memory from the ages of four to sixteen that didn't have both of them in it.

"You're still with Angelo?" he asked me with a hint of disappointment.

I shook my head. "No. I haven't seen him for years. But tonight... I had this job..." My words got stuck in my throat as Liz's empty eyes flashed across my mind. "It was bad," I managed to choke out. "So much shit went down, murder and blood, and now his guys are after me. I need to get out of Siena. I need to run and not look back."

Rhett was quiet, and I assumed he was weighing up if it was worth the hassle of dealing with me for a moment longer. I couldn't blame him. Nice guy or not, there were limits to how much anyone would let a stranger fuck up their night. Especially when that stranger was the enemy of your friend.

Taking another step back, I released a low gasp when his hand shot out and wrapped around my wrist, effectively holding me in place. He leaned in, and I tried not to breathe in his unique, smoky scent. "I don't know your story, Thorn, and it's fucked up that I have to hurt my brother, but I made you a promise." He leaned in even closer so I could hear him over the new song. "You need help tonight, and I can provide it. No strings attached."

No strings attached. That sort of offer came along... never. Well, maybe tonight when I'd been given a job and place to stay by Liz... Look how the fuck that had turned out for both of us. Not that her death was my fault, for once. It seemed we were both just in the wrong place at the wrong time.

"Plus, I'd like to hear your side of things," Rhett added when I didn't say anything. He released his hold on my wrist. "Because I've only ever known you as the devil. The evil in Jace's story. The girl who broke him. But having met you now, I wonder… Shit, I dunno. There're always two sides, right? I want to hear yours."

A cold sweat broke out across my entire body, a visceral reaction to the memories I'd tried so hard to bury. The grief I'd refused to feel. The pain that had almost killed me.

Before I could think about it, I backed away once more, my hands trembling as I lifted them as if to ward off a blow. "I can't…" I choke out. "I can't go back there. Whatever Jace told you… then that's what happened, I guess."

He examined me for a long moment. So long that another song had started and almost ended by the time he spoke. "I can feel your pain," he finally said. "And I can't just ignore it. You can tell me the story when you're ready, but for tonight, let's just get you safe, okay? We can order room service and pretend this awkward encounter with Jace never happened."

Without a single glance back at the table that we both knew was filled with his band mates—even if I hadn't looked that way once—he stepped closer and wrapped an arm around me, pulling me into his side. "Come on, Thorn. Let's get the fuck out of here."

BILLIE

Every instinct screamed at me that this— leaving with Rhett, going back to his hotel— was a *terrible* idea. One of the worst. The second I realized who he was, I should have walked the fuck away and not looked back. But... that was Jace's specialty. Driving those away who didn't fall into his narrative. His cold fury when he saw me *after all these years* just made me dig my heels in.

So, in part, I accepted Rhett's offer to send a giant *fuck you* to the gorgeous man who had made good on his promise to haunt me. Mostly, though, I accepted because I was exhausted. I was cold, hungry, scared, and now reeling from not one but *two* ghosts stepping out of my past within the space of an evening.

When Rhett told me *no strings attached*, I believed him. He radiated that white knight energy that I would never have attributed to a rock star before. He saw how close I was to giving up and was determined to pull me off the ledge.

On our exit from the VIP area, two identical security men appeared out of nowhere. They silently flanked us as we left the club through a back entrance and climbed straight into a waiting car with blacked-out safety glass. Not once did Rhett let my hand go, and I was way past the point of trying to pull away from him. Deep down, under the shock and pain that were dominating my system, was a part of me that *liked* how he held my hand so securely.

I sighed heavily, sinking back into the leather seat as the matching security guys climbed into the front and drove us away from the club. What a fucking night.

"Hey," Rhett said softly, pulling my attention. "Do you like steak? The hotel does a pretty great filet mignon with red wine jus."

That... was not what I thought he was going to ask. "Steak?"

"It really is good," the security guy in the front

passenger seat offered. "Unless you're a vegetarian or whatever."

My lips parted, but no words came out. What the fuck was going on? I was in the back of an expensive, blacked-out SUV, holding hands with a rock star and talking to a bodyguard about room service steak.

No one else spoke, though, so I wet my lips and gave Rhett a small nod. "Sounds delicious."

"You gotta get the brownie sundae, too," the driver rumbled in a low, gravelly voice.

Rhett must have seen my stunned confusion because he grinned when I glanced over. "It's okay to relax, Thorn," he whispered. "Jace isn't here. I won't press you for information you don't want to share. I just want to help *you*. Nothing more. No ulterior motives."

I swallowed hard. It had been a long, *long* time since someone had wanted to help me without standing to gain. Not since... *fuck*. Not since Angelo on the morning of my sixteenth birthday.

I will take care of you, Bella.

"Thank you, Rhett."

He chuckled softly, lifting my hand and brushing a kiss over my knuckles in such a casual gesture it was like we'd been dating for months, not hours. Wait, shit. We weren't *dating*. He was just... ugh. I needed sleep.

"You've got to stop thanking me, Thorn." He glanced out the window as the vehicle glided past the front entry of the Viper Hotel, one of the most expensive and exclusive hotels in Siena.

"Paps are still camped out," the driver grunted, explaining to me for some reason. "We're taking the service elevator from the loading dock."

I supposed those were the kind of precautions people like Rhett—and Jace—needed to take just to avoid being inundated with media and fans. What a crazy life they must live.

The transition from car to elevator, then up to the penthouse level was smooth. The identical bodyguards accompanied us the whole way, casually chatting to Rhett about the concert that Bellerose had played earlier that night. Rhett swiped a magnetic keycard to access the room and held the door open for me.

"Head in, Thorn. My security wants to scold me like a naughty child before they leave us for the night." He flashed me another charming smile. "Room service menu is on the TV; this will only take a second."

I nodded, peeling my hand out of his and taking a few steps inside the room. Wait. Not a *room* at all. This was *the* penthouse suite. Holy crap, it was *enormous*. The living area held a full bar to one side, a plush sofa seating area, massive flatscreen TV, full-size dining table… Most breathtaking, though, was the *view*.

Rhett left the front door partially open as he spoke with the matching bodyguards, reminding me that he was here with me, that I wasn't alone again. Whatever scolding the big guys wanted to give Rhett, it was quick. He stepped into the suite only a minute later, closing the door behind himself and tossing his keycard, phone, and wallet onto the bar top.

"All okay?" I asked, suddenly nervous as I turned away from the view. "Were they…"

"Smacking my hand for giving them the slip back at the club," he admitted with a wry smile. "But I sure as shit won't apologize. If I hadn't slipped my leash, I wouldn't have met you."

I bit my lip to hold back the goofy, smitten smile that tried to creep out. Was I crushing on Rhett already? Uh, major yes. I was smart enough to know nothing could *ever* eventuate out of it… not with him being who he was and me being, well, Billie *Bellerose*. But there was no harm in accepting the flirtation. Just for one night.

"So… penthouse suite at the Viper, huh? Things sure have changed since the days when Jace played concerts in my treehouse, that's for sure." I wrinkled my nose the second those words were out of my mouth. I didn't want to talk about Jace, and I definitely didn't want to talk about our history.

Rhett was crazy perceptive, though, and didn't pick at the scab. Instead, he gestured to one of the closed doors to the side of the room. "My room is through here. We should maybe head in there..."

My mind immediately went to sex. He'd *said* no strings attached, but he was a rock star offering to let me sleep in his bed. Not that I was necessarily against the idea... I was already crushing hard on him, but then there was Jace... and—

"Oh. *Ohhhhh!* Yes, fuck, good thinking." I glanced nervously at the other doors because one of them was probably *his* room. It was the penthouse suite, after all, and they were a band. Rhett wasn't ushering me into his room for *sex* but to save me from running into my hate-filled ex again.

His bedroom wasn't small, by any means. There was a king-size bed, perfectly made, and a private bathroom. Rhett smoothly ignored my awkwardness, grabbing the remote and turning on his flat screen to bring up the menu. "Pick whatever you want; I'm just going to take a quick shower." He paused in the doorway to the bathroom. "Jace won't be back any time soon, if that's on your mind. But Gray probably will be, now that I've bailed from the club. Flo and Tom will stumble in before dawn. I just figured maybe you'd want to avoid the rest of the band."

Fair call. I'd heard some of Bellerose's songs. None of them were kind to me or my story with Jace and Angelo.

Rhett disappeared into the bathroom before I could say thank you *yet again*, and I released a long sigh. The tension in my shoulders ached, so I sank down onto the bed to browse the room service menu.

"Holy shit," I said aloud, sinking further into Rhett's pillows. The bed was *insanely* comfortable. Or maybe that was just because I'd spent years sleeping on mattresses with springs sticking out or on the floor. Either way, my body just *melted*.

The shower had only just turned on in the bathroom; Rhett would be at least a few minutes. Maybe I could just close my eyes... just to calm down and convince my poor, panicked brain that *right now* we were safe. Angelo and his goons were long gone. I was safe here... in the bed of Jace's new best friend and lead guitarist. A man I was already lusting over, despite the shell-shocking events of the night.

Maybe safe wasn't the correct word. I wasn't *about to be murdered* was more accurate.

I'd never be *safe* with Bellerose.

Groaning, I rubbed my eyes with the heels of my

hands, probably smearing what was left of my makeup everywhere. Fucking hell, I should have run to the police, not into the arms of a rock star.

No. *That* would have most definitely ended the night with me in a morgue, rather than lying in a heavenly bed. The Ricci family had the Siena cops firmly in their pocket.

A huge yawn tugged my jaw.

Rhett had saved me tonight, but there was no way I could stay longer. I couldn't repay him by causing friction in his band. I'd make sure I was gone before anyone woke up in the morning. Long gone. But for now... maybe it wouldn't hurt to sleep a little.

When I woke, I had *no* idea where the hell I was. I took a moment to remember, feeling the high thread count sheets around me and the cloud-like pillow beneath my head. As my senses came online, I realized what had woken me.

Somewhere close by, a woman wailed and moaned. She was either being fucked by someone who was seriously rocking her world or she was being murdered. In the suite of a rock band, my money was on the former.

I sat up slightly, still blinking away the haze of sleep, but a heavy, tattoo-covered arm draped over me to pull me back down.

"Ignore it," Rhett mumbled, his face smooshed into a pillow. "Go back to sleep, Thorn."

I bit my lip, listening to the woman's cries become more urgent. Maybe I should just go now while everyone was... preoccupied? But based on how loud the sex noises were, I'd bet they were fucking right there in the living room. On the couch? Or maybe on the dining table?

Ugh. Was it Jace?

"Seriously," Rhett yawned. "They'll go for ages. Better off ignoring it and sleeping. C'mere." His arm around my waist pulled me into his body, and my face somehow ended up pressed to his chest as he fell back asleep once more.

I didn't have such an easy time of it. The longer I lay there in Rhett's arms listening to *someone* in his band put on one hell of a performance, the more turned on I was getting. It was one step away from voyeurism, and I clenched my jaw to keep from making a move on my White Knight.

Eventually, though, the couple in the living room must have run out of energy—or cum—and gone to bed. It was my best opportunity to leave... to slip out unseen and fade back into the night. But Rhett's heartbeat under my cheek pulsed in such a slow, steady rhythm that I drifted back to sleep in no time.

Screw it. I'd deal with the consequences in the morning.

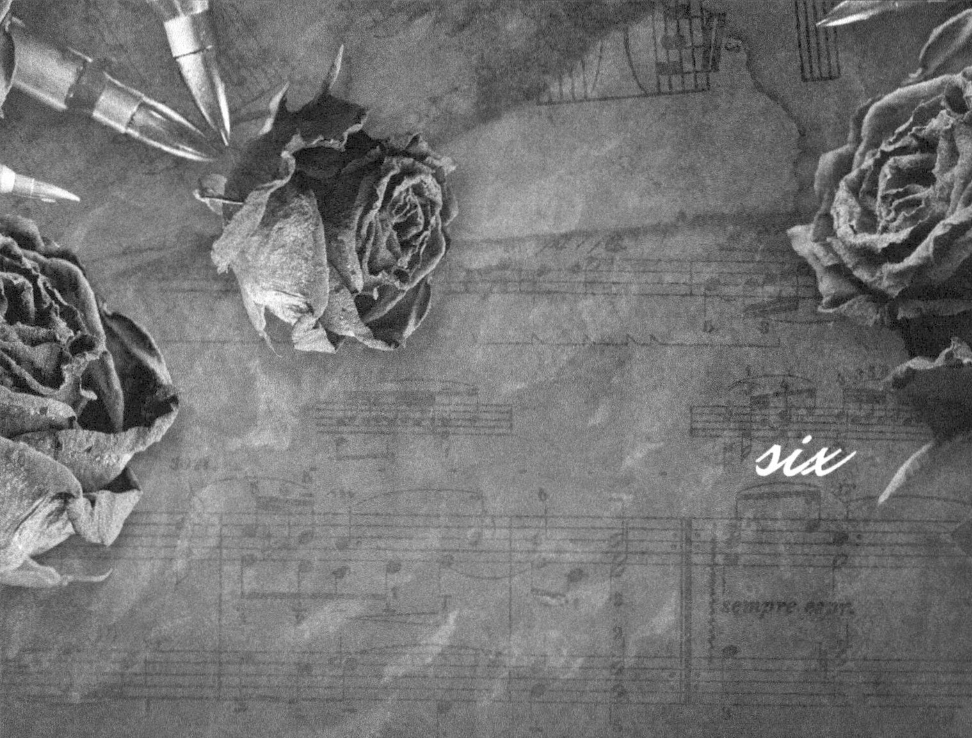

six

GRAYSON

The groupie I'd brought back to the hotel was a stage-five clinger. Bringing her here was a rookie mistake, and I paid for it when I tried to politely send her on her way after we were done fucking. She wanted to *cuddle*. I didn't fucking cuddle. But I was too tired to deal with a whole scene from calling security, so I just let her pass out in my bed. Besides, Jace was busy trying to prove something out on the sofa and didn't sound like he was stopping any time soon.

I couldn't sleep, though. Not with a snoring girl in my bed. Fuck, what was her name? Tracey? Stacey?

As soon as the sun came up, I made a whole show of

getting up to shower. She tried to join me, but I wasn't interested in revisiting that pussy. So I made excuses about an early rehearsal for tonight's show and handed her off to one of our bodyguards to escort downstairs. This *grassroots tour* meant we were more accessible in some ways, in smaller–albeit as sold out as ever–stadiums and venues, but that didn't mean we relaxed the rules.

I ran into Jace on my way back to my room. He had his girl up on the dining table, his tongue halfway down her throat while her hand worked furiously between them, jerking him off. He stopped kissing her long enough to give me a curious glance, then whispered some encouragement to the girl before blowing his load on her tits.

"I'm ordering coffee," I rumbled, not even blinking at the scene. Jace'd done worse over the years. We all had. This kind of shit... we were all just numb to it now. "You want?"

At this time of morning, it was entirely possible Jace was on his way *to* bed, not out of it.

"Yeah, order some food too," he replied, his signature melodic voice in full effect. The girl gave a cringeworthy moan, licking her lips and spreading her knees like she expected Jace to actually reciprocate.

Poor fool. Jace just frowned at her in confusion. "You're still here? You can go now."

The girl's face crumpled into a pissed-off, hurt expression, and her gaze darted to me. "Where's Crystal? Did she already leave?"

I glanced at Jace, then back to the girl. "Who?"

She gaped at me in shock, then slid off the table to grab her purse off the floor, where she must have dropped it when Jace decided to get a farewell hand job. "I guess I shouldn't expect anything better," she muttered bitterly. "Fucking *Bellerose*. The rumors are dead true."

She stormed out of the suite without a backward glance, and I quirked a brow at Jace. "The fuck?"

He just shrugged back. "Don't know, don't care. Get me a burger or something." He sniffed his armpit and grimaced. He only wore a pair of loose sweatpants as it was, probably having just rolled out of bed with that chick. "I need a fucking shower. Do me a favor and wake Rhett up. Make sure he's alone."

Why the fuck would he care if Rhett was alone? Jace had already gone back to his room, so I just shrugged it off and flopped down on the sofa to call our order through to room service. Tom—our bass player's boyfriend and our temporary tour manager—came yawning out of their shared room.

"Why are we all up so early?" he asked me with his face all screwed up in annoyance.

I hated Tom. He gave me bad vibes. But he was tied to Flo, so we were stuck with him for now. "Because we fucking feel like it, Tucker. No one said you needed to get up too."

Tom's eyes flashed with anger for a moment, then a slick smile crossed his lips as he gave a forced chuckle. Like I was *joking*. "Hey, did you see that chick Rhett picked up last night? The one that Jace got his panties in a bunch about?" He sat down on the sofa like we were buddies. We were not.

But I frowned at his question. "What chick?" I hadn't seen Rhett with any groupies. Last I'd seen him, he was sneaking away from the twins to have a smoke somewhere.

Tom leered. What the fuck did Florence see in this sleaze? "Oh, shit, that's right, you had that chick Crystal practically riding your dick in VIP when that shit went down. No wonder you didn't notice."

Who the *fuck* was Crystal? The groupie I'd brought back was Tracey. Wasn't she? Shit, maybe it *was* Crystal.

"She was this tiny thing, not even hot, but Rhett and Jace looked like they were going to come to blows over her. It was *weird*, Gray. They've both pulled girls ten times hotter than this bitch." Tom pulled a packet of cigarettes out of his pocket and sparked up right there on the sofa.

"Take that shit outside, Tucker," I snarled, glaring in disgust at the smoke. "And don't fucking call me Gray." I'd told him this a thousand times; it just wasn't sticking. Sooner or later, he'd end up eating my fist, and then I'd have Flo all over me about making her boyfriend bleed.

At least he took his nicotine cloud out to the balcony, even if he did leave the doors open to try and continue our conversation. I tuned him out as I submitted another room service order, getting coffee for Flo and Rhett. They'd be awake soon enough, given we weren't being especially quiet.

Sure enough, a few minutes later, our magenta-haired bassist flopped onto the sofa beside me.

"'Sup, Gray?" she muttered with a sleepy yawn.

"He doesn't like being called Gray," Tucker called out from the balcony.

I rolled my eyes. Dickhead. I didn't like *him* calling me Gray. Flo was my little sister; she could call me whatever the fuck she wanted.

Florence knew it, too, smirking. "We talking about Rhett's mystery girl?"

"You saw her too?" I grunted. "Where the fuck was I?"

"Knuckles deep in a groupie," she retorted with a teasing grin. "We didn't wanna interrupt. Man, I really thought Jace was gonna punch Rhett. It was *intense*."

I processed that. I guess that explained why Jace wanted to know if Rhett was alone this morning. He always was, though, so I didn't know why Jace thought today would be any different. Rhett banged groupies in clubs, in bathrooms, in alleyways, in cars... He didn't bring them back to the hotel. They were *never* in his bed. He had too many issues for a leap of trust like that.

"Jace has been in a mood for days," I reminded her, shrugging. "You know how he gets when we play Siena."

"True," she agreed, yawning again. "It's like he still thinks the mysterious Billie will just walk up to him while we're in town and be all 'Hey, Adams, remember me?' Like that would ever fucking happen."

Tom snickered, dropping his cigarette butt on the balcony and returning inside. "I'm starting to wonder if she's even a real person. Maybe she's just a metaphor or some shit."

I gave him a narrow-eyed look, letting him know that I generally hated everything that came out his mouth. He gave me an uncomfortable frown back but dropped it.

Our conversation shifted to the concert last night. It

was a good one, but not one of our best. Once again, it came back to Jace being on edge while we were in his home city. I had no doubt tonight's show would be the same, then when we got to New York, he would be like a totally different man.

Jace emerged from his room again some minutes later, still dripping water from his wet hair. He was laser-focused on Rhett's closed door, a deep scowl setting his features.

"Why isn't Rhett out here?" he demanded, shifting his cold gaze my way. Jace fucking Adams didn't scare me, and the fucking punk knew it. I *put up with him,* and that was as good as it got.

My answering glare was hard and unintimidated. "Because he's still *sleeping*, Jace. And we will let him sleep as long as he needs. Won't we?" The threat was clear under my words. Rhett didn't sleep enough on the best of days, and we were *all* worried about him.

Okay, maybe not Tucker. But he was a douche, and no one cared what he thought. Jace, Florence, and I had discussed Rhett's insomnia all too many times to go waking him up now. Just because... what? Rhett got with a girl Jace wanted? Since when did we compete for groupies?

Jace seemed like he wanted to ignore my warning anyway, glaring hard at Rhett's door. His fists clenched at his sides, and his jaw ticked. Eventually, he gritted his teeth and forced himself to cross over to a vacant seat instead.

"You worried he's got that chick in there with him?" Tom asked, never smart enough to read a fucking room. "Rhett doesn't bring them home, dude; he would have fucked her in the back of the car, then tossed her to the twins."

For some reason, this provoked Jace faster than I'd ever seen before. Anger creased his face, and one second he was seated in the armchair across the room, the next he had Tom up against a wall with his hand around his throat.

"Whoa, Jace!" Florence protested, rising out of her seat. "Let him go! What the hell, dude?" She looked over at me, silently asking for me to intervene, but I just shrugged. What the fuck did I care if Tom fucking Tucker finally got his teeth broken? He'd been begging for it.

Jace held Tom there a moment longer, then released him with what seemed to be a whole lot of effort.

"What was that about?" Tom wheezed, rubbing his throat. "What's this chick got going for her that you're so bent out of shape about Rhett sticking his di—"

"She's not some random *chick*," Jace spat, stalking away a few paces to try and calm himself down. Maybe.

None of us spoke, though. There had to be more to Jace's admission, and I for one was happy to wait him out and hear what was so special about the girl Rhett had picked up.

"I need to wake Rhett up," Jace said in a calmer voice, turning back to implore Florence and I with his eyes. "I need to ask him what happened after I left. What happened with *her*. Where he left her. I need to know."

Florence shook her head, beating me to it. "Whatever this is about, it can wait. Rhett needs to sleep. Let him."

Jace gave a hollow laugh, scrubbing his hands over his face. "It really can't, Flo. I *need* to know what happened between them last night." His expression was full of anguish. It was the deep kind of pain that only ever surfaced when he was drawing deeply on his old memories to write about... *Billie.*

"You're fucking with us," I muttered in disbelief.

Jace just winced, shaking his head. "God, I wish I was. That wasn't a groupie Rhett picked up at the club last night. It was *her*. Billie *fucking* Bellerose."

Well. Now I was interested.

I sat forward in my seat, even as Tom sidled up to Rhett's bedroom door. His ear was against it, his face full of glee. I'd never met a guy that thrived on gossip as hard as Tom Tucker.

"Guys, Rhett's awake," Tom reported, smirking over at Jace, "and he's not alone."

Fuck.

BILLIE

Rhett woke the second I tried to wriggle free of his embrace in the morning. His arms tightened, and it was strangely intimate, given we hadn't even kissed. Somehow in sleep, I'd moved closer, curling around him like a koala. Should I be embarrassed by that? Because I wasn't. I was just sad... because our time was up.

"I should go," I whispered reluctantly. "Before..."

Before Jace finds me here.

Rhett gave me another squeeze, then released his arm from around my body. He yawned and scrubbed his hand over his face, mussing up his turquoise hair.

"Might be too late," he admitted with a grimace. "I

don't usually sleep so heavily, but I think the *sneak out unnoticed* boat already sailed, Thorn."

His admission made me sit up, listening. Deep voices rumbled from outside the bedroom door, and I groaned my frustration. How were the rest of the band already awake? They can't have slept more than a few hours, especially whoever was auditioning for PornHub all night.

There was a frantic part of my mind, a part racing and torturing me, that had to know if it was Jace last night absolutely destroying some poor chick's vagina. I mean, it wasn't as if I thought he was a virgin rock star, but knowing he was with other women was the one thing I never allowed myself to think about. I'd already been half on the edge of giving up at times. I really didn't need the visuals.

Seemed I now had the soundtrack.

"We need to talk," Rhett said huskily, voice still laced with sleep. Thankfully, his voice was *almost* enough to distract me from the darker direction of my thoughts. "You fell asleep last night before we had a chance to discuss the next moves to keep you safe. I still don't even know what happened that had you running."

Right. *Right.* What the fuck was I doing stressing over the other asshole in the band when I had the much more pressing issue of the Ricci family hunting my ass down to murder me? Pushing myself up higher, I scooted back until I was sitting straight against the headboard of the bed. Hugging a pillow against me, I debated how much information I should reveal.

"I don't want to drag you into this," I whispered. "It's dangerous. And you don't deserve to pay for helping a damn stranger."

Rhett propped himself up even further, and I tried not to let my gaze drag along the bare muscles and ink lining his naked upper torso. He wasn't completely covered in tattoos, but he had enough that I could spend an hour or two exploring them with my hands... or my tongue.

Tatted-up rock star was apparently the shit that got my lady parts humming.

If only the timing was different. The timing. The past. Every fucking part of my tragic story.

"There're very few people in the world that can get to me," Rhett said, his eyes darkening as concern crept into his tone. "And you've already come back to my hotel. Word gets around about shit like that, so I'm in whether you want me to be or not. Might as well give me the whole story and see if my massive resource reach can help you move forward."

A sad laugh escaped me. "You're too good to be true, you know? A fucking savior."

I'd always been warned about "too good to be true," but I couldn't find it in myself to push him away. Even if a massive fallout and heartache were in the future for me.

Rhett sobered in an instant. "I'm no savior, Thorn. But I know what it's like to be dealt a rough hand. I dragged myself up from—" He broke off and shook his head. "Just trust me when I say that my help comes with no strings, but I'm not as altruistic as it might seem."

I doubted that very much, but I wasn't about to argue with him.

"I got kicked out of my crappy apartment last night," I said in a rush, hugging the pillow even tighter as memories crashed into me. "Couldn't pay the rent, of course. Good jobs are all but nonexistent at the moment. Especially unskilled ones. I don't even know why I came back to Siena, but I was sick of running from town to town."

Big fucking mistake on my part.

Rhett's gaze softened, even as his eyes darkened further, but he didn't interrupt. Instead, his long fingers reached out and grasped my hand, which was still clutching the pillow, offering his strength. Somehow...

some-fucking-how, this guy knew exactly when I needed a boost of strength and comfort.

"I never used to be so pathetic," I blurted out, the words having a double meaning. I was still talking about the lack of job and home, but also about needing his strength because my own was... depleted. Gone. "But the last few years have really kicked me in the tits. Anyway, another chick who lived in my building," I couldn't bring myself to say her name, "heard my eviction and offered me a lifeline. She had a job, good pay, close by. I didn't even know it was one of Angelo's family restaurants until it was too late to back out. Fuck, I wish I'd just dropped my apron and walked out the fucking door."

But then I wouldn't have met Rhett, and maybe it was worth it to have known someone this kind. Even if just for one night.

"Something happened at the restaurant?" he pressed gently, his voice a little raspy. He sounded upset, but it didn't show on his face.

I nodded. "Yeah. We got through the entire shift, and I was about to clock out and head back to my friend's place. She had a special dinner party that was the last booking of the night." The words stuck in my throat as I tried to forget the fear and darkness. "Something must have happened at the booking. I was getting changed, and I heard shots." I had to stop and clear my throat. "They killed her. Her and another man. Probably more. I saw them shoot him in the alley, and then they caught sight of me."

Rhett's grip on my hand tightened almost to the point of discomfort before he must have realized it and loosened his hold. "Then you ran to me?" he asked.

My chest tightened at the way he said *to me,* as if I'd been heading for him deliberately. My guardian angel.

"Not quite," I said with a shake of my head. "They caught me, and I ended up locked in an office by Angelo. They talked about shooting me, but I managed to wiggle out of the window when they left me alone. I ran until I found a crowd, hoping they wouldn't risk shooting someone else by accident."

At this point, Rhett pulled himself up fully on the bed, the sheets pooling low on his flat stomach, and I forced myself not to dead-eye stare at his dick area to see if he was naked under there. I couldn't see any clothes, but I had the sense that he wouldn't have slept naked without checking if it was okay with me. He just seemed the type.

As he scooted back to sit side by side with me, our hands still joined, I heard and felt the long sigh that escaped him. "Angelo Ricci is bad fucking news," I said into the silence. "And I won't let you end up as his next victim, Rhett."

Angelo Ricci had saved my life once. More than once, really. But that was a long time ago. Just like with Jace, he was no longer the boy I knew and loved.

"I need to get out of Siena," I said, trying to focus only on the current situation. "Get out and lay low. I know how to stay undetected; I'm just not sure if they're watching all the roads in and out of this town."

"No doubt. If not them, the cops and state troopers who work for them," Rhett added. "But I already have the perfect fucking idea. I just need to run it by the others."

It was my turn to grasp his hand like it was the last lifeline holding me to sanity. "Please tell me it doesn't involve Jace!"

He shifted to face me, a lopsided smile gracing his lips, the lip ring glinting at me from the small slivers of sunlight making it through the thick curtains. "Leave Jace to me. Bad blood or not, I'm sure he doesn't want to see you dead." A snort escaped me because I wasn't sure he comprehended the true depths of Jace's hatred toward me. Rhett's smile didn't falter though. "I'm just going to propose that you stay on the tour with us until our next stop. We head out of Siena tomorrow. This is our grassroots tour, as a way to give back after the past few record breaking releases, so we're playing a few smaller shows along the way, but then we hit New York, where we play three huge shows. I'm sure you can disappear in a city that size."

Hope bloomed so briefly in my chest. Fuck, I hated hope. The disappointment when it got dashed was near debilitating. But Rhett was right. New York would be the perfect place for me to escape to. If he could work out a way to bring me along on the tour.

Would Jace be able to look past his hatred toward me to help me one last time? To save my life? Eight years ago, the answer would have been easy. Effortless. But now, I wasn't so sure. In fact, I was pretty sure the answer would be *no*.

Licking my lips, I glanced to the closed door behind which those low voices still rumbled. Then my stomach growled.

"You need breakfast," Rhett announced. "You fell asleep before we could eat last night."

I wrinkled my nose. "Yeah, but you've done enough. I can work something out... something that won't cause tension in your band. The *last* thing I need is to be blamed for the hottest rock band on this planet breaking up."

Rhett's brows lifted, and his teeth tugged on that lip

piercing. Was it bad that I was thinking about how badly I wanted to do that myself? Ugh, focus Billie!

"You think it'd come to that?" he asked thoughtfully, then shook his head. "I don't."

My lips parted, but only a frustrated sound escaped. "Rhett... *Zep...*" I gave him a playful smile, and he chuckled in return. "You don't know Jace like I do. You sticking up for me in any capacity would be akin to tossing a hand grenade into the middle of your band. I'm not letting you do that."

He shook his head more firmly. "No, Thorn, *you* don't know Jace like *I* do. Yeah, it won't be pretty; I'm under no illusions about that. But he won't throw you back out there to be gunned down by the Ricci family goons, no matter how much of an argument he puts up."

I swallowed hard. "How can you be so sure?" My voice was small. Weak. But I wanted to believe he was right... because I had no other ideas. Facing Jace right now, *asking* for his help, it'd be like reopening an old, infected wound. But surely that was better than taking my chances on the street with no warm clothes, no money, no place to sleep.

"I'm *so sure*," Rhett whispered back, cupping my cheek to raise my face up so he could hold my gaze, "because every day of my life these last seven and a half years, I've played songs about a girl who broke my friend's heart. A girl he loved so hard he shaped his multimillion-dollar career around her. He hates you, he resents you, *now*. But I've never known a man who *loved so hard*. Regardless of the damage you're both carrying, when it comes down to the wire, he'll protect you."

Rhett's thumb swiped my cheek, and I realized my eyes were leaking. Fuck, I wanted him to be right. The acidic burn of dread creeping up my throat couldn't be convinced, though.

"If you're wrong—"

"I'm not wrong," he cut me off with a firm nod.

I narrowed my eyes. "*If you're wrong*, then I'll disappear. Okay? If Jace doesn't agree to let me hide out until New York, then I walk away, and he can write a whole new bestselling album about the audacious bitch who tried to plead for mercy."

Rhett grinned. "Dramatic, but also probably accurate. It won't happen, though. He'll agree. Trust me?"

I sniffed, biting the inside of my cheek. Trust him? He was a stranger. Worse than a stranger, he was the enemy. But he was also the guy who'd saved me when I was running for my life. He'd literally given me the shirt off his back, then held true to his word in giving me a warm bed for the night. No strings attached.

Sure, he might be a stranger, but so far... yeah, I trusted him. He had yet to prove that I couldn't.

The bedroom door flew open before I could give Rhett my answer, and the breath in my lungs solidified to ice under Jace's glacial glare.

"I fucking *knew* I could hear *her* voice. I thought I was clear with you, Rhett, fuck her once, then throw her the hell out." His sneer was pure hatred toward me. "It's all she's good for, anyway."

That cut deep. But what did I expect? I'd given him plenty of reason to think that about me and held no desire to change the narrative now.

"Careful, Adams," I purred back, finding my sass had returned after a great night's sleep, "your jealousy is showing."

The flash of cold loathing across Jace's face sent a sharp stab of panic through me. Panic and soul-deep regret. But the past was just that. *The past.* It was high time we all moved on... no matter how much it hurt.

BILLIE

Jace's fist curled at his side, and a quick burst of fear zapped through me. Surely, he hadn't changed *that* much, though? The Jace I knew would rather cut his hand off than hit a woman. But eight years was a lot of time. Fame would change anyone, I guessed.

"Jace!" Rhett snapped, climbing out of bed in his sweatpants—aw, damn—and placing a hand on Jace's bare chest. He'd added ink since I last saw him. Not as much as Rhett, but the full sleeve was detailed and definitely suited his new image. "Get out of my room, bro. Seriously. Get the fuck out."

Rhett was a few inches shorter than my ex, but I'd

bet my panties that he could take Jace in a fight. It was just a gut feeling.

"I'm not going *anywhere*," Jace snarled. "Not until *she is gone*. I told you, Rhett, I fucking *told you*—"

"Enough!" Rhett shouted. "Get out." He gave Jace a firm shove, and the taller guy stumbled backwards. Rhett didn't fuck around, just yanked the bedroom door shut and flipped the lock. With a sigh, he turned back to face me. "You sure you don't want to give me your side of the story, Thorn?"

I wet my lips, trying to slow my racing pulse. "I'm sure," I whispered back.

Rhett nodded like he hadn't expected anything else. "Take a few minutes to freshen up," he suggested, nodding to the bathroom. "I'll do what I can to smooth things over. Then we can discuss how to smuggle you out of Siena."

He'd grabbed a t-shirt and slipped out of the bedroom again before I could protest. Groaning, I sagged back against the pillows, covering my face while I screamed silently. There was only one way out of this room, and it was through Jace. So I might as well take a shower and come up with a game plan.

I'd fallen asleep in Rhett's t-shirt, and I didn't want to overstep by helping myself to another one. So I scrubbed myself clean in the shower, making extra sure there was none of Liz's blood left on my skin, then got dressed again in the same clothes.

Thankfully there was a spare hotel toothbrush, so I gave my teeth a solid scrub and raked my fingers through my hair. There wasn't much I could do to make it look good, though. It was as it always was. Unremarkable, mousey, flat. At least it didn't tangle easily, so that was something.

When I'd stalled as long as possible, I straightened my spine, whispered a quick pep talk to myself, and stepped into the lion's den. I'd come up with a game plan while in the shower; I just had to follow through without losing my nerve.

The heated argument between Rhett and Jace halted the instant I exited Rhett's bedroom, and all eyes turned to me. I mean *all* eyes. As well as Jace and Rhett, there was a pink-haired punk girl on the sofa, a skinny guy sitting near her with excitement all over his face, and one other guy.

That guy made me do a quick double take. At a glance, I'd have thought Aquaman was chilling on the couch in a pair of ripped jeans and a vintage band tee. *Hot* Aquaman, not the blond cartoon version. His expression was totally unreadable, his body language relaxed as he inspected me from head to toe.

Whatever he saw, he seemed unimpressed. Bored, even. It threw me off slightly.

"Do you have something to say, or are you just thinking about fucking the rest of my band too?"

Jace's acidic words cut through my distraction, and I ripped my eyes away from Aquaman. However angry Jace had been last night, it was ten times worse now that he thought I'd slept with Rhett. Which, I had. But we hadn't fucked, and that was all Jace really cared about.

I gritted my teeth and forced myself to show some spine. "Yeah, I do. I need to get out of Siena undetected, and Rhett offered to let me tag along with your tour until New York. Is that going to be a problem for you, Adams?"

Jace stared at me, dumbfounded for a minute. Then he barked a sharp laugh. "You're joking, right? You must be joking because I would rather eat broken glass than help you out, Billie."

I folded my arms across my chest, trying to hide the way my hands trembled. The anxiety was gnawing at me so hard I worried I might vomit. But I couldn't show Jace any weakness right now. He'd tear me to shreds.

"Well, your dentist won't be very happy with you," I replied with a slight quiver in my voice, "because I already accepted Rhett's offer. Or did I misunderstand this being a band? Maybe it's just the Jace Adams show, and these guys are your employees." I tilted my head to the side, narrowing my eyes.

He glared daggers back at me, knowing I was positioning him between a rock and a hard place. I might not follow any entertainment gossip about Bellerose, but *every* band had tension over their biggest star acting like he ran the show. Didn't they? Okay sure, I was pinning my tactics on stereotypes and guesses. I had to hope it would work, though. It was the best I had.

"Jace, I'm not sending her away," Rhett said firmly, his expression pained as his friend shifted attention to him. "You didn't see her when I found her. She was covered in blood, and—"

"Blood?" Jace whipped his glare back to me, his eyes scanning me from head to toe. "Seems fine to me."

I gritted my teeth. "It wasn't my blood," I growled. "But it will be, if you don't get me out of Siena. Is that what you want, Adams? You want me dead? Because that'll be what happens if you kick me out right now." I gave a bitter laugh. "He probably has someone waiting for me outside the hotel by now. I'll likely catch a bullet before I make it half a block."

The big guy on the sofa sat forward, his thick forearms resting on his ripped denim jeans. "Who?" His voice was a deep, raspy sound that sent a shiver right through me.

My mouth went dry, my eyes returning to Jace like a magnet. I didn't want to do this... It was only going to make things a hundred times worse.

"No one," Jace sneered when I said nothing. "She's making shit up, preying on your victim complex, Rhett."

"Shut the fuck up, Jace; let her talk." Rhett gave me a reassuring nod, urging me to tell the truth.

My palms were sweating something awful now, and my pulse was thumping so hard I was getting lightheaded. If I didn't tell him... *fuck*. My eyes darted from Rhett to the big man, then quickly over the pink-haired girl and skinny guy who hadn't said a single word since I'd emerged. Finally, I returned my gaze to Jace. I *had* to believe he was still in there somewhere. That he still cared if I lived or died. Even just the smallest bit.

"Angelo," I whispered. "Angelo is trying to kill me, Jace. Please. I need help, just to get out of the city. The second we reach New York, I'm gone. You'll never see me again."

If I'd thought he was cold before, it was nothing on the chill that settled over him as Angelo's name left my mouth. Not just over him, but over the entire room.

At first no one else reacted, but then I noticed some subtle movements. Rhett was closer to me than he had been a second ago, and Aquaman on the couch was sitting straighter, looking a little like a coiled panther about to leap forward.

The only two not moving were punk chick and skinny guy, who continued grinning so hard it was actually starting to creep me out.

"You've got to be fucking kidding me right now. Angelo? You never could leave that bastard's side," Jace seethed. "You made your bed with him, princess, and now it's time to get back in and take it like the *whore* you are."

Against my better judgment, I flinched. I wasn't sure I'd been called a whore so many times in my entire life, but from his perspective—given our history—I supposed it did look bad.

"Whether you believe me or not," I started, finding some of the strength in my voice waning. Why was this happening to me? Seriously. Who had I killed in my last life? Karma was majorly punishing me for *something*. "Last night was the first time I've seen Angelo in almost seven years. Somehow, fate thinks it's fucking funny to reunite me with the worst parts of my past all in one night."

His jaw twitched, and it took him a few minutes to

form words again. "I *don't* believe a fucking word out of your lying mouth." Shocker. "But since you've already conned one of the few people in the world I give a shit about, then I guess it's your lucky day. I won't fight with Rhett over something as *insignificant* as you. But I have rules." His jaw was so tight that those last words came out as a snarl.

I could feel Rhett's heat, and I turned to find he was closer than ever. "What rules?" he asked, his focus firmly on his friend and bandmate.

Jace pulled his enigmatic gaze from my face then, and I let out a ragged breath, my heart slamming in my chest at the intensity of being locked in the eyes of a predator. It was probably lucky he did shift his gaze... My faked strength could only last so long.

"She will need her own damn room. Not yours," Jace started. "Out of sight and with a clear purpose as we make our way across the country." Without looking at me, a sneer lifted the corner of his lips. "You said she's got nothing. No money, clothes, decency, morals..." Funny fucking asshole this one. "She can't do her usual and trade sex for board; I won't fucking tolerate her sleeping around with our crew. So, she's going to work to pay her way. I heard the cleaning crew has an opening."

He thought he was punishing me, but he'd just

handed me a fucking gift. I'd feel much better if I could work off some of the debt I owed Rhett. Already, the thought of *earning* my keep was loosening the tension in my spine.

"No," the turquoise-haired guitarist snapped. "Billie has been through enough. She doesn't have to *work* in order to deserve a helping ha–"

"It's okay," I interrupted quickly, trying to ignore the sour taste in my mouth when he called me *Billie* instead of *Thorn*. When I placed my hand on Rhett's arm, his attention jerked toward me. "I would prefer to work on my way there. It will keep me busy, and I won't feel like I owe you as much. I mean, I already owe you my life, probably, but this goes a small way toward repaying your kindness."

Jace scoffed, and I jerked my head toward him, some of my fire returning now that it seemed I was going to be safe for the next few days. "You better cut that shit," I shot at him, and then for some stupid reason, I decided to remind him of a few factors that might scare the asshole. Even if I never intended to follow through on one threat. "Or I might start exploring the legalities of you using *my* name and *our* life story to make billions of dollars. I also seem to recall co-writing a few songs that somehow appeared on the radio without my permission."

Jace's expression didn't change, but his eyes turned darker. The magenta-haired emo girl gasped, shooting a shocked look at Jace, and Aquaman's brow dipped in a frown. I guessed this was news to them, then.

The skinny creep on the couch leaned forward, though, some of the amusement on his face fading. "Bellerose has everything tied up legally," he said, his voice too smooth. Matched the leer in his expression. That and the overly slicked back hair would have been huge red flags if I'd ever ran into this dude in a dark alley.

"Public perception is everything," I told him softly. "My story would interest many people when it comes to the most famous rock band in the world. Don't you think? Wouldn't Page Six just love to hear all about how Jace had *help* on that single that shot Bellerose to stardom?"

No doubt the rest of the band thought I was an asshole for threatening not just Jace but all of them. Rhett's was the only opinion I could find myself giving a shit about, though, and when I caught eyes with the guitarist, I gave a tiny shake of my head in an effort to reassure him that I was bluffing. The gesture was small enough not to ruin my threat, but he understood and seemed to relax.

He was the only one, though. The skinny creep leapt

to his feet, a frantic look on his face. "Could you give me a minute with the band, *Billie*?" he asked like he was forcing polite words out, sneering my name in lieu of screaming obscenities.

I was tempted to tell him to go fuck himself simply because he gave me bad vibes. But Rhett sighed and touched a gentle hand to the small of my back. "Head back into my room, Thorn. I'll bring breakfast in when it arrives."

BILLIE

The Bellerose "team meeting" took way longer than I'd expected. For a while I just waited, thinking it would be a quick chat around whether Jace had left them all open to being sued for withholding royalties and denying co-writer credits. But eventually I got bored with trying to listen through the door—fucking penthouse had to have solid doors that muffled the words of each speaker—and turned on a movie to watch.

Rhett came in about twenty minutes later carrying a room service tray.

"Sorry, Thorn," he murmured with a pained smile. "Shouldn't be too much longer. Tom is just... being thorough. And our legal team has no sense of urgency; you know how lawyers are."

I shrugged. "Not really, but I'll take your word for it." I licked my lips, smelling delicious food on the tray. "Rhett... you know I was only—"

"Nope," he cut me off, shaking his head firmly. "Don't even say it. I *know* what you were doing, but it doesn't change the fact that Jace screwed you. That needs to be rectified, and I intend to make sure it happens."

My jaw dropped. "What?" My question was a strangled squeak. "Rhett, I don't actually want—"

This time he physically covered my mouth with his hand, even though his eyes were soft. "You contributed to the Bellerose debut album, and you deserve compensation. End of story. It won't get sorted today, but maybe by the time we reach New York you'll be in a stronger position to start a new life."

I groaned, already dreading how much the rest of the band must be hating me. But with Rhett's hand still covering my mouth, it sounded a whole shitload more sexual than regretful. He definitely thought the same because his eyes widened, and his teeth tugged on that piercing at the side of his lip. Dammit. Who knew Jace's bandmates would be *so hot*?

"I should get back out there," he murmured in a

husky voice, slowly removing his hand from my mouth. Did I just imagine it, or did his thumb brush my lower lip deliberately? Shit, maybe I was due for my period; my hormones were going nuts. I couldn't remember my last one, but my IUD meant my period was sporadic at best. I'd missed more meals than I could count in the last ten years to keep up with my birth control, and it was never a regret. The alternative would be way worse than hunger. My world was too fucked up to bring a baby into it.

When I snapped out of my darker thoughts, Rhett was staring at me. Had he said something? Crap, could he see how distracted I kept getting?

"Um, if me being in here is causing more drama than you need, I could just... go for a walk or something," I offered with a weak shrug.

Rhett's brow dipped. "And risk one of the Ricci thugs snatching you? Not a chance. You're fine here; I'm just embarrassed about how Jace is acting. Even if *everything* he's said about you is true—and I'm no longer so convinced—he's still being an asshole."

I shrugged, shifting backwards to give myself a chance to catch my breath. "I'm not shocked. I actually expected worse, to be fair."

Rhett didn't seem comforted but murmured something about wrapping things up quickly. He left the room, closing the door softly behind himself. Not before I caught a tiny snippet of the conversation in the living room, though.

"Shut the fuck up, Tucker," a deep, gravelly voice snapped.

The creep must be Tucker because he gave a slick laugh. "Calm down, Gray, I was—"

His words faded into muffled sounds as the door clicked shut, and I sat there a moment. Gray. That had to be Aquaman's name. What about the girl? I hadn't missed the distrust and judgment in her eyes as she'd silently watched my showdown with Jace. No way was she taking my side in whatever they were discussing out there.

My stomach rumbled, so I got comfy in Rhett's bed and watched an awesome animated show while I ate my breakfast. The food was excellent, but the show was even better. About a girl in an academy for supernatural creatures. If my hate-filled ex wasn't twenty feet away trying to plot a way to make my body disappear down the hotel's trash chute, it'd be the best morning I'd had in a *long* time.

Hell, even with Jace spitting insults, this had been a pretty great morning so far. I could put up with his shit if I got parmesan scrambled eggs and crispy bacon on the regular. And the coffee... yum. So much better than the bitter, watery crap I usually got from a vending machine.

I made it through five episodes of my new favorite show before the door opened once more and Rhett gave me a tight smile.

I arched a brow in question, and he closed the door behind himself. In his hand, he held a small stack of clothes, mostly all black.

"I borrowed some clothes from Florence," he told me, placing the garments down on the edge of the bed. "You guys seem like a similar size."

That was… thoughtful. Or did he just want his t-shirt back? Maybe me wearing his clothes was aggravating the situation with Jace… After all, my ex already assumed we'd fucked last night. Maybe we should have. If I'm going to be condemned, I may as well actually *do* the crime. Right?

"Thanks," I offered instead, sliding my legs out of the bed and brushing some crumbs from his sheets. I grabbed the clothes and slipped into the bathroom to change. Florence had donated a pair of ripped black jeans and a tight black crop top that just barely squeezed over my boobs. I might be skinny—due to my current state of poverty—but my tits had barely budged a cup size since I'd fallen on hard times.

I looked at my reflection in the mirror, releasing a

long sigh. My appearance was perfectly fine from the front. Cute, even. But there was no way I could go out there with my back so exposed. I twisted slightly to peer at my scars in the mirror, then grimaced.

Nope. No way. For one thing, I didn't want to explain to Rhett—or anyone—how I'd gotten them. For another, I badly didn't want Jace to see them. I'd lain in that ICU hospital bed for a *month*, waiting for him to walk through the door. Every time my door opened, I'd foolishly thought it would be him, but it never was. So fuck him. He didn't care *then*; I sure as fuck didn't need his pity *now*..

Pulling open the bathroom door, I braced my hand against the frame to eliminate the chance of Rhett seeing my back. I was lucky he hadn't seen it last night when I ripped my bloody shirt off, but it'd been dark and he'd probably been trying *not* to look.

"Damn," he murmured, his eyes sweeping over me, "you look so fucking hot, Thorn." The instant those words left his mouth, his eyes widened and he cringed. "Fuck, sorry, that was meant to be inside my head. Uh, I meant to say, Flo's clothes seem to fit you okay?"

My cheeks were warm with a blush, and I dragged my teeth over my lower lip. "Uh, yeah. But... could I maybe borrow another t-shirt? I don't... um..." Glancing down at my exposed midriff, I made a gesture to try and explain without *really* explaining.

"Yeah, of course." Rhett stunned me speechless by pulling *his own* shirt—another band tee, this one with the sleeves ripped off—over his head and tossing it over to me.

I caught it, but just gaped at him as he casually reached into his massive suitcase—that he hadn't bothered unpacking—to find another.

"I didn't mean the one you were wearing," I squeaked, the warmth of the fabric in my hand reminding me it had literally *just* been on his body.

Rhett looked over at me with an odd expression, then tugged another shirt over his head. "Yeah, but that color will look great on you." It was such a casual argument that I had nothing to respond. "Unless... was that too far? It's clean, but I can get you a different one." He reached out to take the shirt back, but I clutched it to my chest.

"No, this one is fine," I said quickly, shaking it out and tugging it over my head. I glanced back at the bathroom mirror and released a sigh to see the scars on my back were totally covered.

Rhett stared for a moment, and this time I didn't shift awkwardly under his gaze. The fabric of his shirt was still warm against my skin and smelled of him, the spice of his aftershave with underlying smoke. It was weirdly intimate and did nothing to quell the building attraction between us.

"So… what now?" I asked, breaking the tension before I could do something stupid. Like blow him.

He gave me another lingering look, then swept a hand over his messy turquoise hair. "Uh, I'm supposed to go get you set up with our crew. If that's still cool with you? Because I'm *more* than happy to just hide you in my room."

I grinned, appreciative of the offer. "Nah, I was serious before. I'm *happy* to work in exchange for your help. Although I have no idea what your *cleaning crew* even does, given you're on a road tour."

Pushing my feet back into my worn-out shoes, I followed Rhett out of his room. The living area was empty save for Aquaman—*Gray*—who seemed to be in exactly the same seat as earlier. He wore big noise-canceling headphones with his head resting on the back of the sofa. His eyes were shut, but the drumsticks in his hands beat out a silent tune on his thigh, indicating he was awake.

"That's Grayson," Rhett told me, jerking a thumb toward the big guy as we passed before exiting the penthouse suite entirely. "As for the cleaning crew, uh, you've got a good point. Each venue has its own staff who *clean.* On top of that we have a massive stage crew who drive the multitude of trucks to each venue. You have no fucking idea how many people and how much crap it takes to put a tour on, even a grassroots one. But there's a smaller cleaning crew for the tour buses. We had a security incident a few years ago, and us musicians are nothing if not superstitious. So, for the sake of our own paranoia, we keep our personal cleaning crew small."

The elevator arrived, and Rhett swiped his card to access one of the lower floors. Much, *much* lower.

"And this exclusive cleaning crew just happens to have an opening?" I wrinkled my nose at him. "How convenient."

He cracked a smile. "Trust me, it would have been more convenient if they *didn't* have an opening. Then I would have an excuse to keep you all to myself until we reach New York."

Holy shit. I could have sworn the temperature in the elevator just ratcheted up by twenty degrees because suddenly my palms were sweating. Maybe that was my excuse for the way I shifted closer to Rhett, tipping my head back to meet his... eyes. Yeah. Eyes. I was just trying to make *eye contact.*

The elevator ding and slide of the doors jolted us both out of the little trance we'd slipped into.

Fuck. Had we been about to kiss? That would have gone down *great* with Jace.

"Stupid, fast elevators," Rhett grumbled under his breath, taking my hand in a casually intimate gesture as he led me down the corridor.

My cheeks were so hot they had to be red, and I was grinning like a love-sick fool behind him. I needed to get my shit under control before I embarrassed myself. Rhett probably had girls throwing themselves at him every time he left the hotel; I didn't need to become one of them. A groupie.

Rhett stopped in front of a door and knocked a couple of times. A yawning, dark-haired woman, maybe in her mid-thirties or slightly older, answered and didn't look surprised.

"This is her, then?" She asked the question of Rhett but was already looking at me from head to toe. "She looks like a groupie."

Rhett gave a small growl. "She's wearing Flo's clothes, so careful what you say, Dora."

The woman, Dora, just flashed him a grin. "Calm down, Silver. You got a name, hon?"

I nodded, pasting on a polite smile. "Yeah, I'm Billie B—uh, Billie Thorn. Nice to meet you." I put my hand out for Dora to shake, and Rhett gave a small sigh. He nodded, though, so I suspected I'd just passed some kind of test.

"I'm Dora, team leader. Let's go introduce you to your roommate, Kristie." She stepped out of the room, starting down the hall once more.

Rhett was frowning, though. "She's sharing with Kristie? I thought—"

"You thought we could magically make a vacant room appear in this sold-out hotel?" Dora cut him off, tossing a skeptical look over her shoulder. "Or did you forget the mighty Bellerose is playing in Siena tonight. *The town it all began in.* Half the city is booked out for the concert." Her sarcasm was *thick,* and it made me like her instantly.

I grinned, giving Rhett's hand a squeeze. "It's fine, *Zep.* I would happily sleep in a bathtub if it meant getting out of here unnoticed."

His expression remained tight, but his lips twitched at my teasing name for him. "It's only for a few days," he murmured. "I'll push the lawyers to work faster."

I shrugged. "It's already Friday; you and I both know they won't do shit until next week. It's fine, though. Seriously." Okay, we both knew that the *Bellerose* lawyers were likely on call twenty-four-seven but I'd bet my panties that Tom told them not to hurry.

Dora gave us a curious look, then rapped her

knuckles on another door. The three of us stood there, waiting, but no one answered. Dora heaved a sigh and knocked harder.

Eventually, a half-asleep girl maybe my age, or a touch younger, answered the door. "Fuck, Dora, do you know what time it is?"

"Yes, I do. And I don't care if I woke you up. This is Billie; she's your new roommate."

The girl yawned, scrubbing a hand over her face. Then her eyes widened when she saw Rhett. She looked from Rhett to me, then down to where his hand still held mine... and her eyes narrowed.

"Billie," she repeated, her gaze returning to my face with a touch of... *venom*. "How fun."

No need to wonder about the sudden vibe she was throwing off. I'd gone from roommate to competition in a heartbeat, and she would be out to destroy me at any convenient moment.

Rhett's hand tightened on mine, a small squeeze of reassurance, and then he released me. "I'll have a phone sent to your room with my number programmed in," he murmured as he leaned closer. "You call me if you have any issues."

I nodded, hating that there was a pang of unease in my chest at the thought of Rhett leaving me. I couldn't do that. I couldn't grow attached to a rock star from

Bellerose. All of this magic would be over for me in a few days.

It was time to stand on my own.

As gently as I could, I extracted my hand from his hold and took a tiny step away. The separation felt huge, but every part of me knew this was the right thing to do.

Okay, maybe not every part, but enough that I stayed my course and didn't return to Rhett's comforting warmth.

"I'll check in on you later," he assured me, and I swallowed roughly as I nodded. It was the best I could do.

When he turned to leave, I forced myself not to let my gaze linger on his broad shoulders and visible tatts. It was time now to deal with my current situation: cleaning crew, new boss, and a roommate who was probably figuring out how to stab me in my sleep.

But at least I wasn't dead.

There was always a silver lining. And this time it was more than Rhett *Silver*.

Though that was a nice one too.

BILLIE

"Alright, Billie," Dora said, snapping into work mode despite the sleepiness still filling her brown eyes. "We don't usually start until lunch time—everyone sleeps late after a concert—but seeing as we're all awake and tomorrow is a road day, it's probably best we get started early."

Kristie snorted. "I'm going back to bed. I'll be down at twelve as planned." She shot me a dark look before turning back to her boss. "Just make sure she doesn't touch my stuff."

She swung around to leave, slamming the door behind her. Dora rolled her eyes at the now closed door before she focused on me again.

"I don't have a uniform in your size at the moment, since we weren't expecting any new staff, but you can just wear that for today and I'll get it sorted."

Falling into the role I'd played hundreds of times over the years, I focused on the new temporary job in my life, giving Dora all of my attention. It was always the same; they went over the role, the rules, and what was expected of me.

"Hotel takes care of their rooms, the bulk of the stage crew handle sets and the larger items on the trucks, leaving us to focus mostly on the band themselves. We handle their special requests, and clean their tour buses when we're on the road," she said. "We stock up their fridges, take their laundry, and again, get them anything they've specially requested for the day. We leave tomorrow after the show, so today we will be getting the bus ready for departure. I'll be there to make sure you're cleaning to the standard expected, since I have no idea of your experience."

"I've worked as a cleaner before," I said quickly. "It was in a hotel. Maybe only three-star, but I never slacked on keeping everything as clean as I could."

Dora didn't really seem to care, despite her previous statement, since she didn't even ask me what hotel. "I'm going to get ready now. You can either head into your room or just wait here for me."

"I'll wait here," I said without a second thought. "I don't think Kristie will take kindly to being woken again."

Dora didn't bother to deny it; instead, she just smiled and shrugged. "Nature of the business, unfortunately. When you work for rock stars, everyone is always trying to snag one of them. But we don't ever sleep with them. It's in the rules. In our contract."

Her eyes dragged along the bare skin of my arms, exposed by Rhett's shirt. "I'm not sure of the rules they want for you; I don't think they've got a contract for you to sign. It's my understanding this is just a temporary position? But, anyway, you don't have to worry about Kristie. Her bark is worse than her bite."

Somehow, I doubted that.

Dora disappeared back into her room then, and I cooled my heels in the corridor while trying not to think about the last twenty-four hours. It honestly felt like a lifetime ago I was evicted and ended up in a Ricci restaurant before ultimately finding Rhett. Things really could change in an instant, and the jury was still out whether this change was one that would fuck me up for a long time.

There had been a point when I'd expected to die from a broken heart... not to mention a broken body and soul. As dramatic as it sounded, I'd been destroyed by what happened with Jace and then Angelo and then the… the day I couldn't mentally revisit, as I doubted I'd have the strength to drag myself from the depth of hell a second time.

Running into Jace was a shot I hadn't seen coming, and I could only hope that our time together would be brief enough that once we made it to New York, I'd be gone and so would the pain and memories.

Yeah. Right.

When Dora returned, her brown hair was slicked up in a high ponytail, face makeup free, and she looked very refreshed. She wore plain black pants and a white shirt that had the Bellerose logo on it. Her shoes were sensible black sneakers, and I was glad I still had my own sensible shoes on.

She didn't speak when we made it to the elevators, and I noted that they weren't the main bank that I'd used last night with Rhett. These were larger, looking more like a service entrance. When they opened, Dora hurried in, and I followed.

We remained silent as she hit the button for B, which I assumed was for *basement*. At no point did she ask about me, and I was actually grateful for her lack of "giving a fuck." It was exactly what I needed.

When we stepped out into what looked like a massive underground parking lot, she took a sharp left, and we moved along a small pathway until we reached a nondescript door. It all but blended into the surrounding wall, and I wondered what was on the other side.

It opened as soon as Dora swiped a card over the security panel. When we entered the next space, I couldn't help but look around, worried that we were about to head outside. I wasn't sure what instructions Rhett had given the cleaning crew supervisor, and I'd really hate to get her killed ten minutes into knowing me.

Maybe it was crazy to imagine that Angelo had people surrounding this building, but it was stupid to completely underestimate a family as powerful as that one. Better to expect the worst and be pleasantly surprised, rather than the opposite.

Luckily, on the other side was just a massive parking lot, seemingly just for buses, if the three massive, shiny rigs there were any indication. They were parked in a row before a secured garage door. "These are our buses," Dora said, speaking for the first time. "The largest of the three is for Bellerose." She pointed to the first in the line, and I took in the futuristic looking model. It was black, silver, and purple, and while there wasn't super-obvious branding for the band on it, it still looked like a famous band's bus. The windows down the sides were heavily tinted, and even the front windshield was darker than usual. "The second bus is the rest of their support band, backup singers, and whoever else helps them put on an amazing show. And the third is for security and the remaining crew, which includes us. You'll get a bunk in there since there's one or two to spare."

"Perfect," I said, excited that I'd have a safe space to sleep for another few days.

Dora nodded. "Yep. Come on, let's get going." She smiled wider as we approached the first bus. "You know, I really love when we stay in this particular hotel. They're popular with the band set because of all their security, which includes these bus spaces away from the public. It really makes our job easier. We'll have the entire day to get these three buses ready for tomorrow."

"I've never worked for anyone famous," I admitted. "I can only imagine it leads to some issues when they're being all but stalked by the general population."

Dora snorted. "You have no idea. I've woken up to groupies in my bed before. They don't seem to care who they get close to, all in the small hope that we are the path to Bellerose."

"Seriously?" I gasped. "How do they get past security?"

"It's rare, but it happens. They had an issue for a

year or so with members of their security allowing groupies in for... well, whatever they were exchanging for it. Same with the cleaning crew. It's why they now basically keep the same vetted crew for everything. It's been fairly peaceful since then, but the occasional fan manages to find their way inside."

I couldn't imagine living a life like that. Mine had definitely been hard, but at least I never expected people would use me to get in with my famous friend. No wonder Jace was so guarded. Everyone else in this life was probably just out for his money and fame.

Add that to his already panty-melting face and voi—

No! Billie. Get your horny self together. Jace fucking hated me, and considering he had now been conditioned to think everyone was using him, I knew he'd never trust my motives. Best to just wipe him from mind and get back to the real world as soon as possible.

Thankfully, Dora put me to work soon after. The third bus we entered was stocked up with all the cleaning supplies in a set of cupboards under the kitchen table. "You can start on the second bus," she told me. "And I'll come in and check your work after an hour. I'll focus on Bellerose's since I need it done to the top level. Mr. Adams likes things done to a high standard."

I hid a smirk. Jace'd had just the faintest touch of germaphobia since he was eight, after he'd caught a bacterial infection that made him shit his pants in public. Explosively.

He really should be nicer to me; I had some stories that the media would kill for.

"No worries." And it really wasn't. I didn't need to see where the band slept while on the road. Not to mention where they possibly brought their groupies. They might stop groupies from *sneaking* in, but that didn't mean they weren't *invited*. As demonstrated *loudly* last night.

Shaking off the memories of PornHub screams in HD, I made my way into the second bus in the lineup. Dora spent about five minutes running over the basics, but there wasn't that much to it. Just vacuum, mop, dust, wipe everything down, make up beds with freshly starched linens, and restock the two tiny bathrooms. "We will restock the food later," she said as she headed toward the exit. "Call out if you need anything."

When she was gone, I released a long breath. Weirdly, since this wasn't a legit job, I still had some new-job nerves. It was always the same until I settled into a job and understood how it all worked.

It was nice to be on my own, though, no one looking over my shoulder as I went about my tasks.

Well used to working quickly and efficiently, I got straight into it, taking extra care to make everything shiny. I polished the windows, the table, and walls and made sure the small kitchenette was sparkling too. When I moved to the bunks, I saw that there were ten along both sides of the wall, each not much bigger than a coffin. Lucky I wasn't claustrophobic, if I had to sleep in something similar in the other bus.

There were clean sheets and bedding in my cart of supplies, so I got to work changing out the current sheets that were bundled there, clearly from the last time they slept in here. When the beds were all made, I was starting to get a little hot and sweaty, but after a quick sip of water from the tap, I continued on.

Two hours later, the bus was as shiny as I could make it. The small bathroom had all the toiletries restocked, and I made sure not a trace of dirt or dust remained.

"Billie!"

I turned at the exclamation from behind me.

Dora stood at the top of the stairs, looking around with a huge smile on her face. "I am impressed," she said slowly, still taking it all in. "Nice to see a young person not afraid of hard work."

I almost laughed since she didn't look much older

than me. "I appreciate this job more than I can say." It was literally a life saver.

"Well, *I* appreciate the hard work, even if you are leaving us again in a few days." She glanced down at her watch. "Kristie should be here in a minute with the food and beverage supplies, and then we can break for lunch."

The rest of the afternoon disappeared quickly, and although Kristie and I weren't fast friends, she was considerably less frosty now that she'd woken up properly. Or maybe because Rhett wasn't standing right beside me holding my hand like we were... uh... well, more than strangers.

Dora eventually told us we were done, and Kristie raced off almost before Dora finished her sentence. The support crew all had backstage passes for the concerts, so she'd already told me she was heading to change and do her makeup.

"Are you going to the show, Billie?" Dora asked as we closed up the buses. She made sure all three were securely locked while I waited.

I shook my head. "Nah, it's not my scene. If Kristie is going, I might take advantage of the quiet to take a bath and get an early night's sleep."

Dora smiled as she pressed the freight elevator call button. "Smart girl. I plan to do the same."

The display panel dinged, and the doors to the left side elevator slid open smoothly. Unfortunately, the carriage wasn't empty, and my breath caught as a pair of hard blue eyes met my startled gaze.

Fucking hell.

Refusing to acknowledge the way Jace made me feel, I shifted my gaze to Rhett instead. But he was locked in a heated debate with the girl, Florence, and hadn't seen me. The big drummer dude, who was taller than Jace by an inch, gave me a curious glance as he exited the elevator but said nothing.

"Where are you going, Billie?" Jace barked when I tried to follow Dora into the car they'd just vacated.

Rhett's head snapped around, his eyes finding me immediately as a smile lit up his face.

"Um," I stalled, hoping the doors would fucking close already. "To my room?"

Why the hell that came out as a question, I had no clue.

Jace's responding laugh was totally devoid of amusement or warmth. "Like fuck you are. You're coming with us."

I bit the inside of my cheek, reaching out to stab at the "close doors" button.

"No thanks," I chirped, desperate to keep things casual. "But break a leg and all that."

Finally, the elevator started to close. Finally! But stupid fucking Jace just stopped them with a heavy hand and furious glare.

"I wasn't asking, Billie." The low, angry pitch to his voice sent a deep shiver through me, and my mouth went dry. Shit. He scared me, but also turned me right the hell on.

I had issues, that was no secret. But I wouldn't let Jace Adams push me around like some kind of... slave. Fuck. That.

Rhett's heavy exhale made me frown, and I looked over to him for some kind of guidance. What should I do? How did I handle this volatile, angry version of my childhood sweetheart? Rhett gave me a small nod, silently telling me to just do what Jace wanted. I think.

"Have fun, Billie," Dora muttered as I reluctantly stepped back out of the elevator. "Don't stay out too late."

Without Jace holding the doors, they closed easily and cut off my last chance of escape. Damn it. Worse still, Jace had already turned away, striding through the underground parking lot like I'd imagined that whole interaction. If not for Rhett hanging back and draping his arm over my shoulders, I'd have been questioning if it was all a hallucination.

"Sorry," Rhett said quietly as we followed the rest of

the band over to their blacked-out SUVs. "I have no clue what's going through his head, but I'm selfishly excited to have you at our show tonight."

If I was perfectly honest, I was kind of excited myself. I would never admit it, not even under torture, but I was dying to see Bellerose in concert. To see Jace sing those songs we'd worked on together... back when he loved me. His Rose.

BILLIE

Rhett ushered me into the second SUV while Jace took the first one with Florence and her slimy boyfriend. I was glad for the reprieve but a moment later found myself squeezed between Rhett and the Bellerose drummer, Grayson.

The SUV had another row of seats, which were occupied by a craggy-faced security guard and a guitar case. Apparently, Rhett didn't trust the roadies to bring his baby to the concert venue.

Awkward silence filled the vehicle as our driver started the engine up, following the other car out of the underground parking. I tried to make myself as small as possible, but there was only so small a human being could make themself. And neither Rhett or Grayson seemed to care, so eventually I gave up and accepted the fact that my whole right side was pressed against a man I'd not even spoken to.

"Um, so... hi," I said awkwardly. "We haven't really met. I'm Billie."

His head swiveled toward me, and being so close to him for the first time, I finally noticed a very faint scar on the right side of his full lower lip. "I know."

That was it. Just *I know,* and he turned his face away once more. At a loss for words, I simply stared at his profile for a moment. He had facial hair, not long enough to be a beard but longer than just casual stubble. It suited his vibe, with his slightly longish hair that was tied up in a looped-over ponytail, showcasing the undercut sides. I usually hated long hair on men, but this really seemed to work for him.

Rhett gave my knee a gentle squeeze, tearing my attention away from the silent drummer.

"Don't mind him," he said softly in my ear. "He doesn't like people much."

I gave a small smile in response, showing I wasn't offended. This dude probably believed every horrible thing Jace had said about me, and then some. It also looked like I'd slept with Rhett last night, and I'd done nothing to dispel that assumption.

Rhett distracted me for the short drive to the concert venue, asking about my day with Dora. I answered his questions quietly, not wanting to annoy the whole car with my chatter. Maybe Grayson needed quiet and calm before a show or something. I didn't need to go giving him another reason to dislike me.

When we arrived, the bodyguards escorted us into the backstage area so the band could get ready. They'd apparently already done their soundcheck earlier in the day, so I lurked uncomfortably near the side of the room. My number one goal was to stay the hell out of everyone's way, and I must have succeeded because Jace didn't even glance my way *once*.

Sound crew fitted them all with in-ear monitors, then Rhett beckoned me over as he lifted his guitar from its case. It was impossible to miss the fact that the turquoise accents on the glossy black instrument matched his gelled mohawk perfectly.

"Tom usually watches from the side of the stage," he told me as his long fingers gently stroked over the strings of his guitar. "Will you be okay hanging out with him?"

I wrinkled my nose, glancing over at the greasy creep who was currently kissing Florence. "I guess... But I don't understand why I'm even here. I thought Jace wanted me to stay *away* from you."

Rhett's green eyes shifted over to the moody fuck in question, then he gave me a small shrug. "I have a theory. But we're needed on stage in five minutes. I'm asking the twins to keep an eye on you while I'm on stage, though, okay?"

"I'll be fine, Zep," I teased with a smile that I didn't feel. "Get your head in the music; don't stress about me."

"You heard her," Tom sneered, detaching his squid hands from Florence as a woman with a clipboard called out that it was time to go. "Don't worry, Rhett, I'll take care of your stray puppy."

Rhett didn't seem even slightly reassured—neither was I, for that matter—but Jace barked his guitarists name so sharply that Rhett rolled his eyes and sighed. "If you get bored of our shit music, you can come back here. Okay? This room is totally off limits to anyone but our band security."

"Rhett, *come on!*" Florence yelled into the room.

I smiled and gave him a push. "Go."

He gave me one more worried frown, then shot Tom a warning look before hurrying out to catch up with the rest of his band. The crowd was so loud we could hear the dull roar from the greenroom we were in, but even so, it suddenly felt *very* quiet without the band.

"Listen, I don't care how great your dick sucking

skills are, but—" Tom started, sneering at me, and I put my palm up in his face.

"Save it," I snapped, too tired to put up with his shit. "I'm not here to try and rip off your cash cow, Tom. If it was up to me, I'd be tucked up in bed right now, or did you miss that whole scene where Jace literally gave me *no choice* about tagging along tonight?"

His eyes narrowed into a glare. Then he just stalked out of the greenroom without a backward glance. Fucking *good*, I was more than happy to hang out in here alone for the entire concert. Maybe I could even take a nap while waiting to be allowed to go back to the hotel.

Actually, fuck that. Why was I letting Jace push me around? Yes, I needed their help getting out of Siena without the Riccis catching me, but that was *it*. And that had already been arranged with my temporary position on Dora's team. There was no reason for me to be *here*, at the concert venue.

Of course, I wasn't dumb-shit enough to just wander out on my own and hail a cab—with my zero money—but that didn't mean I needed to just sit quietly while waiting for my master to return with doggy treats.

Stepping out of the greenroom, I glanced up and down the busy hallway. It was easy to spot Rhett's security guys just a short way down the hall, chatting to another black-outfitted bodyguard dude. I gave them a small wave as I approached, and one of the twins nodded in response.

"Hey, uh, Rhett said—"

"To keep an eye on you?" the one on the left finished for me. "Yeah, we got the message. You in some kind of trouble, girl?"

My laugh was shaky and weak. "You could say that. But I was wondering if maybe we could go back to the hotel? I just want to sleep, and this whole rock concert thing really isn't my vibe." I pasted on my very best pleading smile, batting my lashes a little and hoping they would take pity on me.

The guy they'd been talking to scoffed. "You must be the girl we've been hearing about all day. Billie Bellerose herself, huh? I expected someone... taller."

I gave him a frown of confusion. "Um. Sorry for being short?" I didn't like his tone. There was something decidedly unkind about it. "So... could we?" I aimed my question to the twins.

They exchanged a long look, then the one who'd spoken to me shook his head. "Sorry, kid. We can't leave the venue without Rhett's say-so."

The other guy—the one who thought I was short— muttered something about magical pussy before sauntering away down the hall. I wrinkled my nose, scowling at his back.

"That's Roger," the other twin informed me. "He's part of Jace's personal security."

"Ah. I guess that explains his shitty attitude." He must have heard Jace's less than flattering opinions of me today. "I'm just going to stay in there, then." I pointed back to the greenroom. "If that's okay?"

Feeling defeated but not totally surprised, I retreated back into the green room and closed the door. At least it was empty and quietish. Much better than standing at the side of the stage with creepy Tom while my first love sang about how I shattered his heart. Despite my thoughts before, in truth, being here reminded me how painful it would be to willingly subject myself to watching Jace on stage... no matter how curious I was to see Rhett in action.

Still, the greenroom wasn't far enough away to hear *nothing*. Within minutes, the first notes of one of Bellerose's biggest hits rang out, and the crowd went *wild*. I groaned and sank back onto the couch, covering my face with my hands.

Surprisingly, I fell asleep like that. When I woke up again, the clock above the door told me I'd been out for most of the show. The band would be back any minute, and I was *dying* to pee. Ducking out into the hallway, I spotted one of the twins leaning against the wall opposite with his phone to his ear.

He raised his brows at me in question, and I pointed to the restrooms I'd seen further down the corridor. He jerked a nod, and I hurried down there. The whole corridor was empty aside from us, everyone probably out watching the end of the show, so there was no wait to use the ladies' toilet. No doubt there would be a whole horde of fans with backstage passes in there soon enough, though.

When I was done, I nearly ran into someone right outside the bathroom. At first I thought it was one of the twins but realized my mistake when his huge hand circled my forearm way too tight.

"Mr. Ricci has been looking for you, girl." It was Roger, Jace's security guard. But... what did he just say? He was working for *Angelo*? Oh shit.

"Let go of me," I demanded, my voice shaking way too much. Where were Rhett's bodyguards? I tried to look past Roger, but he shoved me backwards, pushing me around the corner and out of sight.

Drawing a breath, I tried to scream, but Roger already had a hand clamped over my mouth.

"None of that," he growled. "We're going to quietly leave the venue without raising any alarms. You'll go back to Mr. Ricci for whatever he wants to do with you, and Jace will thank me for making you disappear."

Panic flooded through me, making my knees weak. It meant I wasn't even trying to put up a fight as Roger practically dragged me along the unfamiliar corridor. *Where was everyone?*

We rounded another corner, and up ahead I caught a flash of turquoise hair amidst a crowd of people. The concert had just ended, and the band was on its way back to their greenroom. Relieved, I batted Roger's hand away long enough to scream Rhett's name.

Except... he couldn't hear me. Dozens of fans were crowded around them, all wearing backstage passes and holding out shit for Bellerose to sign. Of course Rhett didn't hear me; I was just one of many girls calling out his name. Roger knew it, too, snickering an unkind laugh as he dragged me faster, away from my salvation.

"Jace won't let you get away with this," I protested pitifully. My resistance was as effective as a tissue-paper raincoat, and I desperately wished I was stronger.

Roger glanced over at me, unimpressed. "For getting rid of you? He definitely will."

I gritted my teeth because he was right about *that*. "For working with Angelo. He *hates* Angelo, and when he realizes you're on the Ricci payroll, you'll be fired so fast you won't know what happened."

It was sickening. I would be shot in the head to silence me, and Roger would simply lose his job. That thought wasn't even slightly comforting.

Roger whirled around, slamming me into the wall so hard it knocked the air from my lungs.

"You have no idea how badly he hates *you*, stupid girl. You should have heard him today, talking about what a whore you are. How you used that pussy of yours to entrap Rhett. I bet I could do *whatever I want* to you, and he'd give me a fucking raise. *That's* what I think." He crushed my body with his much larger frame. "Maybe I should test that theory out, huh? Been ages since I've had one as young as you."

Revulsion at the meaning behind that statement curdled the contents of my stomach. Was Roger seriously going to try and rape me? Right here in the corridor, practically within earshot of Bellerose's after-party?

Bile rose in my throat, and I didn't fight it. When Roger leaned down to kiss me with his sour breath and dry lips, I let fly. Vomit shot straight out of my throat and into his mouth like something out of a horror movie. He recoiled, and I clapped a hand over my mouth.

Then, out of nowhere, a huge fist cracked into the side of Roger's head and sent him flying several feet before crashing to the floor.

"You okay?" Grayson rumbled, scowling down at me from his six-foot-five height.

My hand was still clamped over my mouth, so all I could do was nod. Grayson scowled even harder, his sharp gaze sweeping over me from head to toe. I was shaking. Hard. Then I saw the blood pooling under Roger's head from where he'd hit the concrete floor.

Swallowing hard, I tried to find some words to alert Grayson before I passed out, but no sound would exit my throat. He seemed to follow my line of sight, though, grunting a curse as he bent down to check Roger's pulse.

"Fuck," he said softly, and my eyes widened so far I worried they'd pop out of my head.

This time, when I peeled my hand away, I managed to squeak out some words. "Is he...?"

Grayson's expression when he met my eyes was totally blank. Guarded and unreadable. "Dead."

Whatever else he said faded into obscurity as blackness swarmed my vision and my body folded into a faint.

twelve

GRAYSON

On instinct, I leaned forward and caught her slight frame. She weighed next to nothing as I lifted her away from the dead fuck and gently set her against a wall, making sure she didn't fall as she slumped over. Once the girl was secure, I turned my attention back to the security guard.

It wasn't the first kill under my belt. My past was littered with carnage—a truth very few knew about me. Not even the rest of the band. Drums had been an escape from my duty growing up, while the rest of the time I was the muscle.

The darkness sent in to extinguish the light.

Bellerose had been my saving grace, and now with the money and fame I had, no one could force me into that life again.

But it didn't mean I'd forgotten my skills... carefully honed over a lifetime. I'd known how to hit this fucker with just the right angle and strength to hurt him badly. The plan hadn't been to kill him, but I also didn't regret it.

Thankfully, there were enough cameras in here that I could easily claim defense of Billie.

Her name settled uneasily inside. There were two parts to her in my mind now: the *before* where she was the manipulative destruction of my brother and the *now* where she was clearly not as evil as she'd always been painted. Either that or she was a fucking excellent actress.

My observation time had been brief, but I'd seen enough to start forming some of my own character assessments, and I really didn't think she was acting. She was too... *sad*.

Not that I'd trust her. I didn't trust anyone. But I wouldn't throw her to the wolves, no matter how badly Jace wanted her out of our lives. I'd had the time to decide if I would step in or not, and there really hadn't been a hesitation in my mind.

"What the fuck happened?" Rhett roared as he

raced over, having just seen us. "What happened to her?" He paused as if realizing that Billie wasn't the only one passed out. "Gray... is that guy dead? Holy shit, that's Roger!"

More people hurried over, but they hung back, forming a half-circle around us. Most of the crew and extras knew better than to get too close to me. "He attacked Billie," I said shortly. I didn't like to waste words or energy, but this would require more than my usual short sentences. "He was going to rape her first and then take her to Angelo. I heard his threats."

A half-truth. It wasn't hard to guess what Roger's intentions had been, considering the Ricci family had put Billie's picture out on blast with a reward for her "safe return," as though she belonged to them. Like a lost dog.

Rhett dropped to the ground beside Billie, reaching down to gently lift her up into his arms. My brother wore a frantic expression, one I hadn't seen in a long time, and I knew that some of his demons would be triggered by this event tonight. A woman in his care getting hurt took him to a dark place that we struggled to get him back from, but hopefully, when Billie awoke and was okay, he'd be able to deal.

Until then, we had a dead bodyguard to worry about.

Tom pushed through the crowd, and when he caught a glimpse of what was happening, including the unconscious girl in Rhett's arms, he immediately started to send the onlookers away. "Thank fuck the groupies are busy with Jace," I heard him mutter. He turned to some of the security. "Make sure they stay that way."

The twins hurried off, but not before Rhett shouted. "You're both fucking fired. Fucking. Fired."

His voice rasped as he repeated the words, but when the twins turned back to Tom, our manager just shook his head. In the end, Rhett had the final say, but we all knew he never made rational decisions when he was upset. Best to wait for the morning.

For now, we'd see if I was about to end up in cuffs.

By the time Tom had cleared the space of everyone except Rhett, Florence, and me, an uncomfortable silence had fallen. "I'm going to need you to tell me right now what just happened," the stupid fucker we'd had to hire because of the label said to me. He pushed in closer in an attempt to get into my face, and as the icy anger I tried not to release too often floated to the surface, his face lost all color, and he backed off in an instant. Okay, so maybe he wasn't completely stupid.

"He attacked Billie," I repeated, fucking hating that I had to speak directly to him. "He was going to rape her and then take her to Angelo. Must have figured he had Jace's blessing. I just hit him once to stop him from hurting her."

No need to mention anything else. No one knew my past or my experience, and I had no intention of changing that any time soon.

Who the fuck expected a drummer to be two steps short of a contract killer in their previous life?

Possibly a skill I'd put into action again soon to get rid of Tom so I didn't have to hear his whiney fucking voice.

"Okay, that's fine," Tom said, breathing deeply as he squeezed the bridge of his nose between his right hand pointer finger and thumb. "We can totally explain this. I'm going to have to call the police and an ambulance. I need you two to get down and try and resuscitate this asshole like we give a shit about him dying."

At that point Rhett spun on the spot and stalked off. "Hey!" Tom called. "We need to wake her up and get a statement."

"Fuck off."

That was the only reply we got before they both disappeared from view. "Yep, later," Tom called. "Later is a good idea—before the cops arrive, though. She needs to be singing the same tune as Gray." Tom's words turned into mutters, sounding half-crazed.

"Okay, I need to handle this. You do exactly what I fucking said. Fake some damn CPR."

He had his phone in his hand and was already dialing, starting to pace as he got emergency services on the line. Flo dropped down then, about to try and give the dead guy mouth to mouth before she recoiled and shook her head.

"Oh, hell no," she muttered. "Is that vomit?"

A yellow sludge dripped from the corpse's lips, and I remembered how he'd staggered away from Billie before I hit him. Huh. Smart girl.

Ignoring Flo's mutters of disgust as she sat back on her heels, I gave a vague attempt at compressions to Roger's chest. The fragility of ribs under my hands reminded me not to press too hard. I didn't need to fuck him up more before the investigation.

The hum of people further down the hall reminded me we weren't alone, but eventually the security got them all out of the way, leaving us to cover up my crime.

A few minutes later, the paramedics we always had at our concerts burst into view, racing across with their equipment. Florence started to fake sob like she was upset, but there wasn't a single tear in her heavily kohled eyes. In truth, all of us were too fucked up to be very upset by the death, especially when it was a piece of shit like this. Security betraying us was old hat, and we were over it.

The paramedics took over from us, slipping an oxygen mask over his face and pulling out a small defibrillator to shock against his chest. They were feeling for a pulse and exchanged a glance when there was nothing, but they continued to try and bring him back anyway.

Wasting time and money on someone who should have been fucking swallowed before conception.

I might have been forced into shit I'd never wanted to do in my past, but I had a line and I never crossed it. My uncle, the one who'd dragged me into his life of crime, knew that, and when I'd gotten too dangerous to be controlled, he'd let me walk away. Not that I'd given him much of a choice in the matter. And now he was dead.

This bastard, though? He'd done this for money and, probably, the thrill of attacking a smaller person than he was. Weak and pathetic.

After about five minutes the paramedics exchanged a few quick words with Tom, and then the police and ambulances arrived. The corridor was cleared completely, and I turned to find Jace standing there alone, the oddest look on his face as he stared down at his former personal bodyguard.

"He attacked Billie?" he finally said, a rasp I hadn't heard before in his voice. "She didn't try to run off back to Angelo or something?"

I loved this guy, but he was straight up a fucking moron over this chick.

"I witnessed enough," I told him shortly. "He attacked her. He was *hurting* her."

Jace's emotions shut down. I recognized the signs. He didn't say anything else, and as the police approached us—two guys and a woman who were first on the scene—he spun and stalked off.

Florence, who was cuddled close to Tom, let her gaze follow Jace's departure, her expression finally revealing real and deeper emotions. She might have terrible taste in men, but she was a solid friend. She worried about all of us.

"We're going to need your statements," the first cop said, his hat pulled down low over his shaved head. He looked to be in his mid-forties but was fit enough that I knew he wasn't lazy. He'd be thorough, that was for sure.

"Don't say a damn word," Tom snapped as I opened my mouth. "We need our lawyers present."

A frustrated sound slipped out from between my lips, but it was low enough that it seemed Tom was the only one who caught it. He backed up from me again, shooting a worried look between me and the cops. "It was self-defense," I said shortly. "He attacked one of our crew, and I stepped in to shove him away. When he went down, he must have hit his head at the wrong angle."

Tom jumped in quickly. "There's video footage, and the crew member in question was knocked out as well and can give a statement when she comes to."

The male cop exchanged a glance with the other two cops before he nodded. "You're all going to have to come down to the station so we can get your statements."

"Not a fucking chance," Tom snapped again, his cool completely frayed. "This is Bellerose. You take them to the police station, and it will be absolute bedlam. As it is, just having you show up to their concert is bad enough. This has to be done with the utmost discretion, or I swear to fuck you'll be paying with your badges."

The cop narrowed his eyes at Tom. He seemed to feel the same about Flo's boyfriend as the rest of us but also seemed smart enough to understand that Bellerose showing up to his station would cause a lot of problems.

"Okay," he said with a firm nod. "I want all of you in a conference room at your hotel in the next hour. We will be in to question everyone, and it'll go from there. I'm not ruling out hauling all of you to the station, depending on what story I get. I'm also going to need the security footage."

Tom nodded, and before I could hear another word, I turned and stalked away.

Seemed it was going to be a long fucking night, and I had some energy to work off before I ended up in cuffs. The way I was feeling now, I'd be dropping bodies again if shit went sideways.

I needed a boxing bag and twenty minutes. Otherwise, I'd be in jail for life.

thirteen

BILLIE

Consciousness returned to me with the force of a freight train. Or a punch from Grayson. I sat up with a sharp, panicked inhale even before my eyes opened. A firm hand pressed against my shoulder, gently pushing me back down to horizontal as someone murmured reassuring words.

Confusion rippled through me as I blinked my eyes open. Why the *fuck* was Jace Adams telling me that I was safe? Shit, I must have hit my head when I fainted.

"What...?" *The fuck?*

Jace heaved a long sigh, staring at me from way too fucking close. His eyes were so familiar, yet so foreign. Barely a shadow of the boy I knew seemed to remain in this man, but for the first time, I caught a glimpse of him. Then it was gone, and he pushed to his feet.

"Rhett!" he barked, his voice hard again. "She's awake. Get her into a car and back to the hotel. Cops want us in a conference room for questioning."

That woke me up properly. "Cops?" I squeaked, sitting up again now that Jace wasn't pushing me back down. My gaze darted around the room, searching for Grayson. Where was he? Was he okay? Did they arrest him? Holy shit, he *killed* that guy!

"Thorn!" Rhett exclaimed, rushing back into the room. We were still at the concert venue, in the greenroom where I'd napped during their show. His hand cupped my face, his panicked eyes searching mine for a moment before he crushed me into his chest with a hug that stole the wind from my lungs. "Thank fuck. Were you hurt? Did he hit you?"

I frowned into his leather jacket, still bewildered and lost for what the fuck was happening. Then I realized what he was talking about, and a slightly unhinged laugh escaped.

"I'm fine," I replied, peeling myself away from his chest just enough so I could breathe. "I fainted. It's so stupid; the sight of blood always makes me faint. Didn't Jace tell you?"

Rhett loosened his grip slightly, giving an annoyed

grunt. "He did, but I figured he was just being a dismissive prick. You were out for way longer than a faint usually lasts, though."

I shrugged. My dizzy spells used to be quick. Basically, as soon as I hit the ground, I was waking up. But the last few years had seen them increase in length. My explanation was simple; I was straight up exhausted and *weak* from irregular meals, so my body took the opportunity for a little nap when it could.

"We need to go," Rhett told me with a grimace. Before I could protest, he'd scooped me up in his arms, and I held onto his neck simply in reflex so I wouldn't fall.

"She can fucking *walk*, Rhett," Jace snapped, his glare like acid as Rhett strode out of the room with me in his arms.

I was inclined to agree, but Rhett just held me tighter and ignored Jace as he carried me. His strides were long, and I decided not to argue. I *liked* being in Rhett's arms, and Jace's irritation about it only made me want to stay.

The drive back to the hotel was quick and silent. Rhett was visibly furious with the identical security in the front seat, and Grayson was nowhere to be seen. I kept my mouth shut, not wanting to talk about what had just happened, and Rhett didn't push me for information. Instead, he just kept an arm around me, and I rested my head on his shoulder.

When we pulled into the underground parking, Rhett totally ignored his security when they tried to speak with him. He even went so far as flipping them his middle finger as the elevator doors closed, leaving them behind.

"It's not their fault, Rhett," I said softly.

He scowled, shaking his head. "Their job is quite literally to prevent harm from coming to their charge. They failed at their job, therefore they shouldn't fucking keep said job."

I released a long breath, choosing my words carefully. He was angry, and I didn't blame him. But his security probably saw me with Roger and thought nothing of it. If Roger was trusted to act as Jace's bodyguard, why on earth would they think he was a threat to me?

"Just sleep on it, Zep. You can't fire them until you have a replacement anyway, right? It would be stupid to just go without security while you're on tour." Maybe calm logic would sink in better than an emotional response. "Where's Grayson, though? Jace said something about cops? Did they arrest him?"

Fuck, I hope he wasn't being charged with the

creep's death. He'd *saved* me; the man needed a medal, not a jail cell.

"No, they didn't arrest him," Rhett replied, a touch of tension dropping out of his shoulders. "Not yet, anyway. We're pretty confident the video surveillance will confirm he was acting in your defense and that it was just an unlucky blow that killed Roger." He paused, frowning slightly at me. "That is what happened, right?"

My eyes widened. "What? Yes! Roger was working for Angelo. He told me himself!"

Rhett nodded. "Good. Just... maybe don't mention the Ricci's to these cops. We don't know if they're on the take or not, but so far they're proving to be sensible in not arresting anyone so let's just keep it that way."

"Understood," I whispered as the elevator doors opened on the ninth floor. It was full of business suites, and Rhett led the way down to one of the rooms, where Florence and Tom were already seated opposite two uniformed Siena policemen.

Tom sent me a nasty glare, but Florence just frowned. Was that a touch of concern in her eyes? Or just tiredness?

"I think we're pretty much done already, don't you?" Tom asked one of the policemen with a pointed look. "The video evidence supports the fact that Mr.

Taylor acted in defense of our employee, and it's in *all* of our best interests that this is closed as an accident."

The cops exchanged a tense look between them, then one sighed and looked over at me. "Miss, we just need to hear the events from your perspective."

Rhett gave me a small, reassuring squeeze, and I haltingly told the police exactly what had happened, from Roger grabbing me outside the restrooms to when I passed out. The only thing I left out was Roger's connection to Angelo Ricci.

When I was done, the cops just took some notes, then gave me a tight smile. "Thank you. Sorry, we didn't catch your name. Mr. Tucker keeps calling you an *employee*, but we need a name for our report."

Tom's glare turned hard, and my mouth went dry.

"Oh, um, Billie," I replied nervously, "Billie Thorn."

Rhett released a long breath and bent down to brush a kiss on my shoulder. I guess the band *really* didn't want my real name getting out into the press, and it would be sure to if it got entered into a Siena police report.

They let us go a minute later, and Rhett hurried me back to the elevator while Tom and Florence stayed behind. I assumed Tom was *managing* the crisis and Florence was just hanging around because they were joined at the hip.

"My room is on the eleventh floor," I corrected Rhett when he stabbed the button for the penthouse. He just arched a brow at me and *didn't* press eleven. "Rhett..." I protested weakly.

"Billie..." he replied, giving me a pointed look.

I frowned. "Don't call me that," I told him softly. "I like that you call me Thorn. It makes me feel like a new person and not such a *problem* for your band."

"You're not a problem, Thorn. I'm starting to think maybe you're the solution." A weird look crossed his face, and I wrinkled my nose as I tried to decipher what in the hell he meant by that. Before I could ask, he cupped my face in his hand and brushed his lips over mine.

Thank fuck I took a moment to wash the vomit out of my mouth already!

Shock made me freeze. He seemed to sense it and started to pull away again, but that was all I needed to snap out of my surprise. Not letting him retreat, I leaned in and kissed him back. Fucking sparks flew, his kiss was that electric, as I wound my arms around his neck and pressed closer. Rhett made the sexiest little groan as I parted my lips, kissing him deeper and letting our tongues tangle. Deep down, I knew I was only screwing myself over. Now that I knew how it felt to kiss Rhett Silver, how could I possibly leave?

The elevator ding made us both flinch. I'd totally forgotten where we were, and apparently, he had too. Except we weren't on the penthouse level, we were a few floors lower, and Grayson stepped in with a dark expression on his face and a sweat towel draped around his neck.

He'd *definitely* just seen us kissing. Shit.

Rhett didn't try to move away, looping his arm around my waist and holding me close when I tried to put space between us.

"You spoken to the cops yet?" Rhett asked, casual as *fuck*.

Grayson just grunted a sound that I had no clue whether was a yes or no. Depending on how long I'd been passed out, I guess he could have seen them before he went to the gym.

Rhett seemed to decipher it, though, and gave a sigh. "Fair enough. Seems like Tom already worked his slick magic anyway. They didn't seem too worried about talking to you again."

"Good," Grayson rumbled. His dark eyes caught on mine in the mirrored door's reflection. For a tense moment he just held my gaze, then his attention moved back to Rhett. "Jace will murder you if he finds out about this."

Shit. He was so right. Guilt flooded through me, even though Jace and I were *ancient* history.

"Bullshit," Rhett replied, though. "He already thinks we slept together last night, and I'm still breathing."

Grayson's brow lifted, and I couldn't seem to stop staring at him in the mirror. "But you didn't," he murmured. "And Jace knows it, deep down. You gotta have a serious talk with him if *this* is a thing now."

By *this* I assume he meant me and Rhett. Together. Was that what I wanted? To be with Rhett, even if it hurt my childhood sweetheart? But even as I asked myself those questions, Jace's hate-filled eyes entered my head. His cutting comments about me being a whore and the way he sneered at me like I was less than dog shit.

A cold anger settled in my stomach, and I realized the answer was *easy*. Yes. Yes, I wanted to pursue this thing with Rhett. I wanted more of those sinful, butterfly-inducing kisses. I wanted to know what his hands felt like on my skin and what it'd feel like to wrap my legs around his slim hips while he—

Short answer. Yes. And if Jace had a problem with it, he could kiss my ass. I was done with feeling like a doormat. He wanted to treat me like the villain in his story? I might as well get a pay-off in the form of Rhett Silver's kisses... and more.

"It's been eight years," I said aloud, answering Grayson, despite the fact that he'd been speaking to Rhett. "Jace needs to get the fuck over it. We all got hurt that day, not just him. It's about time he pulled his head out of his ass and stopped playing the victim. Bellerose wouldn't exist if not for my choices."

Grayson's eyes widened ever so slightly, but his only response was a short nod. Whatever the fuck *that* meant. I guessed I was about to find out, though, because we'd reached the penthouse level.

Rhett kept his arm around me as Grayson unlocked the door and held it open for us to enter. But I separated myself from Rhett once we were inside, hanging back a moment to look up at the big drummer.

"Um, I needed to say thank you, Grayson," I said awkwardly, biting the edge of my lip. "You seriously saved me back at the concert venue. I really appreciate it."

His impassive face stared down at me for a long moment. Then he gave a small sigh and brushed his thumb over my lower lip, which I was biting again. "Don't do that," he rumbled. "You're not an insecure girl; don't pretend to be one."

That was it. Then he walked away like he hadn't killed a man trying to assault me just an hour ago, or that we hadn't just shared the strangest, electrically charged moment. I swallowed hard, forcing my feet to move, but my lip still tingled from Grayson's touch. Weird.

He was wrong about me, though. I'd never felt *more* insecure as I did standing there in the Viper Hotel penthouse with Jace and Rhett both staring at me.

BILLIE

"What the fuck was that?" Jace demanded, the scowl on his face pure venom. "You fucking Gray now too? Color me *shocked*."

The sarcasm was so heavy it crashed down on my shoulders like a lead weight. How was his anger still so fresh?

Rhett wasn't taking it anymore. He reached out and smacked Jace in the back of the head, way harder than playful. "Cut it out, Jace. She's had a rough night; would it kill you to be kind for three fucking seconds?"

A flicker of guilt crossed Jace's handsome face, but then it hardened into hate once more. "Yeah, it probably would. She's like a fucking shark, Rhett. One whiff of blood in the water and she'll tear you to shreds." His glare swung back to me. "What are you even doing up here? Are you suddenly too fucking good to share a room with the cleaning girls?"

My lips parted, shock holding my tongue for a moment. I was too tired for this shit. Giving a humorless laugh, I nodded. "You know what? I have *no* idea why I'm here. Right now I'd rather sleep on the street than suffer your shitty attitude for even a minute longer."

I spun on my heel, retreating back out of the penthouse and slamming the door after me. Rhett shouted my name, then Jace said something that sparked an argument, but I wasn't going to hang around and listen. Fuck that. The elevator was right there, so I got in and pressed level eleven. Just as the doors slid shut, the penthouse opened again and Rhett came storming out like he planned to stop me.

Too late, hot stuff.

I silently let myself into Kristie's room with the key Dora had given me earlier. The shower was running, so I just kicked off my shoes and wiggled out of my borrowed jeans. I had no other clothes, so I'd just sleep in Rhett's top. Okay, fine, I would have slept in Rhett's clothes even if I had other options. What no one knew couldn't hurt me, right?

The evening's events all caught up with me the moment my head hit the pillow. Either I needed to sleep before I could get worked up or let it all out in tears. I chose sleep.

I'd never been a particularly heavy sleeper, always too paranoid to really relax that fully, so it didn't surprise me that Kristie's voice roused me some time later. She was speaking quietly with someone, and my half-asleep brain told me it was none of my business. So I ignored her and went back to sleep.

When my mattress dipped with someone joining me, I startled awake with a gasp of fright. Rhett's arms curled around me instantly, though, his low voice whispering reassurances in my ear as my heart raced with panic.

Normally a jolt like that would be enough to stop me from sleeping the rest of the night, but for some reason, as Rhett's heat and that smoky, spicy scent settled around me, I found myself drifting right off to sleep again.

This time, though, it was the sort of solid sleep I hadn't had in years.

There was no denying it, Rhett made me feel safe in a way that... well, fuck. The last time I'd felt this safe was when I'd fallen asleep between Jace and Angelo, just days before our lives went to shit.

The memories were too painful to dwell on for long, so I just breathed in the scent of my new guardian angel and let restful sleep take me away.

***

THE BLACKOUT HOTEL ROOM CURTAINS MEANT I WOULD HAVE slept the day away if not for the hand slowly tracing across my bare stomach. My shirt must have rode up during the night, and Rhett found the perfect spot to dance those calloused fingers across.

The moan escaped before I could stop it, the sensations too much in my half-awake state.

His hand paused, and I felt him press against my back as he cuddled into me. His lips caressed my shoulder, firing my body in a way that should have been impossible when I'd been dead asleep not two minutes ago. "Kristie?" I murmured, needing to not have a roommate right now.

"Gone," he murmured back.

Thank fuck. His hands stroked lower, and I groaned his name.

His laugh was low and husky against me—he hadn't moved his mouth from my skin, and I was hoping he'd decide to keep exploring as he was. In truth, if he didn't move a little faster, I'd have to take matters into my own hands.

His fingers started to stroke patterns across my skin again, and I couldn't be totally sure, but it felt a lot like he was strumming chords on my body. Using it as his own personal guitar. He was about to hear some freaking music if he kept it up. I might not be able to carry much of a tune, but I had the sense that I was about to scream his name like a goddamn opera singer.

"Rhett," I breathed, more urgency in my tone as I started to wiggle against him. "You have my *explicit* permission to take those fingers to new body parts. Please."

I'd always owned my sexuality growing up. It had taken a huge hit when my heart was ripped in two, but fuck… I was done waiting for life to happen to me. I was taking and embracing *any and all* moments that came my way.

Wrapping his arms around me, Rhett pulled me back against him, and I moaned against his firm hold. "You went through a huge trauma last night," he murmured, his husky tones sending goosebumps across my skin as I squirmed harder. Or at least attempted to. His hold was… yeah, it was doing all sorts of things to me. "Maybe we should wait a few days… give you some time to heal. I'm not going anywhere."

Ah, my knight in shining leather.

The trauma from last night—Roger's attempted assault—was definitely still there, buried amongst the many other shitty moments in my life, but I'd learned that it was these moments that pushed me to live my hardest. It was hardly the first time I'd had a scare like that, either. Right now, there was nothing I wanted more in this world than to lose myself in Rhett Silver.

As I wiggled around, he finally released me so I could turn and face him. Green eyes slammed into me, the color bright and the intensity of his focus enough that I almost lost *my* focus. Almost.

"I promise you that right now I'm not thinking about anything other than exploring this electric connection between us," I murmured, gaze dipping lower to that ring in his lip that he worried at when he was deep in thought. Leaning in, I let my lips press to his, tongue swiping at the ring as I played with it for a beat.

A rumbling groan left Rhett's chest. My good guy was still fighting with himself, but I didn't hesitate to make myself perfectly clear. "Touch me, Rhett," I commanded, my body arching at the very thought. "I have absolutely no doubts about what I want."

Not. A. Single. One.

The moment he gave into his desires was one I'd remember for a long time. With a groan of my name, his lips slammed against mine, tongue pushing between my lips as he took control. Not that he had to push hard, I was opening to his touch without thought.

He tasted so damn good that I was gasping by the time he pressed me back into the mattress, his fingers already working to strip my clothes from me. I'd only slept in his shirt and underwear. Both of which were gone in a flash. For a brief moment, I wondered if my scars were finally going to be an issue between us. Hopefully, he would just ignore them until after this moment was over. Nothing like a little talk of death and fire to quench some lust.

Thankfully, the room was semi-dark and I was on my back, so he couldn't see anything as he pushed himself up on his forearms and dragged a heavy, heated gaze across my naked form. "Fuck, Billie."

I understood that sentiment completely. My gaze was just as greedy as I examined him. He was still wearing his sweats, his top half gloriously naked, and no joke, a thrill went through me to know I was finally going to explore all of his ink.

Just as I was reaching to strip his pants off too, he leaned back down and pressed his lips to my throat, right near my ear, and his tongue tasted my skin before his teeth scraped my earlobe. Tingles raced along my skin and into my center, my pussy already aching and wet. I didn't even have to touch myself to know I was ready for whatever happened next.

Fuck, one taste of Rhett and I was ready.

Scraping my nails across his back, I cried out as he moved lower, dragging my right nipple into his mouth; the feel of his piercing against it was an entirely new sensation. One I hoped to repeat.

Rhett wasn't gentle, but I enjoyed the firm touch, and when he moved to my left breast, I was panting. Fucking panting. My lower body moved as I sought for a release that was just a touch out of reach. But seriously, it wouldn't take much to send me right over the edge.

Rhett shot me a low smile as he lifted his head before he continued to explore, lower and lower, tongue and lips tasting every part of my body he could reach; all the while I gripped the sheets on either side, hoping I wasn't about to combust.

When he reached my pussy, my legs fell open wider as I all but jerked up into his face. Like, *please put me out of my damn misery.* His laugh was low and husky, before he dropped down and licked up in one long slide from bottom to top. A single lap, taking in all of the moisture that had been pooling there.

A cry escaped me, and at the same time he groaned. His head fell back as he stared up at me, eyes hooded. "I get it now," he said softly, the green darker than ever in his gaze. "I fucking get it."

I tried to push myself up, but his firm hand on my stomach held me to the bed. "What do you get?" I huffed out, feeling like my head was spinning from that one, almost orgasm-inducing lick.

"Jace's obsession. The songs. I... yeah, I fucking get it now."

I snorted. "What? Power of the pussy. Seriously." I didn't expect such a typical rock star line from Rhett. But then again, he was a rock star so...

He didn't laugh with me. "It's so much more than that. You're so much more."

Ah. Well, that sounded like my Rhett and not rock-star Rhett.

An extended moment raced between us as our gazes remained locked. I wondered if the mention of *his* name would ruin this moment. Had Rhett just realized that he was in bed with his best friend's enemy? Was he going to get up and walk—

His head dropped again, and with that firm hand on my stomach, he didn't just lick this time. He devoured.

His fingers weren't his only talented part as his tongue rolled around my clit before he sucked it inside his mouth, and the hand not against my stomach slid up to part my folds at the same time.

He slid one finger inside me, moving it slowly, stroking, before a second finger followed. The rough texture of his skin was enough to stimulate all my fucking nerve endings, so I was crying out and riding the sensation as his tongue worked my clit and his fingers my cunt.

The orgasm built low in my stomach, and fairly soon, not even his hand could stop my body from moving. My back arched as that swirl of pleasure inside exploded, sending me near half off the bed as I cried out and gripped the sheets harder. When I managed to release my hold on them, my hands found their way to Rhett's head as he ate me like it was his damn life's work. He took in every drop of my pleasure, his strokes only slowing when I finally stopped jerking against him.

Tugging gently, I tried to move him higher so that we could move to the fucking. That orgasm was mind-fucking-blowing, but I wasn't done. I needed and wanted more.

I also needed and wanted him to feel the same pleasure.

He took his time cleaning me up, *suuuper thoroughly*, and I was panting again by the time he slowly made his way back up toward me.

Lifting my head in a rush, I kissed him hard, uncaring that I could taste myself against his lips. If anything, that only turned me on more. "That was," I breathed heavily, "fucking amazing. We need to… seriously…"

My words kept getting lost as I reached between us, my hand sliding between us. I went to push his sweats down and ended with a handful of hard cock. *Jesus.* Rhett might not be the tallest guy in Bellerose, but he certainly wasn't lacking in any way down there.

I got a single stroke along the silky length, feeling a bead of moisture from the tip, when a heavy knock sounded on our door. We both froze, or at least I did, but I didn't drop his cock. I mean, they weren't in the room yet, right?

Stroking again, I was about to push him onto the bed so I could take my turn tasting him, when a familiar, annoying voice sounded through the door. "Rhett, I know you're in there." Tom was really starting to piss me off. "The bus leaves in twenty minutes. Stop fucking. Get your ass out of bed now. The clothes you requested for your groupie are in the hall."

Rhett let out a curse as he stared down at me. "How

strict is this leave time?" I whispered. A pertinent question, considering I still had a handful of cock. Cock I really wanted to taste. But twenty minutes didn't leave us much time to finish, get ready, and get to the buses.

He shook his head. "Strict. It's all about security, and they hold traffic to allow us out. We can't be late."

Well, fuck. "Want to see if I can work my magic in five minutes?" I suggested with a small, disappointed laugh.

He groaned again, and I tried not to think about all the fucking we weren't going to have time for. At best, I could get him off, which was better than nothing.

"For this first time, I'd rather wait to have a proper night with you," Rhett said, voice lower and more serious than it had been before. "I don't want us to rush. No matter what Tom thinks, you're not a groupie. You're... so far from that."

My heart almost pounded out of my chest; there was nothing but sincerity in his words. He kissed me hard, and I reluctantly released my hold on him, knowing that it would only make it worse to drag it out. We didn't have time, so we'd have to take a rain check.

The next time, nothing would stop us.

He left me to shower first while he retrieved whatever Tom had left outside, and then it was a rush to get dressed and ready before the twenty-minute deadline was up. Rhett and I exited the hotel at the same time as Dora and Kristie, both of whom had a small suitcase dragging behind them. It made me wonder where Kristie had slept, but I was all kinds of glad it hadn't been in our room.

I had nothing except the new clothes I was wearing—jeans, a black sweater, and the new underwear, along with my crappy old shoes. I mean, I did grab Rhett's shirt because I wasn't letting it go, but those suitcases were a stark reminder of my position here.

How little I had and how much I was relying on others to keep me safe, sheltered, and clothed.

It was humbling. Humbling and scary.

fifteen

BILLIE

"She's on the damn third bus," Jace snarled when we all stood in the garage, the huge vehicles already running and ready to go. The rest of the band had boarded bus one, their backup the second, and staff the third. Everyone was just waiting on the three of us, no doubt hoping we'd get our shit together soon.

Rhett crossed his arms over his chest. "Fine. Then I'm on the *damn third bus* too, you selfish asshole."

That gave Jace a moment's pause as his expression fell before anger flared in his eyes again. "Two fucking days, bro! It's taken her two fucking days to lure you into her web like a goddamn black widow spider. If you're not careful, she'll eat you when she's done draining you dry."

Jesus. Dramatic much?

Rhett didn't react as aggressively; instead, he shook his head sadly. "One day soon, you're going to see that it wasn't Billie who fucked shit up. Always easy to blame someone else when the one with the issue is you."

Whoa. Does Rhett have a death wish?

Before Jace could lose his shit—and I knew him well enough to see the bubbling inferno just under the surface of his perfect face—Rhett grabbed my hand and started to move us toward the third bus. The one for staff.

Everyone on there was, no doubt, going to freak the hell out when the lead guitarist of Bellerose spent the next eight hours in close proximity to them. Poor Rhett was going to wish he'd made a different decision, but he seemed determined to stick it out, even after I told him I'd be fine on the third bus. "We will see each other tonight when we stop," I reminded him.

"Not a chance, Thorn."

Damn, that nickname did things to me that I didn't want to admit out loud. Memories of this morning filled my head, and I wondered if we'd have a chance to finish what we'd started before we reached New York.

Before I would have to leave him.

Just as we reached the steps, there was a shout from behind us. "Wait! Just fucking wait."

Rhett grew tenser beside me, but he did turn back to Jace.

"It's safer if we're all on one bus," Jace bit out, coming closer to us, his expression neutral, even if his tone indicated that he'd rather be having surgery without anesthesia than be here having this conversation. "As long as she stays out of my way, we should all survive the next eight hours."

Stay out of his way in sixty feet of space. Sure, easy as fuck. Part of me kind of wished I could just travel with the cleaning crew and avoid all the drama. But for some reason, Rhett had stepped into my corner and never left.

So I wouldn't leave him either.

At that point, Tom poked his head out of bus one. "Can you three hurry the hell up? We have a schedule to keep, and time is money in this business."

Both Jace's and Rhett's expressions hardened, and it was clear there was no love between any of the band members and their manager. Well, except for Florence, of course. She had to be the reason they kept him around. No one was good enough at their job to make it worth dealing with his woeful attitude.

"Billie, are you cool with traveling on the main bus?" Rhett checked in with me before making any decisions.

I nodded, not wanting to cause any more drama. At this point, having Jace and Rhett so close to me had my body, head, and heart a true mess. I'd be a wreck by the time we made it to New York City, but I didn't want to cause more of a rift between the band members.

Despite Jace's opinion of me, I'd never wanted to cause him pain.

Jace left us without another word, heading toward bus one, no doubt content that his altruistic deed for the day was done. Rhett, however, despite everyone waiting on us, took another second to spin me around so he could look down at me directly. He took in my expression closely as he asked, "Are you sure? Once we're on the bus, it doesn't tend to stop except for gas. Security protocols and all that. We'll have hours before our next concert venue, and then days after that before we end up in New York. If you're not comfortable, I'm happy to take the staff bus with you."

How was this guy even real? His words had my eyes burning, and maybe it was just that I'd been in a terrible cycle—treated like worthless trash and half the time homeless—that actually being treated with decency hit me harder than expected.

"I'm sure. I'd rather you be safe, even if I have to endure a little awkwardness between Jace and me." *Understatement of the century.* The only thing that could make it more awkward was if Angelo suddenly joined the tour too.

He examined my face one last time before he gave a resolute nod and reached out to wrap his left hand around my right. We walked hand in hand to the biggest bus, and when we reached the steps, I looked up to find Tom standing at the top. "About fucking time," he snarled, but further words were cut off when Rhett shot a dark look his way. "Just get inside," he finished, before scurrying off like the rat he was.

Hurrying up, I reached the top and had a quick look around. Dora had taken care of the main bus yesterday, so this was my first time seeing the band's personal bus, and I wasn't all that surprised to see how much larger and more luxurious it was than the other two. Everything was done in black, chrome, and gray accents. Sleek and modern. It was fancy, but still... "Why don't you fly and make the rest of your crew use the buses?" I asked as Rhett ushered me forward. "It would be much faster." I was stating the obvious, but I mean, if time was money, as Tom had so eloquently shouted before…

"Flo is scared of flying," Rhett said simply as the doors closed behind us. Moving further into the space, I noticed that the driver was readying to leave. He looked to be in his late fifties, with thinning gray hair and a cheerful smile he shot my way as he welcomed us onboard.

At least one person wasn't pissed by our little standoff outside.

I could hear the other band members chatting in the back of the bus, sounding like they were organizing bunks and getting settled. Everyone except Grayson, who sat behind the table staring at his phone. He looked up briefly to give us a nod but, in usual fashion, didn't say anything else.

This "man of mystery" thing he had going on both intrigued and scared me. I couldn't shake the memory of how he'd touched my lip last night when he'd accused me of *pretending* to be insecure.

Rhett pushed us along the main walkway, and I saw that their bunks were larger with much better bedding than the ones I'd made up on the other buses. "I'm taking the bedroom," Rhett called as he moved us past the bunks. I waited for a protest from someone—

mostly Florence and Tom since they were a couple—but there was no complaint.

I actually thought I heard, just as Rhett opened the door for me to enter before him, Florence say something about him *finally* sleeping again. She sounded happy and not pissed that I was taking the room that was, no doubt, usually reserved for them.

Before I could hear anything else, we were inside, and as Rhett closed the door behind us, I relaxed and looked around once more. "These buses are unbelievable," I said with a laugh. "It's hard to believe how much they fit in here."

He laughed too, seemingly relaxed as well. He released my hand to move forward and drop onto the edge of the large bed. It was covered in a thick, navy blanket, with at least eight plump pillows adorning the head. No lie, it was a cozy-looking bed. I'd only woken up a few hours ago, so there was no reason I should be wanting to crawl my way across and snuggle into the depths.

My gaze dragged across Rhett as he sprawled back before he patted the spot beside him, indicating I should take a seat next to him. *Okay, maybe there was one reason.* We had some unfinished business I really wanted to jump back into. But maybe not on a crowded tour bus with my angry ex.

"We're about to take off," Rhett warned me, and I stumbled forward as the bus picked up speed. Rhett caught me as I landed on the bed, helping me straighten up.

Looking around, since this was definitely not the time to focus on how his hands felt on my bare arms, I noticed that there wasn't much else in this room. The giant bed frame took up most of the space, but I did see a small closet in the right corner. Rhett noticed the direction of my gaze. "I had Tom bring a few more sets of clothes for you. And some toiletries. They should be in there."

Rhett had clearly been planning for me to be in here with him from the start. "You're too good to me," I said softly, glancing down at the new clothing again. "I'm never going to be able to repay you. But thank you."

"It's nothing," he said, and it was clear he meant it. "Don't even worry about tallying this up. It's just one person helping another out. I'd hope you'd do the same if the roles were reversed."

"Of course," I said immediately, and I meant it. I'd always tried to help when I could. "I've never had much, but I have always shared. It's, honestly, how some of us on minimum wage survived during the hard times."

Rhett dropped his hand over mine and squeezed

lightly, and we sat in a comfortable silence for a few seconds as the bus picked up speed, going over a few bumps as the driver negotiated the alley and got us out on the road.

"Come on," Rhett said suddenly, jumping to his feet again and holding a hand out to me. "You won't want to miss the exit."

I had no idea what he was talking about until we were back in the front of the bus, along with all of the band and Tom, each of them staring out the tinted windows. As I leaned forward and peered out, I couldn't help the gasp that escaped.

Fans lined the streets in the hundreds—maybe thousands—cheering and screaming as they waved the buses on. "How did they know you were leaving at this time?" I breathed, shaking my head at how famous they actually were. Sometimes I forgot due to how normal they were in person.

"They follow our tours and wait for hours in the hopes of catching us," Florence said, and I was surprised that she talked directly to me without any attitude. "And this grassroots tour has been planned for over a year, and everyone knows we're playing in all the old venues from when we first entered the music scene. It's been a big deal."

Tom, on the other hand, was still a cunt. "Don't get

used to it, princess," he sneered. "As soon as we get to New York, you're off the tour and we can stop having drama for me to clean up."

Florence smacked him on the shoulder. "Tom," she said in a rush. "Enough, okay. Billie's had a rough few days, and honestly, the last thing any woman needs after almost being kidnapped and raped is another *man* being an asshole to her."

Her voice broke on a few of the words, and I wondered at her story. She hadn't been particularly warm to me, and I'd expected nothing more, really, since everyone here was team Jace. But in this moment, I felt a small female bond forming. When her gaze drifted over her shoulder in my direction, I shot her a thankful smile. She didn't return it, but that didn't matter. Her gesture had already been made.

In a different life, maybe we'd have even been friends.

Jace caught my eye then, his expression blank, but at least he wasn't sneering at me. There was no greater reminder than him of the *different life* I could have had, and it was almost too much for me to handle.

Deciding I was already done with today, despite the fact that it was still morning, I excused myself and hurried back to the bedroom. My soul was screaming that I needed to get off this bus as soon as possible, while my heart reminded me that when we reached New York, it'd be the last time I got to see Rhett.

And Jace.

Maybe this time the goodbye would actually destroy me.

sixteen

RHETT

The tight, closed-off expression on Billie's face as she retreated into our bedroom made my chest ache. But it was quickly eased by the mental reminder she was in *our* bedroom. Hers and mine. Together. Not even Jace had argued when I claimed the only double bed on the bus, and I wasn't stupid enough to think he was suddenly okay with me and Billie being... *intimate*. He'd simply recognized the fact that I could actually sleep when I was with her.

That, in and of itself, gave me hope. Whether it was a conscious thought or not, Jace placed my health and wellbeing at a higher priority than his eight-year-stale heartbreak over Billie Bellerose.

We had two smaller shows to play on the road before we reached New York. That meant I had two nights and three days to convince her she needed to stay. Only two nights and three days to *somehow* repair the burneddown bridge between my best friend and his first love. Except... part of me didn't want to mend that bridge too well. I may have only known her for a relatively short period of time, but I'd be damned if I let Jace steal her away.

"Cut it out," he snarled at me. "If you're going to be all fucking heart eyes over that bitch, I'll change my mind and kick her back to the staff bus."

I swiveled my head toward him and raised one cool brow. For some reason, I was more than ready to throw down this morning. "For one thing, Jace, you're not in charge around here. Lead singer does *not* make you our *leader*." He recoiled with a stricken look on his face, but I was far from done. "For another, you need to cut the insults when it comes to Billie. Pretend all you like, bro, but you loved her once. You loved her so much you literally named our band after her. So you're not fooling anyone by calling her *bitch* and *whore*. All you're doing is proving how painfully not over her you are, and frankly? After eight years, that's just sad."

Flo gasped, but I kept my eyes locked on Jace. His

eyes hardened, his jaw tensing as he digested my words.

"You have no idea what you're talking about," he replied in a hoarse voice.

I laughed coldly in response. "You're right. I don't. All I know is what *you've* told me, what you've told all of us, and now I'm seriously starting to question how biased that version of events really was."

He swallowed hard, seeming to lose a fraction of his cold fury as his eyes darted to the closed bedroom door. Then he gritted his teeth and refocused on me. "Like I fucking said. You have *no* idea. She fooled *me* once before too. Then she left me for my best friend and never looked back. Don't be stupid, Rhett. She'll do it to you too."

There was something off about his tone, though. Something that hinted there was a *whole* lot more to the story, and I narrowed my eyes.

"You've clearly told the story often enough that you believe it all to be true," I said calmly, "but seriously ask yourself this, Jace. If Billie really ran off into the sunset with your best friend, why is she so fucking terrified of him finding her now? Why does she say she hasn't seen him in *almost* as long as she hasn't seen you, huh?"

His brow dipped in a scowl and his jaw tightened, but he said nothing back.

I sighed, then reached out and flicked him in the forehead. "Wake up, Jace. She's just a girl, and you're an asshole who can't pull his head out of his ass long enough to see she needs *help*."

That flick enraged him—or maybe it was my observation—and he rose out of his seat with fists clenched.

"That's enough," Grayson snapped, closing the journal he'd been writing in and shooting us both a hard look. "Sit down, Jace. You're not fighting him."

Tom cleared his throat, nodding like a fucking bobblehead. "Yeah, exactly. We can't show up with bruised faces, or rumors will start. Especially after that incident last night." He gave Grayson a long look, but Gray just ignored him as he pulled a pair of drumsticks from his jacket.

"Jace, I heard you working on something new this morning," Flo offered as a change of subject, pasting a smile on her face that urged us all to kiss and make up. Or at least retreat to our corners and save the violence for another time. "Can we hear it?"

Jace was still glaring daggers at me, though, and I couldn't seem to quell the fury burning inside me. He was right, I *didn't* have the whole story, but Billie was the only person who could tell me the rest, and she'd been pretty clear that she wasn't going to share. She didn't seem to have any desire to change Jace's song, no matter how off-tune it suddenly rang.

But those scars on her body told a whole different story. I hadn't said anything this morning when I'd noticed a few ropey burns on her sides, but they told me there was darkness in her past. Just like in mine.

I loved Jace like family, but he was way, way off the mark about her. Finding that evidence of pain literally burned into her flesh had confirmed that for me, even if she wouldn't say what had happened out loud.

"No," Jace replied to Flo after a long, tense silence. "It's not done."

A scathing insult sat on the tip of my tongue, desperate to be unleashed. I kept it to myself, but shit... maybe his muse would sing if he found out I'd tasted Billie's sweet cunt this morning. After all, *everything* he wrote was about her, whether he admitted it or not. The fact that he was suddenly writing again—when he hadn't written anything new for almost a year— couldn't be a coincidence.

Grayson's drumsticks tapped out an unfamiliar tune on the tabletop, his head tipped back and his eyes closed like he was listening to something in his head. Flo and I exchanged a confused look, then she reached out and poked Gray in the ribs.

"Hey, grumpy-guts. What was that?"

He opened his eyes, giving a shrug. "Just something stuck in my head."

"Like... something you wrote?" She gave me another look that was easy to interpret. Despite the fact that Grayson frequently wrote in his journal, he never shared.

Tom Tucker, the oily fuck, snorted a disparaging laugh before Gray could answer. "Grayson doesn't write songs for Bellerose. That's Jace's job. And do I need to remind you that you're supposed to start recording your next album as soon as this tour ends? Grassroots is for the nostalgia of the past hits, but now it's time to think of the future ones."

We absolutely did *not* need reminding. And so far, we had a grand total of *zero* songs to record. He wasn't wrong that Jace wrote all of Bellerose's lyrics, but after that first album that had shot Bellerose to stardom, all of us had contributed to the melodies. Jace worked better when he was collaborating. When it was all on him alone, the music turned too hollow and melancholy.

Which only added weight to Billie's accusation that she'd been a part of those original tracks. Shit, he'd really screwed her over. We'd been living it up with our multimillion-dollar contracts, and she'd been fucking *homeless.*

That thought turned my stomach, and I pushed up out of my seat.

"Hey, Rhett, where are you going?" Tom demanded, looking up from his phone like he was our permanent manager or some shit. Shit, I really regretted the day Brenda Dove—best band manager in the business—had taken an extended maternity leave and the label put fucking Tucker on as our tour manager. Usually, Brenda chose our tour manager and they were a hell of a lot more tolerable than slimeball Tom.

"I need some fucking space," I muttered over my shoulder, already halfway to the bedroom. I needed some space away from Jace because it was hard to swallow the fact that his broken heart had caused Billie such hardship. It was hard to sit there and pretend that we were okay, when the opposite was true.

"Rhett, don't—" Flo started to protest, but Jace cut her off.

"Leave him," he snapped. "Maybe if he gets his dick sucked, he'll stop being such a sour little bitch."

My fist curled at my side and my teeth ground hard, but I refused to take the bait. Instead, I slipped into the one and only bedroom on the bus and found Billie curled up in the middle of the bed. My heart ached and my gaze instantly softened as I closed the door behind me and flicked the privacy lock. She was tucked up in a tiny ball on her side, wet tracks cutting telling lines down her cheeks and a scrap of purple fabric balled up under her head.

Sighing, I realized how utterly paper-thin the bedroom door was.

Wordlessly, I kicked off my shoes and climbed onto the bed to wrap the little ball of Billie up in my arms and hold her close. My lips against the back of her neck, I pressed little kisses to her skin until she relaxed into my embrace.

"I don't want to do this to you guys," she whispered, her voice so broken it made me want to storm back out there and punch Jace for real. "I've hurt Jace enough already; I can't be responsible for taking another friend away from him."

Christ. She'd heard all that and still worried about hurting him? Billie Bellerose was a fucking saint.

I didn't respond immediately, not wanting to make it seem like I was dismissing her concern. But ultimately... Jace was a big boy. He just needed to start acting like it. So I just lay there with her for a while, dancing my fingers down her bare arm and tangling our fingers together. Sniffing, she held up our interlaced hands and kissed my knuckles.

That innocent brush of her lips shot straight to my cock, and I bit the inside of my cheek to keep my mind out of the gutter. Not while the entire fucking band was within earshot. Not when I wanted her anything *but* quiet while I fucked her until she couldn't stand up.

Ah crap. That was the opposite of keeping my mind out of the gutter. I needed to shift away slightly so she wouldn't feel the *hard* evidence of where my thoughts had just roamed.

"Can I ask you something?" I murmured, resting my chin on her shoulder.

She glanced back at me, a small frown on her brow. "Um, sure. I guess..."

I smiled. "Very confident response, Thorn."

Her lips tilted in amusement. "Ask your question, Zep."

I hesitated, wondering if I was pushing things too far, too fast. But the *need* to know was eating away at me. So I wet my lips and went for it. "How did you get your scars?"

She went stiff in my embrace, so I hugged her tighter. After a moment she gave a small groan and rolled over to face me, her cheeks pink. "I hoped you hadn't noticed," she admitted in a soft whisper. "You didn't say anything at the time..."

I grinned, letting the filthy thoughts shine through. "I had other things on my mind, Thorn." Then I pulled her closer, hitching her leg over my hip so she could feel my hard dick against her crotch. "Still do, if we're being totally transparent. But I just want to know what happened... Did someone do that to you?" *Was it Angelo?* If it was, I'd stop the bus right now and go after him with my bare hands. Jace would back me up, too, I knew it.

She wrinkled her cute nose and shook her head. "No, nothing like that. It... I was in a fire." Her teeth worried at her lower lip, and she studied my eyes like she was trying to decide how much truth to offer up to a man she barely knew. I got it, I did. But it didn't stop me from wanting her to just hand over the keys to her mind. And heart.

"What kind of fire?" I asked gently, trying to squeeze just a *little* more information out. For no other reason than I wanted to *know her*. I wanted to understand what made her tick, what made her shed tears over a guy who was happy to leave her homeless to avenge his hurt feelings. Okay, in fairness to Jace, I didn't honestly think he understood how dire her circumstances had been that night. He was just too stubborn and too self-centered to really *look*. Based on what he'd always told us, he genuinely believed she'd chosen money over love, since the Ricci's were rich and he'd been all but a starving artist. He probably had never imagined her struggling in the time they'd been apart.

She gave a small sigh. "A house fire. My family home, the one next door to Jace and down the road from Angelo... They think it was an electrical fault or something, but... it was the middle of the night and none of the smoke alarms went off. My bedroom was upstairs, and when I woke up, the fire had already cut off the exit." She paused, wetting her lips as her gaze darted away. "I got out, barely, but my parents didn't make it. They never even woke up before the smoke got them."

Holy shit.

"I spent a month in ICU... I didn't know they were dead until two weeks after their funeral."

Wow. Talk about insult on top of injury. I couldn't even imagine...

Jace couldn't know about this, right? If he'd just ignored that sort of loss, hurt feelings or not, then he wasn't the man I thought he was.

"My parents were shitty humans; I chose not to attend their funerals," I admitted, making her startled gaze dart back up to meet mine. "But it sounds like you really loved yours, so I'm sorry for your loss."

A soft, sad smile touched her lips. "Thanks, Zep."

"How long ago did it happen?" I asked gently,

slipping my hand under the fabric of her shirt to stroke the bumpy burn scar on her spine.

She stared at me for a long pause. "Eight years ago," she whispered. "Eight years and one month."

Just a month after the last time she'd seen Jace. Shit, she would have only been sixteen, the poor thing. Before I could comment on that fact, her mouth was against mine, and I eagerly kissed her back. She wanted a distraction, to shift those sour emotions away, and I was all too happy to oblige. We'd keep it quiet, and what Jace didn't know couldn't hurt him. Fucker.

BILLIE

Turned out that eight hours on a bus until we reached *Forster* could go really fast when one was holed up with a sexy rock star. There was no way we could have sex in this room with its paper-thin walls—if I could hear them arguing, they'd *definitely* hear me moaning.

That thought had given me a moment of panic that they might have heard me telling Rhett about the fire, but he quickly reassured me that when we spoke quietly, we couldn't be overheard. Not unless someone had their ear pressed to the door. I wasn't so sure I'd put that past Tom, though, so I needed to be more cautious.

Two nights and three days. Rhett told me that's how long we had between the two small shows and making it to New York. Surely, at some point in that time, we'd find ourselves properly alone.

With*out* the ghosts of my past looking over my shoulder. Fucking Jace was taking up too much real estate in my mind as it was, and if I was totally honest... so was Angelo.

When a knock sounded on the door a couple of hours before we were supposed to arrive, I rolled over to find Rhett sound asleep, his face calm and peaceful. Awake, the demons lived in his expression, but right now, he was free from their hold.

Making sure not to disturb him, I dragged myself out of bed and grabbed his shirt on the floor to pull over my nakedness. Just because we hadn't had sex didn't mean we hadn't had *fun*.

Running a hand through my scruffy hair, I wondered who I'd find on the other side.

My heart pounded harder in my chest as I reached for the handle, and I wondered how I'd react to Jace right now. *If it was Jace.* Fuck. Why was I even thinking about that guy at the moment. Rhett made me feel safe and content, and he played chords on my body that would stay with me forever.

Jace broke me just as badly as I'd broken him, and I had to remember that.

With a huff, I yanked the door open, a glare descending across my face only to be replaced with shock when I realized it was not Jace at all.

It was Florence.

"Hey," she said softly, her gaze dragging along the shirt and down to my bare legs before it shot to the bed where Rhett continued to breathe softly in his sleep. She remained locked on him for many seconds, and I wasn't even surprised that a shot of jealousy licked through my body.

The look on her face was love. She loved him.

"Thank you," she whispered, and I blinked like my grasp on English was slipping. I had no idea what she was thanking me for.

"For what?" I finally said, trying to pull myself together.

"Giving him some peace. It's been too long, and I die every night hearing him rage and scream in the few moments of unbroken sleep he gets." She was dramatic, but I wouldn't expect less from a rock star. And the subject was worrying enough to have my head snapping around to Rhett.

Maybe I was dramatic too, but I choked on my next breath as I tried to imagine the reasons for his torturous sleep. "He's been fine with me," I said, shock lacing my tone. Turning back to her, I shook my head. "I don't understand."

Florence shrugged and laughed sadly. "None of us have a great past. It's the reason we're such amazing musicians—we have tragedy in our souls that bleeds into the music. And when you listen to our songs, you feel our pain. You feel... everything."

I couldn't argue with that. It was the reason I could never listen to Bellerose's music. It broke me even further, and I was barely keeping my shattered pieces together as it was.

Clearing my throat, needing not to be in this heavy moment with a chick I wasn't even sure liked me, I changed the subject. "Did you need something from Rhett?" I asked. "I can let you know when he's awake."

She shook her head. "No... no. I actually knocked to see if you'd like some food. I know Rhett grabbed you both some sandwiches earlier, but... I mean. Yeah. I made some extra." She shrugged. "Whatever. Not a big deal."

She stumbled over words and floundered around before a stubborn look settled across her features. She'd let a little too much of her softer side out and was trying to repair the damage, but I was not someone to ever use that against her. Hopefully, she'd see that.

With one last look at Rhett, I decided he was calm enough that I could leave him. "I'd love some food," I told her with a quick smile. "Thanks for thinking of me. I'll just throw some pants on."

Her lips twitched briefly before settling back into firm lines. "Good idea. Most of the others are sleeping, but who knows who we might run into on this tiny shit heap."

A sad sigh escaped me, but I reeled it back in before I sounded too pathetic. "I'll be right out," I said in a rush, and when she nodded and turned away, I moved silently back into the small space and found my jeans on the floor. Dragging them on, I moved just as silently out before closing the door softly.

Rhett clearly needed to catch up on a lot of sleep, and I tried not to think why a small warmth buried deep in my chest at the sound way he slept today. That warmth was followed by pain as I thought of the scars he had that weren't as visible as mine. I needed to do better at supporting him as he'd done for me.

If he wanted me to, of course.

But for now, I was having food with Florence Foster.

It was still hard to believe that this was my life right now.

In the dining area, she was already seated behind the table, a huge charcuterie tray before her. I only knew what the fuck a charcuterie tray even was from working in restaurants, and I'd never had the luxury of eating from one.

There was a huge selection of cheeses, dips, cold cuts, and small sandwiches. "Wow," I said, only half in the booth as I took in the delicious spread of food. "I've never seen anything this impressive before."

Florence eyed me closely, probably trying to figure out if I was being sarcastic, but there was no hiding the awe and sincerity in my voice. "There's so much here too," I added, before I lowered my voice again, dropping it down from a cartoon character with an "excited" speech bubble over their head.

She finally chuckled before grabbing my arm and all but pulling me into the space next to her. "I get so hungry after shows. We burn like a thousand calories dancing, singing, and playing our instruments under all of those lights. This is my version of a miniature buffet —which is my favorite way to eat."

My favorite way to eat was anything not from the garbage, but I wasn't about to say that out loud. No doubt she would think I was trying to gather up sympathy points.

"Thanks, Florence," I said instead. "It looks amazing."

She turned to examine me once more, and I was

starting to get her personal popularity in Bellerose. She had a piercing sort of stare that somehow looked right through you, but also made you feel like her best friend.

It was weird, but I kind of liked it.

"Call me Flo," she said as she released me from her gaze. "My friends all do."

I nodded, unsure why the hell my throat was all clogged up like I'd just been given a puppy. This was how sad my life was, that the simple act of friendship was enough to bring me to tears.

Thankfully, the food was a wonderful distraction as Flo dove in and I followed just as quickly. I watched the way she piled up food on a cracker, starting with dip and then cheese and meat, eating it up like a little cracker sandwich.

We took our time trying out the various selections, and for the most part, focused on food rather than chatting. But the silence wasn't uncomfortable.

"So, what are your plans once you reach New York?" Flo asked as she chewed on a piece of apple, a second piece in her hand ready to go when she swallowed the first. For a tiny chick, she could impressively put the food away.

"The city itself is too expensive for me to stay in," I said, knowing this without even having to check. "I'll head for a fringe area with enough population to blend in and enough jobs that don't ask for identification or social security. It might take a few days, but I'll find something. I always do."

"You really think that Angelo would track you half way across America? I mean, why would he bother?" She didn't sound skeptical exactly, but I could see her confusion.

Playing with a dried apricot, I started to tear it between my fingers, my appetite gone now. "Hopefully not, but I won't underestimate him. We have a checkered history too, and I'm not sure he'll just let me walk away this time. Or his family. They're powerful, and Angel wasn't the only one to see me that night."

My nickname for him slipped out before I could help it, and I swallowed down the bitter memories of the days I had his love and protection as well. Just like with Jace, there was no going back to those happier days. None of us were the same *innocent* people any longer. And in no way did that refer to sexual innocence... Nope, that wasn't the case. It was our souls that had been innocent, without the tarnish and scars we all wore now.

Just like with Rhett, not all of my scars were visible.

"We'll help in whatever way we can," Flo said, breaking me free from the darker thoughts. "You don't have to do everything alone. I doubt Rhett would even let you go it alone." As she leaned over and grabbed more food, it sounded like she muttered, "Or let you go at all."

Deciding to answer as if I'd heard her correctly, I was completely honest for once. "I'd love to stay here in the protective embrace of Bellerose. Rhett was right when he said you might be some of the few people in this country who could stay out of the Ricci family's control. But..." I shrugged as I took a deep breath. "I can't do that to you all. Not to Jace or Rhett, who will probably beat the shit out of each other on a daily basis. Or the rest of you, who might end up in danger because of me. I'm no saint, but even I couldn't live with the guilt if any of you got hurt because of me."

Flo waved me off. "Girl, we're Bellerose. We thrive on this drama and have a shit ton of security. You should at least think about it—"

"Florence," the whiny snarl cut her off mid-sentence. "What the fuck are you doing?"

The animation in her face died off a touch as Tom stumbled into the kitchen area wearing just a pair of sweats, showcasing his skinny frame. Why the hell a chick as awesome as Flo was with a fucking loser like this was beyond me, but I wasn't about to judge.

Flo pushed up from her seat then, scooting out of the booth. "Heading back to bed now," she told him in a rush, before shooting me one last smile. She took Tom the fucker's hand and led him toward the bunks, leaving me alone with half a charcuterie board and a lot of mixed-up feelings.

It wasn't until I glanced up at the clock on the wall that I saw I'd been out here for almost an hour. We were going to arrive at our destination in another hour, and I realized... I was content.

This time with Rhett and then with Flo had calmed some of that trauma always churning inside.

I just wished she hadn't brought up staying, because I couldn't let myself fall into this.

My future wasn't here with Bellerose, no matter how right it felt.

eighteen

GRASON

Squishing my six-and-a-half-foot frame into the bunks never resulted in much sleep, but with another show tonight, I had to try. Of course, that plan went to shit when I heard their voices. Flo and Billie were in the dining area, and even though they were keeping their voices down, this space was too small to hide their conversation completely.

I caught enough of it to get the vague idea. Billie was making a weak attempt at acting like she wasn't shit-scared to be on her own again, and Flo was trying to convince her to stay with the tour a bit longer. Which was... strange. Why did Flo care? Tom had made no secret that he disliked Billie and wanted her gone. As much as we hated it, Flo didn't often cross Tom. He was too much of a manipulative shit for that.

We weren't worried that he was hurting her; none of us would stand for that, and it'd be impossible to hide in our close quarters. But he *was* controlling and generally an insufferable fuck. He'd taken advantage of Flo when she was in a bad space, and now she couldn't dislodge him.

As if my thoughts summoned him, Tucker muttered some curses and climbed out of the bunk that he was sharing with Flo.

"Florence." He'd cut her off mid-sentence with a teeth-grating whine. "What the fuck are you doing?" Was he seriously so insecure that he couldn't let Flo make a friend? Hah, what was I thinking, of course he was.

Flo muttered her response, and the two of them returned to their shared bunk. There had to be fuck-all space in there for them both, but there was a spare bunk above if they wanted it. I waited, listening for Billie to return to Rhett's bed. He was sleeping so deeply I could hear his quiet snores through the bedroom door. Lucky fuck.

After several minutes of silence, I had to assume she wasn't going back to sleep. I needed to rest myself, but between Rhett snoring, Jace mumbling in his sleep, and the wet, rhythmic sound of Flo jerking Tom's shriveled dick, I wasn't holding my breath.

Silently, I climbed out of my own bunk and slipped into one of the cramped bathrooms. Maybe if I gave her a few more minutes, she'd be gone before I went out to the front.

It was quiet enough when I finished up and washed my hands that I was surprised to find her still sitting at the table. She was all tucked up in a ball, staring out the window at the passing scenery. and didn't even seem to notice me standing there.

She was... interesting. I took advantage of her distraction for a moment to study her, taking in the sadness in her face and the defensive, guarded body language. Then I started feeling like a creep, so I sat down to grab some prosciutto from the charcuterie board.

Billie startled, her head whipping toward me and her eyes huge. But when she saw it was *me*—rather than Jace, I would guess—she noticeably relaxed. It was odd, to say the least. I knew what kind of effect I had on people; I was intimidating and my reluctance to speak made people nervous. But not this girl. She seemed *calm* sitting opposite me.

"Hey, Grayson," she said softly, her voice doing

unexpected things to me as she said my name. "Did we wake you up?"

I shook my head, reaching for a chunk of cheese. "No."

Ah, good one. Really inviting conversation, huh? Idiot.

She didn't seem put off by my grunt. "I'm surprised everyone is able to sleep at all in the daytime. But I guess when you know you need to be up half the night, you have to rest whenever you can." A small frown touched her delicate brow. "Flo mentioned something about Rhett not sleeping much...?"

I shrugged. "Until you, yeah." See, I could manage more than one word answers occasionally. Go me. Personal progress and all that shit.

She stared at me for a long moment, that tiny frown sitting on her face. She *wanted* to pry more information out, but that was Rhett's story to tell, not mine. So I just grabbed some more cold cuts from the platter and put them in my mouth. Salty and delicious.

When she, no doubt, realized I wasn't offering up any more details, she gave a sigh and rested her cheek on her knee. Her legs were still tucked up in front of her, those thin arms wrapped around them. How long had she been living rough, I wondered.

Tom Tucker—the fucker—was doing everything possible to ensure Billie never saw a cent out of

Bellerose royalties, but I was pretty sure she wouldn't take it anyway. Her threat had been hollow, made out of desperation. So long as we saw her safely to New York, she would disappear without a dime. If Jace had taken even one second to step back and distance himself from his hurt feelings, he'd have seen it too.

She wasn't here to ruin his life and break up the band. It was just a case of wrong place, wrong time. Or right… depending on whose perspective it was.

Reaching out, I pushed the charcuterie closer to her. "Eat," I ordered. "You're so thin you might snap." That was basically a full sentence. My therapist could go fuck himself.

She gave a small gasp, her eyes rounding and a blush touching her cheeks. It made me morbidly curious to know what was going through her head. What had I said that would make her blush? That she might snap? I severely doubted she was thinking—like I now was—about how I'd break her in half in bed.

Before I could do something fucking dumb—like ask how she preferred her orgasms, from hand, mouth, or dick—the bus slowed to a stop and our driver pressed the intercom button.

"Roadblock," Mark said over the little speaker, "looks like state troopers."

Billie sucked in a gasp, and my immediate instinct

was to protect her. "Wait here," I muttered, pushing up from my seat. They wouldn't be able to see her through the window, the tint was dark enough, but I had to stop them getting onto the bus.

Slipping out of the door, I closed it quickly behind myself, just in case the open door was seen as some kind of invitation. Mark was right about it being a roadblock. Barricades closed the road entirely, and several State Trooper cars lined the shoulders, lights turned on.

We were within eyesight of the state border on a quiet road, not the main highway. Our buses typically took "scenic routes" to avoid traffic jams and paparazzi, so these guys looked bored, to say the least.

"What's the problem, officer?" I asked as politely as possible when one of the uniformed cops strode toward us. Mark had come out of the bus, too, but was content to let me do the talking. A glance over my shoulder told me the rest of our entourage had caught up and were waiting behind our bus.

"Apologies for the delay, sir," the officer replied with a yawn. "We're looking for a person that is suspected to be trying to skip state lines." He plucked a photo from his pocket and held it out. "Have you seen this woman?"

Maintaining my expressionless face, I reached out

to take the photo from him. It was taken from a CCTV camera, showing Billie in a white blouse with a black apron tied around her waist. She carried several plates of food expertly stacked up her forearm, clearly in the middle of a waitressing shift. The capture from the video had grabbed her when she'd tipped her head toward the camera, almost like she was looking right out of the photo at me.

"Nope," I lied, handing the picture back. "She a fugitive or something?" I was curious what bullshit the Ricci family was disguising this as. The fact that the cops weren't immediately searching our bus for Billie said that Roger *hadn't* called in before trying to take her. They weren't aware that she was being sheltered under the Bellerose entourage. That was good.

The cop huffed a laugh. "Or something. Don't be fooled by her pretty face; this woman is the lead suspect in a restaurant shooting two nights ago."

My brows hitched with legitimate shock. "She's wanted for murder? Of who?" I was pushing the line, but my curiosity was burning hot.

The officer was bored enough that he didn't seem to mind my question. "Couple of nobodies," he shrugged, hitching his utility belt under a heavy gut. "Waitress and a restaurant manager. Problem was, it was a Ricci restaurant. They want her *found* if you catch my meaning." He leaned in to tell me this in a conspiratorial tone, and I forced a shocked look on my face.

"So they want this girl found but not arrested?" That probably meant they wanted her dead. Why, though? Why did the Riccis care if Billie had seen them shoot some waitstaff? It wasn't adding up. One girl's word against a mafia family surely wasn't a threat.

The cop gave another shrug. "They deal with shit their own way. Anyway, you mind if my guys check your buses? Just in case she stowed away or something." He had to be some kind of hardcore Bellerose fan to be spilling this sort of info. He also wrongly assumed I gave zero shits about the police corruption he was so blatantly admitting to.

I ground my teeth with irritation. "Check the next two, but not this one." I jerked a thumb to our main bus. "The band is asleep. You don't want to be blamed for Bellerose putting on a shitty show, do you"—I squinted at his badge—"Officer Smithers?"

One of the younger officers hurried over with a hesitant smile on his face. "Are you Grayson Taylor? Holy shit, man, you're my idol. Could I get your autograph?"

I twitched a brow at the paunchy cop in charge, Officer Smithers, and he gave a sigh. "Yeah, alright I doubt she'd be dumb enough to hide out with a high-profile tour like yours." He huffed a wheezing laugh, and I forced myself to join in.

The younger cop pulled out a marker pen and had me sign a notebook that he pulled from his belt, then we were free to go. They moved the barricades to allow our buses through, and I watched from a window as we passed.

Only once the lights of the cop cars had faded behind us and we crossed the border into Ohio did I release my pent-up breath and relax. Only then did I realize Billie was still sitting exactly where I'd told her to stay, her face so pale she was ghostly. It made the small sprinkling of freckles over her nose stand out more prominently.

"You okay?" I grunted, returning to the table with her half-eaten charcuterie.

She shook her head, wetting her lips. Damn, she had great lips.

Ah shit. Now I was thinking dirty things about little Billie Bellerose again. What was it about this girl?

"Did that cop say they think *I* murdered Liz and Gary?" Her voice was husky and panicked, and I finally clicked that she'd been listening in while I spoke with Officer Smithers.

I wasn't one for sugar-coating shit, so I just sat back down and grabbed a piece of salami. "Yep."

Her sharp inhale startled me, and her eyes swam with wetness. "I didn't!" she protested, shaking her head, "Angelo and his guys did! I saw them do it and they were going to kill me too and then—"

"Chill, little hedgehog," I cut her off, trying not to laugh while she was clearly so panicked. "No one is buying their bullshit." I needed to change the subject before she started crying. "Are you coming to the show tonight?"

Her mouth opened and closed a couple of times, her brow furrowed like she was trying to catch up with my question. "Um, do I have to?" She winced slightly as she said that, and I bit back a grin.

"I think Rhett will want you there," I murmured, focusing on my food. "For safety."

Right. Rhett *wanted her there for* safety.

Since when was I such a blatant liar? I mean, sure, that wasn't untrue... but it wasn't why I was asking. But she really didn't seem excited by the idea of a side-stage view of Bellerose in concert, and that threw me off my game.

Not that I had much game. Chicks threw themselves—and their fucking underwear—at me; I never needed to work for it. Even more so now, thanks to my resemblance to the new Aquaman.

"You don't want to?" I had to ask.

She wrinkled that cute fucking nose. "Not really. Can you blame me? A whole concert about how much Jace hates me and how badly I betrayed him? Not really my idea of a good time. But I guess..." She bit the edge of her lip again. Fuck, why did that nervous gesture drive me insane? "I guess for the sake of safety I could just wear earmuffs and read a book or something."

That mental image made me huff a laugh out loud. Billie gave me a startled look, and awkwardness crept over my skin like a rash.

"Um," I replied, sounding dumb as *fuck*. "Okay. Whatever works. I should..." I gestured toward the bunks, then gave up and exited before I could scare her any further.

Fuck. Tiny little Billie Bellerose with all her adorable prickles was making me feel like a damn teenager again.

BILLIE

The room felt about ten times larger when Grayson left to go back to the bunks. He was a huge guy, there was no denying that, but even more than that, his presence filled every space. For someone who barely talked, there was a charisma and sense of danger that surrounded him, and I found my focus drifting his way, even when he was busy doing something else.

Something like protecting me from a fucking roadblock.

Those state troopers hadn't suspected I was onboard, so they hadn't pushed anything, but it was clear the Ricci family was stepping up the search for me to the next level. I'd heard enough to know there was a photo of me. There was an accusation of murder...

Liz's lifeless face flashed across my vision, and I had to swallow hard multiple times to stop myself from vomiting across the table. The charcuterie board almost made an appearance again, but somehow, I managed to keep it contained.

Fucking fuck. They were too powerful. Would I even be able to disappear in a city as huge as New York? Would I have to change my appearance and name completely this time? Or would I end up on the streets trying to keep myself clothed, fed, and unmolested?

Exhaustion pressed on me until I slid halfway down the chair and slumped forward, my head hitting the top of the table.

My life wasn't supposed to be like this. This had not been in the fucking plans. It was true what they said: Life could change in an instant, so embrace every day. I didn't do enough embracing when I was safe and loved.

A cleared throat had my head jerking up. Jace stood there in the very spot Grayson had been a few minutes ago, and the dread-slash-anticipation I'd been holding onto all day about seeing him surged up in another stomach-churning wave of nausea.

Our gazes locked for a moment, and even as the voice inside my head screamed at me to look away, *run away*, that tonight, with everything else, I couldn't handle the venom in his gaze, I couldn't bring myself to break the stare.

It had been too long since I'd stared into those depthless blue eyes, tracking the minute color changes as his mood went from playful to sexy to alpha. He had the ability to be all three in the same moment, but his eyes always gave away which part of him was the most in charge.

This late afternoon, in the low light of the bus, his eyes looked almost black.

A color I'd never seen until the day I broke both our hearts.

"I deserve an explanation," he said suddenly, husky tones lower than usual.

The demand was so unexpected that it took me at least two minutes to respond as my brain scrambled to make sense of what he was wanting.

"An explanation?" I finally bit out, anger surging to life inside of me. "You think *you* deserve an explanation? After the fucking life you went on to live while I was struggling every damn day! It was almost ten years ago, Jace! There is no explanation I could give you that would make up for the fact that you never checked on me, even once, in ten fucking years."

At some point I'd surged to my feet, half bent over

in the booth, so I could snarl those words at him and probably wake the bus. Jace's head snapped back at the venom in my words, no doubt expecting poor, pathetic Billie again. But fuck that noise. I was done being any man's punching bag.

"I was sixteen years old, Jace," I told him, my voice quieter. Calm. As I forced down my anger and pain. "You gave me no grace and just assumed the worst. I'm not the only one with blame here."

Easing out of the booth, I sidled beside him, trying not to focus on the way the heat from his body seemed to slide across my skin when we were close. He smelled the same too, but also different... This was a form of torture I was ill-equipped to deal with.

The Jace before me was both *mine* and one I had no true knowledge of, but I knew one thing for sure: if I wanted to keep my sanity, I had to hold onto my anger. Anger I could deal with. It was the other emotions that would destroy me, and in truth, I couldn't give him the explanation today. Not with so much pressure and pain in the room. I'd break, and I had no time to break when I was running for my life.

Making my way back into the bedroom, I opened and closed the door silently, despite the way my hands visibly shook. When the door was secured, I leaned back against it, trying to calm the racing of my heart before I climbed into bed with Rhett. Only I never got the chance. Warm, strong arms wrapped around me, and for a moment, I collapsed into Rhett's hold, allowing him to take some of my pain.

It was selfish of me. This guy had more than enough pain of his own to deal with. But soon I'd be alone, and I wanted the comfort that had been denied to me for so long. "You're not alone," he whispered before he scooped me up into his arms. "I don't care what Jace needs. I don't fucking care if this breaks the band up; I won't let you deal with this shit alone. Do you hear me?"

He was whispering the words against my skin near my right ear as he brought us back to the bed and gently set me down. I was shaking, and I had to be stronger than this, but I'd always had visceral reactions to Jace. In all ways.

"I won't break you up," I managed to say before my throat closed over. I wasn't going to fucking cry. Not when I'd flooded half the damn town with my tears at sixteen. When they'd finally dried up, I'd told myself that I was done crying over Jace Adams. He hadn't exactly fought to stay with me, and I had the sense that he'd buried himself in alcohol and pussy to move past us, not tears and ice-cream like me.

Rhett slid closer to me, dragging the blankets up

over us, even though it wasn't cold. Somehow, he knew I needed more comfort. I needed to feel surrounded, and as his arms closed around me and pulled me back against him, I wondered why this guy had put up with my shit for even the couple of days that he had.

His trauma had him trying to save others. I saw it now. My reference to him being a knight in shining leather had been a somewhat joke, but I was fairly sure he truly had a savior complex. I was just his next project, and that was okay because I didn't have the means to fight for myself today.

Today I would let him "save me" because tomorrow that meant I could save myself.

I MUST HAVE DRIFTED OFF, SLEEPING THROUGH THE STRESS, SO when I woke sometime later, the bus was stationary and I was alone in the bedroom. Blinking and yawning, I pushed myself up and saw that the clock read almost 8:00 PM.

Holy crap, I'd slept much longer than I thought. The guys would be going on stage soon, and I wondered if Rhett had left me alone. Not that he shouldn't have, of course. I was a big girl and could look after myself. But it just seemed uncharacteristic of him, and I hoped that he was okay.

Could the Ricci family have gotten to them somehow? But if they had, I certainly wouldn't have been left to sleep peacefully in this room, so there had to be another explanation.

The room was quite dark, outside of the small light from the clock, so I stumbled a bit to get out and find the door. Once I opened it, light flooded in, and I heard multiple voices that I must have missed in my initial waking and panic. Pausing to listen—since I was trying to avoid being murdered, it felt prudent to figure out who was in the bus—I strained to hear any familiar tones.

It sounded like multiple men and one woman, at least. They were chatting and laughing about nothing in particular, and I blinked as I crept farther out of the door and rounded the corner. Two more steps and I was along the hall and in the dining space.

At least ten faces turned and stared at me, and I almost burst into laughter.

They were all huge, men and women, squished into seats, on the floor—even a couple sitting on the stairs of the bus. When I appeared, they grew quiet, and I ran a hand through my hair, knowing it was, for sure, a hot mess. "Uh, hello," I said softly. "What's happening?"

A woman with her blonde hair back in a tight bun jumped down from the kitchen bench and hurried toward me. Like the rest, she was dressed fully in black, and I saw a gun holstered at her side. She wasn't using it or pointing any weapon in my direction, so I went on my instinct that these were not Ricci goons.

"Sorry," she said in a rush. "We were too loud and woke you. The band will have our heads."

Before I could ask again who the hell they were, she handed me a cell phone. It was one of those expensive, sleek numbers that I'd see other members of the band use. "Rhett wants you to call him ASAP. You should have a few minutes before he goes on stage," she said. "He wants to explain everything."

I swallowed roughly. "Okay, thanks. I'll just..." I gestured behind me toward the room. "Yep. Thanks."

Backing away, still unsure what was happening and feeling a tad uneasy with twenty eyes locked on me, I made it to the room and closed and locked the door behind me. Not that it would stop bullets if they started to rain in on me.

Opening the phone, I stared down at the many icons with no idea what I was supposed to use. My old phone literally had numbers and call and hang-up buttons. No fancy screens or access to the internet. Finally, I found a green icon that looked like a phone, and when I hit it, I realized I didn't know Rhett's number.

A few minutes later, I found the address book, and the only number entered was *Sexy Lead Guitarist of Your Dreams*. He might be a fucking saint, but he definitely had the confidence of a rock star. Both were equally sexy in my opinion. After I hit the number, the phone started to ring in my ear, and he answered before the second ring finished. "Thorn!" Noise blasted me at the same time, and it was clear he was right in the midst of concert chaos.

"Hey," I said awkwardly. We hadn't done the talking-on-the-phone thing yet. I was much better face-to-face.

"Sorry I wasn't there when you woke," he pushed on in a rush, and it was getting harder to hear him as the background ruckus increased. "But you needed the rest. I was just going to skip out tonight, but I don't like to let the fans down."

"Definitely not," I said quickly. "I'm totally fine, but there're... there're a lot of people on the bus. Is that right?"

His next words were drowned out for a touch, before he seemed to move away from the main stage where I could hear him clearer. "We pulled security from different trusted sources, and none of them are permitted to take you anywhere alone. We're hoping that by using multiple security companies, the Ricci family won't have had time yet to get to all of them. They have strict orders to bring you across as soon as you wake up. If you hurry, you'll make the first set."

I was about to argue and say that I'd just stay here locked in the room with more security than the damn president to watch over me, when he added. "I won't be much use on stage tonight if you're not close by, you know, where I can see you and know you're safe."

Dammit. I couldn't do that to him when he'd been so good to me.

"I'll get ready and be right there," I told him, forcing a smile to my face so it would be reflected in my words. "See you soon."

"See you soon, Thorn," he replied.

"Thank you," I whispered just as he hung up, so I wasn't sure if he heard or not. But it needed to be said. This guy was too damn good to me, and I would never be able to thank him enough.

For now, it seemed step one was to get my ass over there and support him.

Time to figure out what clothing he'd provided so I could add a little rock star to my waif look. I needed the armor to go into battle once more.

While Jace told the world about the bitch who broke his heart.

Might as well add that to the alliteration I had going on. Billie Bitch Bellerose.

Had a bit of a ring to it.

twenty

BILLIE

Rhett was damn good at what he did. No, scratch that, he was fucking *epic*. From the moment he stepped out under the spotlights, his talented fingers working the strings of his guitar, he was a total *star*. Jace fucking who? Okay, that was an exaggeration—they were all pretty damn incredible out there—but my heart couldn't handle acknowledging anyone but Rhett.

I kept my eyes on him, soaking up the sound of his guitar and blocking out the rest. Or that's what I tried to do. A few songs in, they started playing one of their early hits, one of the first Bellerose tracks to hit number one on the Billboards that had earned them a platinum record.

Swallowing hard, I wrapped my arms around myself and really, *really* tried not to hear the lyrics. But it was impossible to push them out of my head when I knew them so fucking well. It was a song that I'd collaborated on, as had Angelo. It was one that Jace had started writing when the three of us were *happy*, and one he'd finished, *changed*, right after I broke his heart.

What had started as "Precious Rose," a song Jace had literally dedicated to me and how much he *loved* me, had been released six months later as "Poison Roses."

I'd always been Rose to him, like I was Bella to Angelo. And now I was Thorn to Rhett. How utterly fitting that my name had sharpened and grown ugly... just like my heart.

Acid curled through me as Jace's deep, husky voice filled my head. *A poisoned Rose, beautiful and cruel, stolen away by fallen Angel, you played me like a fool.*

Pain lanced through me as I accidentally locked eyes with Jace on stage. His stare was both smoldering hot and glacially cold at the same time. He didn't look away as he sang that cursed song, and I broke first.

Closing my eyes, a hot tear squeezed out from between my lashes and rolled down my cheek. I thought I was done feeling guilt and regret over Jace and Angelo, and here I was crying like it'd happened yesterday. This plan, hiding out with Bellerose, it was a huge mistake. Who did I think I was? I didn't have a fraction of the mental fortitude necessary to pull this off without losing my mind.

It was all *still* so raw, so painful.

A tap on my shoulder startled me, and I spun to find a roadie standing behind me, holding out a pair of headphones and a book.

"Um?" I raised a brow in confusion.

The guy shrugged. "Beats me. Grayson asked that we get these for you before the show, but I got caught up fixing some shit with the amps. Sorry." He handed his delivery over and was gone again before I could question him further.

Curious, I put the headphones on as I looked across the stage to where Grayson was wailing on his drum kit. His expression was laser focused, like he didn't even know he was on stage playing to tens of thousands. All that mattered was his connection with the music.

When the soft headphones covered my ears, the sickeningly true lyrics of "Poison Roses" and haunting cadence of Jace's singing voice faded out. It was replaced by just a drum solo, a rhythmic beat that immediately calmed me down and dried up my stupid, pointless tears.

Grayson tipped his head my way, but a shadow cast over his face, so I couldn't figure out if he was looking at me or not. Either way, I gave him a nod of appreciation and mouthed my thanks, just in case he was. Then I sank my butt down onto one of the chairs tucked in the wings and opened the book.

It wasn't a new one; the spine was well cracked and the pages fluffy on the corners like they'd been thumbed countless times. To my surprise, it was a romance... or at the very least, it was a love story. Whether it ended happily or not remained to be seen, and I abhorred people who read the ending prematurely. If I was going to take the journey that someone—Grayson maybe— had clearly taken dozens of times already, then I wanted the whole experience, no spoilers.

With the noise-canceling headphones on, the calming drumbeats drowning any residual noise, it was easy to lose myself in the book. It wasn't something I'd have picked for myself, but I was fascinated to see what Grayson chose as a favorite read.

I made it about halfway through the book about firemen who jumped from planes into the depths of raging wildfires—which I was starting to think might have a sad ending—when the concert ended. I only noticed because Jace "accidentally" bumped me on his way off stage.

I flipped my middle finger at his back, but he didn't see it. Dick.

"Hey, Thorn," Rhett greeted me with a huge smile when I tugged my headphones off and looked for him. "What did you think? Pretty bad ass, huh?"

Arrogance was a surprisingly good look on Rhett Silver, and I eagerly accepted his embrace when he reached for me. He'd already handed his guitar to a waiting roadie, so his hot hands went straight to my ass, lifting me up so his mouth could crush against mine.

For a moment, I forgot where we were. I forgot who we were and who Rhett's best friend was. But reality was quick to smack me in the face in the form of Tom Tucker.

"You're within full view of the backstage pass holders right now," he sneered, "and I saw more than a few phone-camera flashes. I thought poor little Billie was supposed to be hiding her location."

I cringed, burying my face in Rhett's sweaty tank top, but he didn't put me back down. Hell, he gripped me even tighter. But maybe that was because he was using me to shield his rapidly hardening dick from prying eyes.

"Give her your hoody, Tucker," Rhett demanded instead.

Tom gave an indignant sound, but Flo elbowed him, and he reluctantly took it off. Flo seemed to know what Rhett meant, draping Tom's hoody over me so I could hide my face while we passed the backstage groupies.

"Like it fucking matters *now*," Tom muttered under his breath as he and Flo walked ahead.

"Rhett, put me down," I protested when he started walking with me still wrapped around him like a fucking squid. "Come on, this is insane; they're going to think—"

"That I'm seeing someone? Good. I am." He strode forward, uncaring that the screaming girls were calling his name in desperation. Panic made me just cuddle tighter and hide my face under Tom's hoody. There was no time to do anything else.

Rhett didn't put me down again until we were in the greenroom with the door firmly shut behind us. Then Jace lost his *shit* before my feet even touched the ground. Fantastic.

"What the *fuck*, Rhett? It's not enough that you're banging my ex on our goddamn bus, now you're going *public* about it. What happened to Billie hiding, huh? Or was that all just bullshit cooked up to manipulate us? Maybe her pussy lost its magical appeal and she needed to resort to cheap tricks just to—"

The rest of his rant was cut short when Rhett punched him square in the face.

I sucked in a sharp gasp, and the whole room went silent. No one spoke, no one moved. Then Grayson started laughing.

Jace's eyes damn near popped out of his head as he pressed a hand to his face and swiveled to stare at his drummer. Apparently I wasn't the only one shocked to hear Grayson laughing. Or maybe not outright *laughing,* but he was definitely chuckling.

"Calm down, Adams," he muttered with a smirk, grabbing a beer from an ice bucket and holding it out in a peace offering. "You've been asking to get punched for days."

Jace glowered but reached out to take the beer. Grayson held onto it a moment longer though, leaning in close to say something in Jace's ear, too quiet for anyone else to hear. Whatever it was made Jace snap his venomous glare my way, then stalk out of the greenroom without another word.

"What... the fuck?" Flo asked as the door slammed behind him. "Rhett, you can't just—"

"Smack some sense into him? Yeah, Flo, I can. And

I'll do it again, too. The way he's been talking about Billie is unacceptable. About any woman. Period. And if it takes physical violence to make him see sense, then so be it." Rhett was totally unapologetic for his actions, but the gentle way he looped his arm around my waist seemed to be seeking forgiveness.

Tom sneered. "Oh, it's unacceptable because suddenly your dick is invested?"

Rhett stiffened. "It's unacceptable because Jace isn't that guy. He doesn't call women *whores* or accuse them of manipulation or imply that they orchestrated an assault situation. He's not acting like himself, and he needs to be smacked out of it before that petty hatred seeps into his soul and leaves an indelible stain."

Goddamn musicians were all poetic fucks.

"Agreed," Grayson grunted. Grabbing himself a beer, he collapsed into the couch and gave me a curious look under his long lashes. I had his book in hand, having managed not to drop it when Rhett picked me up, and his headphones were looped around my neck. He didn't say anything about it, but I could sense he wanted to ask whether I liked the book.

And I did. A lot. Not just because it was gripping—it was—but because he had *listened* when I said I didn't want to attend their concert. He cared. And now I wanted to understand *why*. But then that thought made me nauseous with guilt because I was quietly attracted to Grayson while Rhett, my dark knight, had just punched his best friend to defend my honor.

Shit. Maybe Jace was right about me after all.

"He had a point though," Tom whined. "Yesterday little miss Billie was so paranoid about her anonymity that she was prepared to be our maid, and now she's happy to be outed as Rhett's girlfriend?"

Wait, what? Rhett's girlfriend?

"That's not—" I started to say, shaking my head. "I'm not—" Shit. *Shit.* "We're just—"

"No one is *outing* Billie as anything," Rhett drawled, shrugging the whole thing off and smoothing past my obvious panic. "Her face was covered; no one saw her. She's just an unidentified woman that the gossip mill can go nuts over, but *no one* will guess who she really is unless one of us confirms it. Right?"

Florence winced, holding up her phone. "Sorry, Billie. Too late for anonymous..."

Detaching myself from Rhett, I raced over and grabbed the phone from Flo's hand. Sure enough, Flo had just been tagged in the background of a fan's Instagram image—an image of me and Rhett kissing like we were madly in love. While it might not show my *whole* face, it was enough that I could recognize myself. Enough that Angelo would too.

"Maybe Angelo isn't a Bellerose fan?" Flo offered in a weak attempt at levity.

I gave a bitter, choked laugh as I gripped her phone like I could somehow erase the image with the power of thought. "Oh, trust me, he's not. But... how long until this crosses his radar anyway?"

Rhett gently took the phone and handed it back to Flo. "It doesn't matter, Thorn. We're out of Illinois now; the Ricci family can't possibly have the entire country in their pocket. With the new security, it wouldn't matter if we put out a formal press release with your full name; he can't touch you."

I swallowed hard. I wanted to believe him, but shit... I'd been let down so much that I didn't like to depend on *anyone* anymore.

"He's right, you know?" Florence added, giving me a gentle smile. "We won't let the Riccis get you."

For some fucking reason, my eyes shifted to Grayson. Did he agree?

He said nothing, but the intensity of his gaze and the slight dip of his head filled me with calm reassurance. I was safe here with Bellerose. At least from Angelo. Jace... well, he was a different kind of danger. One that all the bodyguards in the world couldn't protect me from.

BILLIE

Despite my initial panic at seeing me kissing Rhett all over Instagram, the other shoe never dropped. At least not for the rest of that night. Everyone decided that the mood had soured enough to skip their usual after parties, and we all retired to the bus early. That meant the convoy could set out early and take us to the band's next scheduled stop before New York.

It was a relief to be back on the road. Every mile we put between me and Siena, the better my chances of escape became.

Rhett seemed to sense that I was panicking on the inside, so he just snuggled me—clothes on—while the bus drove us to the next destination. When I woke in the early hours of the morning, it took a minute for the confusion about where I was to wear off. Then, when I remembered, I was confused why I was awake, considering we'd only fallen asleep after midnight.

I was alone. That must have been what woke me... Rhett had gotten up before me.

Worried, I slipped out of the bed and shivered. One of his hoodies had been dropped on the floor, so I grabbed it before slipping silently out of the bedroom. The bunks were all quiet, the privacy curtains closed. Soft snoring came from one as I passed, and I smiled, wondering who the snorer was.

Rhett was slouched on the little sofa in the bus living area, his guitar across his lap and headphones on. His fingers moved on the strings, but no sounds filled the bus. That explained the headphones, I guessed.

He paused to write something in the notebook open on the table, then glanced up to see me approach.

"Hey, beautiful Thorn," he whispered with a grin, "come join me."

Wishing like fuck that my desperate need to be at his side wasn't there, I forced myself to move slower. But it was a small space, and within a few seconds, I was seated on his right. As our bodies made contact, some of the darker emotions settled in my gut, and I refused to analyze the why of that. Or what I might suffer once we reached New York and I had to leave.

No matter what Rhett said, there was no other option than for me to disappear. Not just for their safety, but because of Jace. I couldn't long-term do this with him, and I refused to break up this band.

That was not a sin I would carry. Not when I already held too many.

Rhett, either sensing my bad mood or needing to finish what he'd started, didn't say anything as he continued to strum his guitar. This close, I could pick up the faint vibrations, and as I sank into his warmth, calm infused into me slowly. Strum by strum, chord by chord. I couldn't even hear what he was playing, but whatever it was, it seeped into my soul.

My eyes must have fluttered closed at some point, and I didn't even realize it until I felt the soft brush of his lips across my cheek. As my lashes lifted, I was met with a blast of dark green. His gaze was locked on mine, the guitar resting on the small table now as I captured his full attention.

It burned differently, being caught in Rhett's gaze. His fire was less obvious than Jace's had been, but when it caught alight, the heat was just as dangerous. Just as tempting.

"Did you finish your song?" I rasped, before

attempting to clear my throat.

Rhett's smile was a slow tilt of full lips, and fuck if the song was gone from my mind only to be replaced with memories of our time in the bedroom. Despite Jace's venom, there had been no sex yet, but I was so fucking ready to know what it would be like with Rhett.

"It's a work in progress," he said, voice pitched lower than normal, maybe to keep from disturbing the others on the bus or maybe because he was feeling all the same things I was. I had no idea why when lust... need... want filled your chest, it also stretched into your throat until it felt like you couldn't speak or breathe.

"How long have we known each other, Billie Bellerose?" Rhett asked me, and there was a flicker of what almost looked like uncertainty or confusion on his face. "How can it only be days, when it feels like I've never existed until we met."

It was rock star corny, but the sincerity in his gaze, the depth of emotion in his voice, took away any "corn" that might have existed in that statement. And he was right.

"Do you believe in soul mates?" I asked him before I could think about it.

His eyes widened, and I hurried on because that got way too deep for people who had—as previously stated —only known each other for days. "I don't mean that there's *one true love and only one true love for you in the universe.*" My words were a jumbled mess as they spilled from me. "I mean that souls have lived before, and that in other lives, there were people who meant everything to them. More than one person. If they find those people in their next life, then it can feel like they've known them forever. Have you ever wondered if that's why it feels that way?"

Holy shit, I needed to *shut the fuck up right now.*

My breaths heaved in and out for a few seconds as I shook my head to try and clear the tangled web of my thoughts and emotions. Before I could freak out further, Rhett's hands landed on my cheeks, covering my face in his warmth, and he kissed me. Hard enough that a small moan escaped me right before he gentled it, exploring my mouth with his own.

His hands slid across the back of my head and into my hair, tangling and tightening to pull me closer, even as the kiss deepened. I lost all concept of time and location. I didn't care where we were or what was happening outside of this space, as long as Rhett never stopped kissing me.

His lips were warm and he tasted faintly like toffee. I knew he occasionally snacked on these small hard candies that he thought no one else noticed him hoarding, and I had to figure that was what he'd had before I came out of the room. The taste combined with Rhett had me wanting to start up my own fucking stash of the little suckers.

"My soul knows yours, Billie," Rhett murmured against my lips as we finally came up for air. "We made music in our last life together, I know it."

A flash of pure joy lit my insides. It had been a long time since people *got* my eccentricities, the odd ways I saw the world and thought about the love I had for music and life. The last time had been Jace and Angelo, and the pain of that still haunted me to this day.

Rhett opened a new part of my soul, and I was both exhilarated and terrified about what that meant for my future.

His eyes traced across my features like he was trying to figure out the inner workings of my mind, and since I was about done with thinking for the minute, I was the one to lift myself higher and slam my mouth to his. This time the kiss was more intense, Rhett taking control in seconds, his tongue demanding entry, which I willingly gave him.

When his fingers wrapped around my hips, it took a split second for him to shift my position so I was straddling his waist. It happened so quickly that my head spun for a beat, or maybe that was just the way he kissed me like I was the only woman in the world.

We all deserved kisses like this. Ones that had your head spinning, your knees weak, and... Well, other parts of my body were definitely humming. My hips started to grind against the hard length beneath me, Rhett's hands—still on my waist—flexed against my skin, and I was really hoping to feel more of that strength on my bare skin.

There was something about the way he touched with enough firmness, just shy of pain, that had me panting and desperate for more. Rhett was holding back with me, and I was so ready to experience the moment he fully let go.

That firm touch continued as he slid his hands across my thighs, and since I was wearing just his hoodie and panties beneath, he had all the access he needed to stroke across my center. His fingers glided through the moisture already pooling, and at his touch, my pussy spasmed hard. Needy bitch that she was, we were ready to jump on Rhett's cock and take it for a whirl.

Only this was a tour bus and there had been someone asleep back there. Something told me sex with Rhett would be a loud, adventurous activity, so we'd have to settle for some foreplay again.

As his fingers traced across the center of my cunt, pushing the thin material of the thong inside me, my moan was muffled against his shirt as I leaned into him. Rhett's chuckle had a small groan attached to it, and like he couldn't help himself, he yanked my panties to the side and slid two fingers roughly inside me.

My body was more than ready, taking his offering as I rode his hand like it was my favorite fucking dildo. Shit, no dildo would ever compare to the rough texture of his fingers, strong strokes, and perfect positioning that Rhett had going on. He curled those fingers to hit my G-spot near instantly, and I almost screamed at the pulse of pleasure that shot all the way to my toes.

Tingles sliced across my body with each slide of his fingers, and I was so wet that it was no longer a silent experience, the sound of him *finger fucking* me audible to us both.

Hopefully not to anyone else in the bus though.

Rhett's lips slid down my chin and across my neck to stop just above the neckline of the hoody. At the same time, I used my thigh muscles to lift my body a little higher to give him even greater pussy access. Not that he'd been lacking in any way, but from this angle, his fingers pushed harder into me, and I lost my fucking brains jerking my hips against him.

The orgasm was there; I could have tipped over the edge at any point, but like the greedy asshole I was, I tried to drag it out as long as possible.

But Rhett was too good to let me coast in the pleasure for long. Two more strokes and the spirals in my stomach reached their peak, and as he sucked against my throat, a small cry spilled from me.

For some reason, as the orgasm exploded, my pussy clenching hard around Rhett's hand, I found my eyes shooting open to lock gazes with Grayson.

He stood in the junction between the hall and the living area on the bus, shirtless, with those hard, broad muscles on view. His expression was blank, and most people would think that he was unmoved by what was happening, but I could see the dark and stormy nature of his gray eyes. They scorched me, boring into my fucking soul—how many rock stars did I know in my previous life?—and I couldn't prevent a cry from escaping. Something about Grayson's gaze burning into me while Rhett's hands destroyed my body had me coming harder than I'd done in a very long time.

Rhett stole my attention back briefly when he lifted his head and slowed his fingers inside of me, and by the time I looked up again, Grayson was gone.

For a brief second, I wondered if I'd imagined the entire thing.

Fucking hell, I was in some serious trouble, and this time, it had nothing to do with Angelo and his murderous family.

RHETT

Never in my wildest dreams did I think touring by bus would be so damn enjoyable. Then again, I doubt I ever could have dreamed up a girl quite like Billie Bellerose. Holy hell, she was unreal. No wonder Jace was so fucking bent out of shape about losing her, even if that had been a whole-ass century ago. I hadn't even known her a week and I knew no way I'd ever forget my beautiful Thorn.

When I'd woken up with her in my arms and music in my head, I knew I had to get it written down. Like it was fairy dust that would disappear if anyone spoke before I got it out. Then she'd joined me, and all the pieces slotted together in my mind.

Maybe I was an asshole... Okay, no *maybe* about it, I was definitely an asshole. But I'd heard Gray get out of his bunk. I'd seen him hesitate in the shadows when he saw Billie sitting there with me. In my defense, I'd given him a chance to come out and announce himself before things went further, but *he* chose to be a creep. So it was his own damn fault that he'd witnessed Billie shattering like something out of a wet dream.

Really, when I think of it like that, Gray should be thanking me. He thought he was so fucking secretive and mysterious, but every time he looked her way his whole face turned into one of those anime characters. Heart eyes. The big grump was crushing on my girl, and I wasn't even mad about it. I mean, of course he was; she was fucking awesome.

"So, what's the plan today?" Billie asked as I handed her a coffee from the tray I'd collected from a roadie. We'd just arrived in Philadelphia for our last show before New York, and I was already trying to figure out how to sabotage the bus before we got to the Big Apple. I couldn't stand the thought of her leaving so soon.

What had she asked me earlier? Do I believe in soulmates? I didn't a week ago, but I definitely did now.

"We have to head to the stadium for soundchecks and shit," I replied, selecting my own coffee from the tray and sliding into the sofa seat beside her. She hummed a contented sound as she sipped hers, and I smiled. The roadies had included her order—an almond latte, double foam—without me asking today. I liked that.

A groan came from the bunks, followed by a thump. Billie raised her brow in question, but a moment later, Jace stumbled out still half asleep.

His barely open eyes snapped toward Billlie, and she froze with her coffee halfway to her perfect lips. An uncomfortable feeling twisted through me as the tension between them built. My soulmate or not, Billie and Jace weren't done. Shit. What had she said, again? *People* we knew in past lives. Plural.

Right when I thought Jace was about to kick off again with his insults, he scrubbed a hand over his face and reached for his coffee. Then he just sat down on the couch bench opposite us.

"What's that?" he mumbled, nodding to my notebook, still lying forgotten on the table.

I shrugged. "Just had a melody in my head that needed to get out. Maybe it'll fit those lyrics you've been writing." I was poking the bear, but I couldn't help myself. All his songs were about Billie in some way, shape, or form. Whether he admitted it or not. The fact that he'd started writing again now that she'd stumbled back into his life... No way that was a coincidence.

Jace didn't take the bait, though. "Maybe."

"Speaking of songwriting," I pushed, "have we heard back from the lawyers about Billie's royalties? As much as I like having her here, I'm sure she would rather it be her choice to stay. Not out of desperation."

She gave a small squeak of surprise beside me, and Jace's sleepy eyes swung her way.

"You want to stay on tour?" he asked, his tone flat and unreadable. "Why?"

Her spine went stiff, like she was bracing for a fight. But Jace... something was off with him this morning. He wasn't as combative or angry. Maybe I should have punched him in the face sooner, if that's all he'd needed to treat Billie with respect.

"I didn't—" she started, wetting her lips. "I wasn't asking to—"

"But you don't *have* to ask," I quickly cut her off. "I think I've made *my* feelings pretty clear by now. I want you here. I want you to stay." *With me.*

She softened slightly, melting into my sideways embrace, but I couldn't ignore the way her eyes darted over to Jace like she wanted to know what he thought about that idea. I groaned internally because he was my best friend and I loved the crap out of him… but I wanted Billie to be *mine*, and only mine.

Something told me that wasn't going to be possible, though. Especially with the way her face heated as Grayson came out of the bunk area to join us. She hadn't said a *word* about him watching while I got her off with my hand, but she'd definitely seen him.

"Morning," Jace muttered as Gray dropped down on the sofa beside him, coffee in hand.

Grayson just grunted a response. His gaze rested on Billie while he sipped his drink, and I stifled a sigh. She was the center of everyone's attention. Did she know?

Flo and Tucker—the fucker—broke the tension, coming out together like they were joined at the hip. Because they were.

"What are we talking about?" Tom asked after Flo had said good morning to everyone.

Jace yawned, running his hand over his hair. "Rhett was asking whether our lawyers have sorted out Billie's royalties for the first album yet." Again, totally expressionless. What the *fuck* was going on in his head right now?

Tom's eyes widened, and his jaw flapped a moment. I knew why, too. Jace was supposed to front up about *which* songs she was owed royalties for, and last time Tom had asked, Jace blew his top and stormed out. I hadn't pushed the issue because I wanted to keep her a little longer, but... I'd rather win her favor by being the one to offer her freedom, not force her captivity.

Flo clearly knew it too because she cleared her throat and changed the subject. "So, what did you think of the show last night, Billie? You caught a few songs before someone gave you headphones, right?"

My girl nodded, wincing slightly, her gaze flicking to Jace *again* before she answered Flo. The girls settled into polite conversation about the show—what little Billie had seen before Gray's minion delivered headphones and a fucking romance novel—while I narrowed my glare at Jace.

He stared back at me for a moment, then tipped his head toward the door of the bus, silently asking me to step outside with him. I gave a small nod, then brushed a kiss over Billie's cheek as I murmured I'd be back in a minute. Then I followed Jace... as I always did.

We'd barely even made it twenty paces from the bus when he sparked up a joint and took a drag. Maybe that explained why he was so fucking chill this morning?

"What's up?"

He didn't answer straight away, just offered me the joint, which I accepted.

"This thing..." he finally said, his eyes downcast as he kicked gravel, "you know, between you and Billie."

I scoffed, handing back his joint. "Yeah, I know *this thing*. What about it?"

Jace's eyes snapped up, glaring at me. Then he shook his head and looked away, taking another drag. "You don't fucking get it, man. She'll break your heart."

Logically, I knew part of him was genuinely concerned for me, for his best friend. But part of him, a *bigger* part, was just seething with jealousy.

"Then so fucking be it," I replied, holding his gaze when he looked back over at me. "I'm serious, Jace. If she breaks my heart, then you can have a good laugh and say *I told you so*, but I don't give a fuck. You know what they say, 'better to have loved and lost than never to have loved at all. Or whatever it is.'"

Jace looked like I'd just slapped him. "You *love* her? You don't even *know* her!"

I winced. "I wasn't saying..." But, wasn't I? "I dunno, man. Maybe I do. I just know that I've *never* felt like this. And yeah, you're right. I don't even know her, and I *already* feel this way. So doesn't that mean something?"

My friend was quiet a long time, and I kept my own mouth shut. It wasn't until we had nearly finished sharing the joint that Jace spoke again.

"You will," he said softly, his voice dripping in regret. "Fall for her, I mean. If you haven't already, then you will when you really get to know her. Rose is fucking special. She's... she's just one in a million. But you can already see that, so you're a smarter asshole than I was."

Words failed me, and I swallowed hard.

"But that was then, and this is now, and no amount of *special* changes the fact that she ripped my beating heart clean out of my chest and stomped all over it." His smile turned brittle, and his laugh sounded forced. "I'm gonna hit up some groupies and spend the afternoon balls deep in some anonymous pussy. Maybe I can even get some girl-on-girl shit going on... Care to join me? Like old times?"

I scowled, and he just laughed, tossing his head back like he was really trying to make us both believe the levity of the joke.

'Kidding, Rhett. Kidding." He snickered as he pulled out his phone, probably already sending out booty calls. Shit like that would have been a great time last week. Now it just seemed *sad*. Had Jace always been masking his heartache with his man-whoring ways? Or was this a new twist thanks to Billie's return?

I sighed and pulled out my own phone as we wandered back to the bus. As soon as I saw the thousands of notifications on Instagram, I remembered the photo incident of last night. The fan upload of me and Billie kissing like we were in love.

Clicking into the image, I smiled. Oh man, I was such a sap because I screenshot the image, cropped it, and saved it to my wallpaper. Fuck it, my phone was passcoded; no one would see it but me.

Just as I was about to close the app and leave the notifications for our PR team to handle, my eyes caught on a username in my message requests.

"Hey, Jace?" I called out, dread curling through me. "This might be picking at the scab, but did Billie used to call Angelo by a nickname? Like, uh, *Angel*?"

Jace spun around to face me, his brow set in a scowl. "Yeah. Why the fuck would you ask me that?"

"Shit," I breathed, opening the message. Panic fluttered in my chest, and I turned my phone for Jace to see it.

His eyes widened almost immediately, and his face paled at least six shades. "Fuck."

My thoughts exactly. Because there in my inbox from a username *BellasAngel* was a clear warning.

Ricci family wants her back, dead or alive. Don't be a fucking idiot, Silver. Ask Jace what happens to anyone who gets in the way.

twenty-three

BILLIE

Something was going on, I was sure of it. Rhett had been acting really strange ever since he and Jace went for a private chat first thing in the morning. They'd come back smelling of weed and looking like they'd both seen a ghost.

Neither one of them were talking about it, either, but I could swear there was double the usual security protocols at the concert venue when we arrived later that night.

"Flo, hey." I caught up with the cute punk-rock bassist as we made our way through the busy backstage corridors.

She paused, offering me a smile. "What's up?"

"That's kinda what I wanted to ask you," I replied with an awkward laugh. "Why do I get the feeling everyone knows something that concerns me but they're not *telling* me?"

Flo shrugged, but not before I caught a flicker of guilt cross her face. "Maybe ask Rhett, babe. I gotta go, you know, get my head in the zone and shit. But, um, maybe just stick close during the show, 'kay? So the boys don't stress and mess up the lyrics."

Her suggestion was great, if not for the fact that Rhett suddenly seemed too busy to talk. Weirdly, so was Jace. Not that I'd be inclined to reach out to him, but it seemed awfully suspicious. The only person *not* avoiding me was Grayson, and I was still too damn mortified to seek him out after he'd seen me getting thoroughly finger-blasted by Rhett this morning.

So that was how I wound up pacing the greenroom like an angry tiger while they played their show. Fuck their *need* to keep eyes on me; if they couldn't respect me enough to let me in on whatever was going on, then why the hell should I suffer through another Bellerose concert? Like fucking ear-torture.

Okay, that wasn't fair. They were fantastic musicians. I just wished their lyrics were even slightly vaguer so I could pretend that I wasn't the hated subject in all of them. Jace was really milking the whole art is pain shit, that was for sure.

"Terry is going to grab some coffee," one of my new personal security informed me. "You want anything?"

I jerked my head in a terse negative. "No, I'm fine." Then winced at my own tone. "Thanks."

The heavyset guy just arched a brow. "I'll grab you one, anyway. You seem... tense."

Irritation flared hot through me, and I parked my hands on my hips. "I *am* tense. You must know something, Clint. Why did Rhett increase security tonight? What happened that no one is telling me?"

Clint seemed unconcerned with my temper, shrugging one broad shoulder. "We're kept informed pretty strictly on a *need-to-know* basis. For this job, all we *needed to know* was that there had been an attempted abduction on you, and we've been brought in to ensure it doesn't happen again." He gave me a long look. "Is there something more we should know?"

I sighed and shook my head. "No, that's the gist of it. Except that if he'd succeeded... the guy who tried to take me, I mean. If he had gotten away, I'd be dead right now." *Or worse, whatever that might be.*

Shivering, I wrapped my arms around myself. Clint just gave a stoic nod.

"Well, then it's a good thing my team is here now.

As for why there's extra security on tonight, I couldn't say, except that it wasn't Mr. Silver who placed the order, it was Mr. Adams."

Clint was gone again before I found my tongue, but even then I had nothing to say except *what the fuck?*

The only logical conclusion was that Clint was mistaken and the orders had come from Rhett... because Jace couldn't give two shits whether I got taken or not. Hell, he probably still thought I was making the whole thing up for attention.

Whatever, at least I could give him more material for his music if I died.

Eventually, I got bored enough with my pacing that I poured a glass of champagne from the bottles laid out for the band and settled down with Grayson's book about smoke-jumpers. Before I knew it, I'd finished the bottle *and* the book and only had a few minutes until the concert ended.

Whether it was the alcohol or the warm fuzz of a good love story, I was in a *much* better mood by the time the band returned to the greenroom. It was a shame that mood soured so quickly when Jace immediately got up in my face, demanding to know where I'd been for the last two hours.

"Oh, so it's not enough that you've built your million-dollar career on hating me, you seriously want me to sit there and listen to it live? You're fucking delusional, Adams." I was tipsy as fuck. Okay, sure, I was more than tipsy, and I swayed somewhat as I tried to stand up to him. Whoops, that sort of ruined the tough girl act, huh?

Jace's eyes widened like I'd slapped him, and Tom *Fucker* sneered. "*Multi*million," the asshole corrected.

Jace snapped a death glare at his... what the fuck was Tom, anyway? He wasn't a manager. He was... a parasite. Hah, that was fitting. Tom Tucker was like a leech, sucking money and fame out of Bellerose and offering a whole lot of nothing in return.

"Are you drunk, beautiful?" Rhett asked with a lopsided smile, breaking the tension by literally standing in front of Jace. His sweaty, tattoo-covered arm wrapped around my waist, pulling me close, and I gratefully let him hold me up.

"Maybe a little," I admitted. Then hiccupped.

Jace muttered something about being *irresponsible,* but Rhett just kissed my forehead and laughed. "I don't blame you, Thorn. Let's get back to the bus; I'm dying to shower."

"It'll have to wait," Tom interrupted, shaking his greasy head. Huh, I hadn't noticed before that he looked kind of like an oily meerkat. Big head, skinny body, no shoulders or jawline. Sexy did not apply to

Tom Tucker. If I hadn't already gotten to know him, I'd have assumed he had an amazing personality to snag a babe like Florence. But that *definitely* wasn't the case.

Here's hoping he at least had a huge dick, but looking at his size-seven boots, I'd have to guess that wasn't the case either. Poor Flo...

Oops, I'd tuned out what the fucker was saying. Something about a meet and greet that fans had bid on in a charity auction or... something.

"Oh, come on," Rhett groaned. "They only want to meet Jace and you know it. They won't even notice if the rest of us don't show up."

"Not true," Tom replied with a smug look on his face. "One of the auction items was specifically for a ten-minute date with the one and only Rhett Silver."

Rhett's jaw twitched with tension, and I could sense he was about to tell Tom where to shove his meet and greet, charity or not. But that would be bad for his career, bad for PR, and ultimately not going to win me any favors with the rest of the band. So I leaned into him and tipped my head back to kiss his throat. It was all I could reach unless he leaned down.

"I'll go with Clint back to the bus," I offered.

Rhett scowled. "You could come—"

"No, she can't," Jace snapped, shaking his head. "Everyone at the meet and greet has a camera."

I winced, thinking about how much of a mess that Instagram kiss must have caused today. Crap, maybe *that* was why Rhett and Jace were acting all cagey today? They'd been dealing with the fallout of my actions?

Rhett and Jace shared a long look, basically confirming my suspicion, then Rhett sighed.

"I'll stay with her," Grayson rumbled, shocking the pants off of me. "Not like anyone came to see me, anyway." He gave a nonchalant shrug, then tipped his head toward the door. "You coming, Prickles?"

Rhett appeared to relax the moment Grayson offered to stay with me. The security might be from him —and Jace, apparently—but there was no one he trusted more than his fellow bandmate.

"Coming," I trilled, and it didn't escape my tipsy notice that Grayson actually smiled. Maybe it was the suggestive word, or more likely it was my distinct lack of intonation. I couldn't sing for shit, but I was excellent with song lyrics and putting music together. Just because I couldn't sing didn't mean I couldn't *hear* the music. Not everyone could be Jace Fucking Adams and have the full musical trifecta. Some of us had to sing in the shower and for fun.

Rhett gave me one last kiss on the lips. A brief brush, but it was enough to heat my already fired-up blood. When he released me into Grayson's hold, the massive drummer steadied me on my feet but then proceeded not to touch me for the rest of the walk to the tour bus. The band had their own private area, and at this concert, there wasn't even a crowd surrounding the gated zone for their tour buses. The silence and fresh air were welcome, and it cleared my head a touch.

Only a touch, though, because I was feeling the energy racing between Grayson and me. It might have been an awkward energy, based on the fact that he'd seen a lot of my O face this morning or maybe it was the fact that he was fucking sex on legs and had probably saved my life.

If Jace could know my inner thoughts, calling me a whore would be the least of his insults, but in this moment, I couldn't find a single fuck to give. Angelo might kill me next week, so today... I was living for whatever came my way.

"Where are your thoughts?"

My head jerked toward Grayson, and no shit, he looked surprised too that he'd just asked a question. "My thoughts?" I parroted back like a fool because my head was suddenly spinning again.

Grayson straightened and faced forward again, the bus only a few meters away now as security trailed us.

"You're quiet a lot. Most chicks I know talk my ear off. You don't do that."

"Not even when my life was golden did I chatter a lot," I replied softly, "except when I was exceptionally nervous."

Come to think of it, I should be exceptionally nervous with this enigmatic and beautiful man—talented, rich, and famous. Despite his words from before about no one wanting him at the meet and greet, we all knew the truth: women lost their minds around him. It was Grayson who kept them away with his scary persona.

Tonight, though, he was calm, and that inspired the same in me.

I felt like I could just exist with him, no stress, no expectations.

Possibly, he still hated me based on Jace and the one-sided story he'd heard for years, but if he did, he was able to keep that to himself.

"I finished the book you gave me," I said as he opened the door to the bus. He looked like he was about to enter first and case the place, but the security stepped up then, and Grayson appeared to reluctantly let them do their jobs.

"What did you think?" he asked, his focus on me now reminding me of the last time those gray eyes had been locked on my face. The heated-wine blood inside of me swirled again, quite violently, and I reached out and casually placed a hand on the side of the bus.

"I loved it," I said, forcing my voice to sound calm. "The romance captured me from the first moment Jetta shot Roman in the leg before he managed to carry her away. Something about the enemies-to-lovers trope just does it for me."

Grayson looked like he was about to reply, the smallest twitch to his lips as he opened his mouth, but we were interrupted by security before he could say anything. "Bus is all clear," Grace, the blond female on the security guard roster, said with a no-nonsense voice. "We scanned for listening devices and explosive residue. Nothing to report."

Grayson nodded. "Great, thank you. I'll ask you to wait outside now until the next shift arrives."

She wasn't surprised by this, returning his nod with one of her own, and then the dozen or so security exited, meeting up with the few who'd been scanning under the bus as well. Grayson held a hand out to indicate I should go on ahead of him, and once we were inside the bus, door closed and locked behind us, I was starting to feel my nerves raise their heads. I hadn't been alone with Grayson like this before, when we knew we couldn't be interrupted for at least an hour or so.

This was probably going to be a really fucking bad idea with wine still churning in my system.

Really fucking bad.

GRAYSON

Despite her calm expression, her nerves were clear in the way she crossed her arms tightly across her body and the tense way she held her hands. Small cues, but it was enough that the change from outside was glaringly obvious to me.

It wasn't in my nature to try and ease her discomfort, but for some fucking reason I found myself wanting to. "Would you like to shower or change into something more comfortable?"

Her eyes went super wide, and I wanted to kick my own stupid ass. I'd meant that purely platonically—she was involved with my best friend. But my words could be taken suggestively, and by any other woman I'd brought onto this bus, they would have been.

"I'm just going to order some food," I added flatly, hating the awkwardness more than I hated chatter. I wasn't equipped to deal with this shit.

Thankfully, Billie just went with it. "That would be great," she replied softly. "I always need a few minutes to decompress after... all the songs." She swallowed roughly, and I fought the urge to reach out and smooth those rough edges she exposed at times.

Not that she needed me to since she managed to tuck her vulnerabilities away with ease once more. "See you in a few minutes," she told me as she straightened and strode down the hall, the curve of her hips swaying slightly as I followed her path until she disappeared from sight.

It was fucked up that I was as captivated by Billie as Rhett. Not that we hadn't shared chicks before in the band, but it had been years. Rhett wasn't into the casual thing these days, and I was *only* into casual. There was a lot broken in my soul, and no chick deserved to be immersed in that shit. Best to just let them think I didn't give a damn.

Fuck, who was I kidding. Most of the time I didn't.

After sorting out the food—the order had already been placed since we were always starving after a show

—I settled back into the booth, having to spread my legs to try and fit their length into this small space. Trying to relax, I worked really fucking hard at ignoring the sound of the shower.

A drink sounded nice at this point, and I only had to lift myself up to reach the cabinet above. I pulled down a bottle of whiskey and some crystal decanters. The drink and food would help release the tension riding my chest, and it wasn't just that Billie fucking Bellerose was naked in my tour bus. It was that fucking text from Angelo that Rhett had shown me before the show.

That motherfucker thought he could threaten her and there'd be no repercussions?

Not a hope. He had no idea the challenge he'd just placed at my feet, and I would tap into any and all resources to ensure that Billie never ended up in his presence again.

Even if I had to kill him myself.

I barely knew the girl, but no one deserved to live in fear like that. Besides... she was cute as hell and Rhett would be devastated if something happened to her.

Closing my eyes and leaning my head against the back wall, I lifted the glass and took a sip, enjoying the slow burn of forty-year-old Port Ellen scotch. I was selective with my drinks. Shit, I was selective with everything in my life. Even the limited number of groupies I chose to indulge in were all heavily curated. I'd learned the hard way what happened if you weren't selective.

I'd never go back to that life again. And I couldn't let Prickles end up in the same position as I had been in. Survival mode was not for the faint of heart, and powerful entities owning you was the death of a soul.

The scent of Rhett's body wash, mixed with the sweetness that was all Billie, reached me a few minutes before she spoke. "Shower's free," she said softly.

Opening my eyes, I tried to ignore the way the water made her hair darker and somehow more gold as it hung freely around her face. She was wearing gray sweats, and her face was completely makeup free. Her fresh-faced look was too fucking tempting, so I focused instead on the dark circles under her hazel eyes. "You need to rest," I told her roughly, straightening and dropping my half-drunk glass on the table. "Take this time before everyone gets back."

She ignored my gruff tone, pushing forward to slide into the seat next to me. The space was small, and it shrunk even further as the heat of her skin reached me. We weren't touching, and it took too much control to stop myself from reaching out for her.

"I haven't told Rhett," she continued, before she reached out and picked up my glass to take a sip, never flinching as the golden liquid hit her tongue, "that I'm struggling to sleep alone at the moment too. It's like… when I close my eyes, I just see Liz dead. I see those bastards shooting at me. I feel that security guard's hands wrapping around my body, bruising me as he tries to drag me to my death."

I wanted to leave the bus and murder everyone who'd touched her. I was mentally creating a list. The sort of list no one wanted to be on. Roger had already been taken care of, but there were others now.

"I'll sit with you," I found myself saying. Fuck. I really should have gone out on my murder spree because I was in too much fucking trouble here. "You can rest easier."

Wide eyes met mine, and her hand shook just slightly as she lifted the glass and drained the last of the whiskey. Before I could say anything else, she raised her body higher and leaned in to press her lips to my cheek. "Thank you," she breathed.

Heat flared under that touch, and my cock responded instantly, rock hard and straining to escape my pants. Damn it to hell. This was not smart when my control was shot around her.

Shifting back, she remained close, her hands on the table as she pushed herself high enough to reach my face. The moment extended, and her pupils dilated before she leaned in to kiss me again. This time on the lips.

Every part of me craved this touch, just to see if she'd taste as fucking sweet as she smelled, but I was already in too deep with Billie. I'd have to settle for killing those who'd wronged her, and then I'd walk away.

Leave her to the more deserving, like Rhett.

That lucky bastard.

BILLIE

He dodged my lips at the last second, his expression flattening, and I honestly wanted to die of mortification. What the hell was wrong with me? What was I thinking trying to kiss Grayson when I was also involved with Rhett?

I might be living like these were my last days, but that didn't mean I got to hurt the people who cared about me. "Shit, sorry," I gasped, wishing I could blame the wine and whiskey for my behavior. I would have, except I'd been feeling this pull to Grayson from about the first moment I saw him.

When I'd walked out of the shower tonight to find him sprawled in the booth, legs in that sexy man-spread so he could fit them in the space, I'd been unable to think clearly.

Mortified. I was completely and utterly *mortified*. Not only had I just tried to kiss a man who was best friends with the *other* man I'd been kissing recently, but he'd rejected me. It was safe to say I'd totally misread that entire situation. Stupid, arrogant me had thought he was *interested*.

Ugh. I knew drinking so much would bite me in the ass.

"You're drunk," he rumbled as I pressed the back of my hand to my mouth and scooted my ass out of the seat. "Billie—"

Fuck, we're dropping the nickname already? That was quick.

"You're right," I cut him off with a forced laugh. "I am drunk. Let's just pretend this *never* happened, okay? I'm just gonna go get some air and sober up."

Not waiting for his response, I hightailed it off the bus and nearly collided with Grace, stationed right outside. She gave me a startled look, then her gaze darted past me and her expression darkened to murderous.

"I'm fine!" I squeaked before she could ask anything. "I just need some air. I won't go far."

Drunk, yes, but I wasn't a total moron. I was well aware that Rhett—or Jace—had assigned security guards for my *protection,* so I was fully prepared for Grace to follow me and that was fine. Hell, it was good. The last thing I needed while drunk, confused, and horny was to be snatched by a Ricci family goon.

With that in mind, I headed back to the concert venue, hoping to find a quiet corner somewhere to wallow in my humiliation.

Thank *fuck* we would be in New York tomorrow. Then I would never need to see Grayson again.

Shit. Then I would never see *Rhett* again... or Jace. *Shit, shit, fuck, shit.* Why did that thought hurt like a knife through the chest? The pain of it was so palpable that I gasped and staggered, but a pair of strong hands caught me before I hit the concrete.

"What the—" My protest cut off with a gasp as I realized those were *not* Grace's hands.

Grayson set me back on my feet, then quickly manhandled me around the corner, out of sight of our security. A flash of panic tripped through my chest, making me hiccup. But then Grayson backed me up against the wall and planted his hands on either side of my head, caging me in.

Unable to avoid his intense gray gaze, I sucked in a deep breath and flattened myself against the wall. "W-what are you doing?" My voice was all breathy and sexual. Crap.

"You didn't let me finish," he growled. "You're *drunk*."

Anger flared hot within me, chasing away my nervous energy at our proximity. "I'm *aware*," I snapped back, narrowing my eyes. "Can I go now?"

Grayson gave a frustrated shake of his head. "You're *drunk,* so I don't want to take advantage if it's something you'll regret in the morning. I don't want you waking up tomorrow in Rhett's arms, feeling guilty for kissing me."

As if I would.

Okay, sure, I'd probably feel all kinds of guilty, *but* we would be reaching New York soon. After that... well, could I really be blamed for taking my opportunities while I had them? Rhett and I weren't dating, no matter how intense the thing between us was.

"But I think you misunderstood my chivalry as rejection, so let me clear this up for you." One second he was leaning over me all intimidating and sexy and growly, the next he was kissing me.

Shock held me frozen for a hot second, and my brain exploded into a puff of feathers. Then I melted against him, returning his kiss like we were long lost lovers. He kissed more aggressively than Rhett, more dominantly and all consuming. He stole the air clear out of my lungs as he devoured my mouth but didn't once put his hands on me.

All too quickly, he broke away, and I gasped for breath as my fuzzy eyes tried to focus.

"W-what?" I mumbled again, thoroughly confused.

Grayson's mouth twitched into a micro-smile, and he leaned in to kiss me again, a quicker one, like he was savoring the taste of my lips. "Now you can honestly say *I* kissed *you*. No guilt required."

He pushed off the wall, and it suddenly felt like an entire canyon had opened between us. I instantly wanted to grab him and pull him close, but a shrill scream cut through the night air.

Fear shot through me, and Liz's dead face flashed into my mind. She'd never screamed, but that kind of blood-curdling shriek couldn't be anything good. *Could it?* Based on the way Grace and the other security guards came racing around the corner and the protective way Grayson positioned himself in front of me? No, I would guess not.

"Grayson, what's going on?" I demanded when it became clear that he was shielding me.

"I don't know," he snapped back, tension tightening

all his muscles up in a way that *really* shouldn't be as sexy as I was finding it... given the circumstances.

I had way too many emotions going on, and the wine was starting to make me queasy. So I wasn't feeling real patient for caveman bullshit. "Well, let's find out. What is in that direction?" I pointed the way Grace and the other guards had just taken off. The direction the scream had come from.

Grayson swiveled his head to glare at me. "The meet and greet area," he grudgingly told me.

Blind fear coursed through me, and I ducked out from behind his broad frame. I had no fucking clue what I thought I was doing or where I was even going. All I knew was that I couldn't stand there when something was happening at the meet and greet. People I lov—cared about were there, and I would not wait to see if any of them were hurt... or worse.

Grayson reached for me as I started to sprint. His long limbs managed to scrape across my shirt, but the one advantage I had in life was my speed. I had a lot of experience escaping from situations that were less than safe. Grayson clearly hadn't expected that, and he just missed keeping hold of me.

"Billie," he barked, and I heard the warning in this voice. Something told me I was going to have a few stern words coming my way later, but for this minute, I was in panic and flight mode. Heavy footsteps sounded behind me, and I was thankful when a few minutes later Grayson and some of the security caught up to me. Extra grateful when he didn't attempt to slow me down again.

It was almost as if he knew I needed to see for myself, and he had decided to tag along and keep me safe. Well, not just me, his best friends were also at the meet and greet.

Okay, yeah, he'd have no doubt been going whether I'd taken off or not.

Not everything was about me.

No one spoke as we ran, and the tension pounding through my veins gave me the adrenaline to sprint without puffing like the unfit human I was. Running for my life on occasion had made me fast, but in general, I did not run for fun. Cardio outside the bedroom could fuck right off. And then keep fucking. Thankfully, if we'd heard that scream from the bus, the area couldn't be too far away. Even with the way sound could travel.

If we didn't reach the area soon, though, I was going to embarrass myself by gasping for breath in front of Grayson, who I was fairly certain didn't even need to breathe at all. Was his chest moving?

Fucking robot.

His gaze caught mine, and no doubt he wondered

what the hell I was staring at. My brain was a fuzzy mess when I was stressed, and I hoped he would assume that was the reason I acted like a weirdo at times. Like the kiss.

Fuck. I'd been kissing Grayson while Rhett was possibly being murdered. Dramatic as that sounded, it slammed into my chest hard enough that I stumbled and almost fell on the graveled path.

Grayson's arm whipped out in a flash as he caught me, and I knew that my *speed* I'd been so proud of actually had nothing on his. The only reason I'd gotten away before had to be because I'd taken him by surprise. "I kissed you, remember," he growled as he straightened me.

We were still moving, and the only reason I hadn't eaten shit again was he still had a hand wrapped around my right bicep, keeping me upright and propelling us along. "How the fuck did you know I was thinking that?"

He faced forward so I couldn't really see his expression. "You wear your emotions on your face," he finally said a beat later. "It's odd. Usually those who live on the edge of homelessness...on the edge of being on the streets, lose that innocence."

At this point it was almost as if he was talking to himself, the words turning to low mumbles, and I found myself temporarily forgetting the danger we were running toward as his tone captured my full attention. There was nothing innocent about Grayson, and I wondered if maybe, *just maybe,* that reference had been as much about him as it was me.

But how? How had this incredibly capable and famous drummer of Bellerose lost his innocence? When did it even happen? I had to assume it'd been before he joined the most famous band in the world. I'd never looked into Bellerose or any of its member's origin stories, even though I knew there were multiple documentaries about their rise to fame. It had been too painful to even hear the name, let alone take in more information, but maybe now I was ready to find out. Especially since Bellerose was so much more than just Jace now.

The darker emotions this band used to illicit in me had shifted into something lighter. Something that filled my soul rather than hurt it.

In truth, I was actually desperate to know more about Rhett and Grayson. About how they'd come to be part of the Bellerose world. Almost as desperate as I was to feel that rough, dominating edge to Grayson's kisses and the talented touch of Rhett's calloused hands.

You know, providing he was still alive, and that was where my goddamn focus needed to be.

As we rounded the corner near the venue, there was a small crowd of fans standing there and waving banners, unperturbed by the scream that had rung out before. At this point I was super grateful that we were almost at the area. My chest was hurting hard, while my legs protested the rapid pace the security and Grayson had set.

"Is this the meet and greet?" I asked in a breathless rush.

"No," Grayson said shortly. "These are the fans that just hang around in the hopes of seeing us walk to our tour bus. The meet and greet is through that fence."

I looked where he pointed, past the dozen or so giant trucks parked up until they were reloaded with all of Bellerose's staging and sets. I noticed the two security on the fence were tense and speaking rapidly into the comms they wore. I wasn't sure if it was a good sign that they hadn't left their post yet, but clearly something was going on still.

The fans lost their shit when they realized it was Grayson, screaming his name and jumping up and down like they were super jacked up. He didn't even look their way, running forward to the two men clad completely in black at the fence.

"What happened?" he snapped.

"One of the fans pulled a gun," the first one said. He ran a hand over his black hair, which was shaved short to his head. "They've asked us to remain here and keep others from entering. It's a hostile situation they're working through."

"Since you work for me," Grayson said, leaning in so no one else would overhear; I was the only one close enough, "it's in your best interest to let us through."

The guard almost looked like he was going to argue and then must have decided it really wasn't worth the aggravation. Even if he hadn't been their boss, Grayson wasn't the sort of man one argued with. "Go on through. We'll make sure no fans can follow."

He used a key from his pocket to unlock the huge bolt that held the gate closed and stepped aside to let us through.

Our pace was somewhat slower, and I saw the way the security fanned out around us, covering our back and side as Grayson and I moved toward the meet and greet.

From what I could see, most of the fans looked to be on the ground, hands covering their heads, and it was eerily quiet.

Or at least I thought it was until we ended up much closer, and I finally saw what the situation was.

A small woman stood in front of the band's table, and she had a handgun pointed right at Rhett.

My heart almost stopped before it slammed into gear again so hard that it hurt.

It took a few seconds for my ears to work, as panic and stress crashed my senses, but the moment they did, I realized that she was shouting at him.

"You betrayed me!" she screamed, her hand shaking. "We were meant to be together, Rhett! You and I are *fated*, and now you're..." Her rant trailed off in a devastated wail.

Grayson had stopped all of us just before the light, his hands shifting side to side so that the security knew to halt as well.

"You betrayed me *with her*!" Her last scream was the loudest, and the truth hit me like a fucking truck.

This was about the photo. The photo of Rhett kissing me.

Holy fuck. I had to do something.

twenty-six

BILLIE

Somehow, in the few seconds that followed my realization, my brain went through an entire range of scenarios of what I could do to stop this from happening. I could live with a lot of bad shit going on in this world, even being homeless and on the run for the rest of my life. But I couldn't lose anyone I cared about again. I was so fucking broken from the last time, and Rhett didn't deserve this.

Grayson said something to me then, and I blinked at him, trying to figure out what he'd asked. Leaning in, he repeated himself. "It's not the Ricci family, right?"

My head was shaking before words could emerge. "No. No. This is about the photo."

Despite all the scenarios from before, I found my body reacting on instinct. I straightened and took a step away from Grayson. He blinked at me, no doubt wondering what the hell I was doing.

I didn't even know, but I had to try something.

"Hey!" I screamed.

The chick had been so focused on Rhett, who'd had both hands up in front of him, trying to reason with her, that it took another shout before her eyes flicked in my direction. This was also the moment that Rhett and the other band members noticed I was there.

Not that it mattered. With whatever flawed reasoning I had going on, I had to save them. Even if it was the last thing I ever did.

"It's me you're angry with," I said, lowering my voice a touch. Grayson moved toward me, no doubt wanting to step in front of me, but I didn't give him the chance.

Knowing I had to act now, before Grayson or our security tackled me to the ground, I raced toward the gun-wielding girl. When I was ten feet from her, I ground to a halt, and she looked somewhat shocked as she stared at me. She was very pretty, with blond hair and huge blue eyes. She had very dark eyebrows and eyelashes, which should have stood out against her light hair and skin tone but instead, framed her beauty perfectly.

Beauty which morphed into something dark and twisted at the realization of who I was.

The gun was pointed at me a beat later, and this time, her hands didn't shake. Her pose had everyone else in the vicinity frozen. I felt Grayson behind me, but he was no longer trying to grab me.

"You," she said, and now her voice was calm. Almost detached.

"Back toward me, Billie," Grayson said, voice low.

"If she moves, she dies," the girl said, her smile weird and unnatural. She was also crying, silent tears I hadn't noticed at first tracking down her cheeks. "Why did you take him from me?"

I didn't pretend to misunderstand her.

"Rhett is his own person. I'm not even important. It was just a kiss of adrenaline after a fantastic concert."

A derisive snort sounded from the table behind her, and I took a split second to remove my eyes from the threat to see that Rhett and Jace were half out of their chairs. If I had to guess, I'd say the only reason they hadn't charged her yet was the worry that their actions would trigger her to shoot me. Or maybe they figured I'd brought this on myself, and I was on my own.

Either way, it almost appeared that they were

frozen in midmotion, their bodies twisted as if they were about to launch over the table and head toward us. Noticing my distraction, the chick shifted her gaze to the table, and Jace spoke up quickly.

"She *is* fucking nobody," he said with a sneer. An all too familiar sneer. Ouch.

In typical Jace fashion, he captured her attention fully with just that perfect tone he was born with. This deranged fan might have been wigging out over Rhett, but she wasn't immune to Jace's charms either, as she leaned closer toward him, the gun falling a touch so it was no longer angled directly at anyone.

Before another word was spoken, someone grabbed me roughly and I was hauled away and all but handed off to someone. "Get her the hell out of here," Grayson said, and his voice was so coldly empty that it sent a chill down my spine.

Whoever had me was moving so fast that I didn't see much outside of Grayson, like a silent panther, lunging for the chick and managing to steal the gun from her in seconds. At least it looked like that, as they got smaller and smaller in my vision until I finally focused on the guard sprinting away with me.

"Put me down!" I demanded, desperate to get back there and *help*. Logically, I knew I was way underqualified and would probably get myself killed in the process, but shit, try telling that to my primal need to protect the ones I loved.

"Not a chance," was the reply from the guy carrying me over his shoulder. From this angle in the darkness, I couldn't see who it was, and it really didn't matter. They were stronger and better trained. There was no way I could escape, and as the rush of playing hero died off, I found myself slumping and trying not to hyperventilate.

She'd pointed a gun at me. She wanted to *shoot* me. I'd seen it clear as day in her eyes, but Jace had somehow distracted her. Why had he done that? What if she'd been mad at the distraction and shot him instead?

Arrogant fuck had been banking on the *Jace effect,* and it could have ended completely differently. So totally differently.

Bad blood or not, that bastard was getting yelled at when he ended up back here.

It felt like we reached the bus far faster than it had seemed when we went to the meet and greet, but maybe that was just due to me zoning out for half the journey.

When the guard set me on my feet, I recognized the blond hair and hard face that was somewhere in its forties, but I wasn't sure of the owner's name. Trace, maybe? Or Tony?

"The others will be back shortly," he said, pressing his hand to his ear. "They need to stay on site until the police arrive and deal with all the paperwork. I've been instructed to lock you on the bus and stand guard."

I wanted to glare and demand my independence— not in a stupid way, but it was good to remind them I was a living breathing person with my own rights. My own choices.

But I'd just had a gun pointed at me again. I'd almost died again.

I was too tired to fight "the man" tonight. That would have to wait for tomorrow when the shock and fear wore off a bit.

"They're all definitely safe, right? No one got shot or anything?" There was a flatness to my voice that would worry me, but I'd already detached from the situation. From reality.

"Safe," he confirmed. "Shooter's been detained by our team, and police are still on their way. Slow fucks."

I nodded a couple of times and then moved toward the bus stairs. He let me go first, which was odd, and when I tried the handle, I found it was locked.

"New automatic lock on these now," he told me,

reaching for keys and opening the door. "Practically impossible to break into. You'll be safe inside. I'll remain out here and keep an eye on the area until the others return. *Don't* leave the bus, no matter what. Understood? This beast is bulletproof; it's the safest place right now."

I nodded again, and there was a very distinct possibility that part of me was broken.

"Look, more guards are already here," he said, and I turned just enough to see half a dozen jogging in our direction. "I told you it was all handled."

Yeah, he certainly had.

Without another word, I entered through the open door and let it close behind me. The solid deadbolt lock clicked loudly when it slammed back into place. We'd left the door open when I returned with Grayson earlier, so I hadn't noticed it. I had to admit, it was nice to know they weren't messing around on security.

Moving slowly, I rubbed my hands across my arms, trying to find some warmth. It wasn't cold in the bus, but I felt chilled to my bones as I all but limped up into the dining area.

My frazzled mind locked in on the shower... maybe that was what I needed before the band got back here. People took showers when they were in shock, didn't they? Something about the white noise and warm water was supposed to help.

Making my way through the bus, I just couldn't get my body to function normally. I was somehow moving both too slow and too fast. Just as the bathroom came into view off the side of the hall, a shadow moved, and this time I was *definitely* too slow.

Strong hands grasped my forearms, wrapping almost painfully around them and forcing some clarity into the fog in my head.

So much for the bus being impossible to break into.

BILLIE

The bus was semi-dark. I'd been in such a brain haze that I hadn't turned any lights on. Fuck, no wonder I was so easy to—

"Bella." Angelo's voice cut through my jumbled thoughts like a Damascus blade. It stole the breath from my lungs and turned my knees weak. He didn't let me to crumple to the floor, though, his grip tightening to offer me support. Or hold me captive.

"Angel," I gasped, my voice *weak*. His timing couldn't be worse if it was orchestrated. Wait, was it? "Did you set that up? Was that shooter chick here with you? Angel, she wanted to *kill* me! I saw it in her eyes when she—"

"Bella, shut up," he snarled, giving me a little shake. I needed it. "That had nothing to do with me; I just took advantage of the timing. I needed to talk to you without..." He trailed off, and his white teeth flashed in the shadows as he grimaced.

I got it, though. "Without Jace seeing you?" I asked, still breathy.

Angelo didn't reply for a long moment, then his grip on my arms eased and he sighed. "Of all the people I *never* expected you to turn to..."

"I didn't," I snapped, shaking off a touch of my initial confusion. Wrapping my arms around myself, I took several steps backwards, away from Angelo and towards the door. Maybe if I was fast enough...

"I'm not here to hurt you, Bella," he said with a groan, clearly anticipating what I was about to do. "If I was, you'd be dead already."

A shiver of fear ran through me, and I took another step back. I thought eight years had changed Jace? He had nothing on Angelo. I barely recognized this menacing, tattooed mobster looming over me in the darkness. Almost as tall as Grayson, he was built like a linebacker, and even in the semi-darkness, I could picture his bronze skin and dark eyes so clearly.

"So why are you here?" I asked, forcing more strength into my voice. Curiosity was getting the better of me, and deep down, I just wanted to see if the boy I loved, the Angel who'd saved me after I broke Jace's heart, was still in there. Somewhere.

He gave a frustrated sound, running a hand over his head. His hair was so short now, not like the shaggy mop he used to wear as an eighteen-year-old boy. "I wanted to talk some sense into you, Bella. What the fuck were you thinking, hiding out on tour with fucking *Bellerose*?" He spat the band name—*my* name—with such hatred it made me flinch.

Gritting my teeth, I lifted my chin higher. Light from outside came through the windows—it wasn't totally dark—so surely he'd see that I wasn't cowering in fear. At least not on the outside. "You hardly gave me a choice, Angel. You're a fucking murderer, and you think I was going to just hang around waiting to be killed? Hell no."

He didn't say anything back, not straight away. That scared me more than anything because, surely, a more natural reaction would be *What? Kill you? I was going to take you out for a succulent Chinese meal then walk you home under the moonlight.*

Okay. Maybe not *exactly* that, but I felt like he should be a little quicker to correct my accusation of murder. But as the moment of silence stretched, a cold dread built within me.

"That night," he said slowly, like he just planned to ignore the big old *murder* elephant in the room. "My father believes you might have overheard something important. He wants you alive, Bella."

I scoffed. "Until he finds out I *didn't* hear anything, and then what? He'll let me walk away? Doubtful." Angelo's father was a ruthless man and had *never* liked me. No way would I be walking away, even if I could be useful.

Angelo didn't disagree with me, either. How comforting.

"I didn't hear anything," I repeated, drawing a deep inhale. "I was in the bathroom when you started killing people, then when I saw an opportunity to run, I did."

Angelo shook his head. "You waitressed that whole dinner service, didn't you?" I nodded. "And you waited on a table of three Italian gentlemen between eight thirty and ten, correct?"

"I have no fucking idea, Angel; it was a busy night in an *Italian* restaurant." Now I was getting irritated.

He made a frustrated sound. "You did; we checked the tapes. Those men—"

"I don't care," I cut him off, desperately not wanting any more information about that night. It was bad enough that I'd witnessed several murders, I did *not* need the reasons. "I do *not fucking care*. Whatever your asshole father thinks I know, I don't. And I'm sure as shit not being killed to appease his paranoid delusions of, what? That I'll go to the cops? Report him as a murderer? Unless things have drastically changed, I doubt that would be more than a vague inconvenience to the mighty Riccis."

Angelo gave me another one of those tense silences in response. Fuck, I hated that. He'd always been the quiet one of the three of us, but he used to wear his emotions on his sleeve to the point that Jace and I could practically read his mind. Not anymore.

"I'm surprised Jace has forgiven you," he said in a change of subject so swift it made my head spin. "His lyrics seem to imply that heartbreak is still fresh for him."

My brows hitched. "You listen to *Bellerose*? The songs aren't all about *me*, you know. I'm not the only one who broke his heart."

"I remember," he murmured and slipped back into tense silence. He hadn't tried to grab me again, nor was he holding a gun in my face. I didn't feel *safe*, far fucking from it, but I also didn't fear for my life. "You need to come back to Siena. If you don't..."

"I thought you said your father doesn't want me dead," I retorted to the clear threat in those three words.

"Yet," he corrected. "But do you really want Jace to get hurt because of you? Again? Haven't you done that enough?"

I inhaled a sharp breath through my nose. "You're seriously going to come here *alone* and threaten to hurt one of the most famous men in the entertainment industry to get your way? There are a dozen guards just outside this bus, Angel; I could scream once and have them swarming this place."

For the first time since I'd backed away from him, Angelo moved closer. He didn't touch me, but he was close enough to, making me tip my head back to meet his dark eyes. "But you haven't, Bella. You could have screamed the moment I grabbed you, *but you didn't.*"

A deep shiver ran through me, and I grasped for straws. "I was in shock after nearly being shot by a crazed Bellerose fan. My wits are slowly returning, though."

His lips tipped in a cold smile. "Sounds like I've overstayed my welcome. Think about it, Bella. You won't always have twelve guards in yelling distance, and I won't always be alone. The Ricci family doesn't like loose ends, so take my advice and *don't become one.*" He reached out and tucked a folded piece of paper into the pocket of my ripped jeans. "I'll be waiting. Next time we have to have this chat, blood will need to be shed."

Oh, shit. I was going to ignore that. He was joking, right?

"Not to spoil this whole mysterious Batman thing you're aiming for tonight, but how do you plan to get out of here unseen? The second you walk out that door, my security guys will grab you. Idiot." I tried really hard to keep a straight face as I said that, but there was something so fucking stupid about this whole plan. He really hadn't thought it through.

Angelo just smirked. "If they're still there, maybe."

That sent a jolt of worry through me. Why *wouldn't* they be there? Panicked, I crossed to the window and leaned down to look outside. When I recognized Grace and Trace—or Tony—as well as several other familiar figures, I gave a sigh of relief.

"They *are* still there; thanks so much for that heart attack, Angel." I straightened up, turning back to face him.

Except... I was talking to thin air. Angelo was nowhere to be seen.

For a moment I just stood there, staring at the space of empty air where he'd been *just* standing. Then I started second guessing myself. Had I just imagined that *entire* thing? Was it some kind of shock-induced delusion brought on by nearly getting shot *again*?

"What the fuck, Billie?" I muttered out loud. Then, because I was freaking myself out, I looked around. Maybe he was just taking a pee? But no... the bathroom was empty, as were all the bunks and the bedroom and... "Oh, holy shit. Seriously?"

Looking up, I saw how he'd escaped. The skylight above the bed—the one I'd been sharing with Rhett— was wide open. Angelo really was pulling some Batman shit.

His last warning echoed through my head. *The next time... blood will be shed.*

twenty-eight

BILLIE

"Where the fuck is she?"

The shout was harsh, and it came from Jace. Two guesses who the *she* was in this scenario.

Right. Like anyone would need two.

One of the security guards must have told him that I was on the very bus I'd been ordered to get on, because not even a minute later, a few entry lights lit everything up, and I could clearly see the raging tower of musician storming toward me. His energy hit me first, like it always did with Jace. For years I'd convinced myself it was his ego that surrounded him, but it was more *his presence.*

A presence I wished was anywhere other than this tiny bus when I'd been dealt two shocking blows already tonight.

That shower I'd been hoping would calm my frazzled nerves hadn't eventuated, and after I'd finished dealing with Angelo followed by Jace, I doubted it would help anyway.

"What the fuck were you thinking?" he shouted, mere inches from my face as he leaned over and let his rage flow free. The juxtaposition between his personality and Angelo's couldn't have been more obvious than it was in this second.

Opposites attract happened in more than just romantic relationships.

"I was thinking that I wasn't about to allow any of you to get shot because of something I'd done." *Dickhead.*

"Thorn, come on," Rhett said, and it was nice to know he was behind Jace, even if I couldn't really see him around the angry lead singer. "I kissed you knowing full well that we could be seen by fans. This is all on me, and I never, ever want you to put yourself in danger for me again. I will literally—"

"Smack your fucking ass so hard you won't sit down for a week."

That came from Grayson, who sounded like he was the third in the line of Bellerose's band members who wanted to yell at me.

Was it bad that, even in my shock, a mental image of Grayson's hand on my ass made my legs weak? Was I suddenly into that? Yes. Yes, I was.

Jace, of course, ruined the vibe before I could think it over any longer.

"You're a fucking manipulator," he spat, finally leaning back from my face as he crossed his arms over his chest. "But let me give you a little piece of advice, sweetheart. Getting yourself killed doesn't get you the money or the man. Tone it down next time; you reek of desperation."

I gasped as he pushed past me, his wide shoulders pressing me against the wall as he claimed the bathroom I'd been heading for when he'd come storming in. As soon as he was gone, Rhett's arms closed around me, and he yanked me hard against his chest.

I was surprised to feel his arms tremble as he tightened them across my back, holding on like he was never going to let me go. "You scared me half to death," he whispered against my neck, pressing his lips to my skin. "The only reason I didn't jump and run for that bitch was the chance she'd manage to shoot you before I got to her."

It warmed me that my first instinct had been right. At least about Rhett. Jace... well, it was still up in the air, but he had been the one to distract her long enough for Grayson to go into superhuman action. Speaking of...

My eyes met Grayson's as Rhett leaned down into me farther, and I managed to lift my head enough to say, "Thank you," to the big ninja.

Grayson's eyes were hard. His face was hard. His arms were crossed over his chest too, and every muscle stood out starkly like he'd just done a massive workout and those muscles were pumped as fuck. If I didn't know this guy and he came at me in a dark alley, I would probably shit myself and then die. Because *damn.*

"We'll talk later," he warned me, and then he was gone—not the way Jace had pushed past, but back along the alley and out of the bus like he needed some air.

We'll talk later almost fell into the same category as *the next time blood will be shed.*

Both were threats. Still, one was much more appealing than the other.

Pushing aside the dangerous, dominant men now

suddenly filling my life, I focused on Rhett, who was still holding me like his sanity depended on it. We were pressed as close as two people could be, but I tried to pull him even closer. To offer comfort. Rhett had been the one with the gun pointed at him first. I could have lost him tonight.

"It was the worst feeling in the world when I saw her standing there with that gun on you," I told him, my voice catching as my throat clogged up. Fuck, was it getting short of air in here, or was I on the verge of a panic attack again? "I didn't even think before I pulled her attention; I just knew I had to do anything to keep you safe. To keep you all safe."

He finally lifted his head, eyes rimmed in red and so green they were almost blinding. "If anything happened to you..." he said slowly as his hands moved from my back to slide up my sides until he cupped my face, holding me steady. I couldn't escape that blinding gaze. Not that I wanted to. "It would have killed us all anyway. The pain... Just, next time remember you might be breathing for more than one person."

"Rhett," I gasped.

He kissed me, a swift press of his lips to mine, and I surrendered myself to him. The fuzziness that had been clouding my head since the meet and greet was completely smashed by Rhett. His heat and energy consumed me, and I groaned against his mouth, that desperate kiss destructive to my equilibrium.

When he finally pulled away, hands still gripping my cheeks—gently this time—we were both breathing heavily. "We're pushing back our arrival into New York one day," he told me between puffs of air. "We're going to stop at a hotel about an hour from here that we use quite regularly. It has enough security, and Tom found some rooms for us. All of us need a night to relax and not be on the fucking bus from hell."

"Will we have a room alone?" I asked him, trying to keep my tone casual. I think I failed epically, as his pupils dilated and the green darkened slightly.

"Very much alone. No roommates, no bus mates. No *Jace*."

He wasn't keeping his voice down, but the shower was still running, so hopefully Jace missed this conversation. Meanwhile, I was wondering if maybe the gun-wielding superfan had done me a huge favor. A night alone with Rhett, hiding from all the stresses of the last few days and the possibility of leaving them in the next few days, was an absolute godsend.

"I can't wait," I said, lifting myself to kiss him again. He gave me the lead this time, and the kiss had less of a desperate quality, but it was no less hot.

Rhett groaned against my mouth. "We need to stop

now, or we won't make it to the hotel. I'm not usually into putting on a show…"

"Yep," I said with a small laugh. "Let's just be on our best behavior. An hour is barely anything, right?"

"Just sixty minutes," he said, voice lower as he leaned down closer.

"Three thousand six hundred seconds," I breathed. I'd been time obsessed when I was younger and had lots of random time facts useful for moments like these.

"And then we have the rest of this night alone, with the bus not departing until nine tomorrow."

Hours. Hours alone with Rhett, and fuck, I was starting to think this one hour, sixty minutes, or three thousand plus seconds was going to go as slow as a fucking snail.

Distractions entered the bus a minute later, with Florence, Grayson, Tom, and the bus driver all getting on and the door closing behind them. More lights flickered across the space, and it was so blindingly bright that it took me a moment to orient myself. Rhett moved to the side as Flo raced for me. "Thank you," she cried as she wrapped her arms around me. "Thank you for trying to save my brothers. That was so brave of you."

"Stupid," Grayson rumbled, not mincing words. I

wasn't offended though. It *had* been stupid with zero plans before action.

Flo turned around and glared at him. "Shut up, ass. Anyone who risks their lives for people I love will always have my gratitude."

Grayson's face didn't soften, even though I knew he cared for Flo too. She wasn't perturbed though, just wrinkled her nose at him before turning back to me. "Even though we're getting into the city a day later, we'll still have all morning before the concert, and I'd like to take you out for a girl's shopping trip to say thank you."

I opened my mouth, but she continued before I could say anything.

"Not just as a thank you," she quickly amended. "It's been a long time since I had another girl to hang out with, and I think we could both use the retail therapy. My treat."

It had been a long time since I'd had that too, and even though I'd never take a dime of her money for shopping, the day hanging out together would be more than enough for me. "I'd love that," I said with every ounce of sincerity I felt.

"You'll have so much security with you it'd hardly be worth it," Tom sneered from where he'd sat himself at the table. "Just order your stupid clothes online or through stylists and forget about trying to be normal. You're a celebrity, babe, you should act like it."

Florence shot me a small smile. "Ignore him; his bark is worse than his bite."

All parts of him were the worst, but I didn't say that to her.

She left then to take her position attached to his side, and Rhett wrapped an arm around my shoulders, once more drawing me close. "We're about to leave. No food tonight since we're in a rush, but we can eat at the hotel." The bus roared to life, the massive engines thrumming below us as the driver got settled in for the drive. "The other buses will be right behind us too with security and staff."

"Perfect," I said before his words triggered a thought. "Uh, you know I haven't really been cleaning or doing my job since we got on the road. Should I maybe be reporting to Dora at the hotel to see what she needs done?" It would kill our vibe for the night, but freeloading wasn't my intention. Florence's comment about taking me out for a girls' lunch was a pretty huge reminder that I had no money and was supposed to be working for Bellerose.

I really should have been more proactive in seeking out Dora or even Kristie, having seen both only in the distance over the past few days. There had just been so much going on, with the Roger incident and the rest, that I hadn't even thought about it.

"It's too dangerous for you to be without security," Rhett told me, "and you'd make it harder for them to do their jobs. Everyone is in agreement on this. We can settle debts later if it makes you feel better, but right now the priority is just to keep you safe—especially now that I've painted another target on your back."

The bus lurched forward as we started to move, and since I couldn't argue with that logic, I didn't. My presence had already put the band in danger, and they were surrounded by security. Their staff didn't have the same privilege.

Not to mention Angelo had gotten to me even with all the extra precautions. I already knew that random chicks like Liz were expendable to him, and I would not have that on my conscience. Just thinking about Dora being killed made my stomach hurt.

A flicker of guilt hit me. I hadn't told any of them that Angelo had been on this bus, and I couldn't figure out why I was holding the information back.

Was it a nostalgic feeling of old love I'd had for him that kept me silent, or was it the fact that the psycho bastard would kill anyone who came after him and I wasn't exactly sure how Grayson—or the others—

would react to the knowledge that he'd been in this bus?

Not just in the bus, but with an opportunity to take me out before anyone even knew he was there. Sure, he'd made some vague threats about his father wanting me, but there had to be more to it than that.

What was Angelo hiding from me?

Or a more important question: Would I live long enough to find out?

BILLIE

All the best laid plans for a night of hot rock star sex flew right out the window when our bus hit a series of brutal potholes only half an hour into the drive and popped two tires. Luckily, we had spares between our bus and the next one, but it was a *slow* process to get them changed, and with all the excitement of the night—between nearly being shot and Angelo's creepy visit—I was dead on my feet.

I didn't remember getting to the hotel sometime before dawn but had a vague memory of Rhett carrying me off the bus and tucking me into bed. And holy shit, what a comfy bed it was too. In just a couple of nights

I'd gotten used to the somewhat thin mattress on the bus, but the hotel bed was like a damn cloud.

When I woke, Rhett was curled around me, his breathing deep and even, and I gave myself a moment to just relax there. He made me feel so safe and *adored*, which I hadn't realized I'd needed so much. He was so unafraid of his feelings, so confident in expressing his affection for me... It was both unfamiliar and nostalgic at the same time.

I could see why he and Jace were friends. Rhett was how Jace used to be: carefree, optimistic, valiant. Yes, part of the attraction for him was probably my vulnerable position. Rhett clearly held onto some trauma from his past, and I sensed that partly drove his *need* to protect me. But that didn't detract from how intense the sexual chemistry was between us.

Even now in his sleep, his hard dick pressed against my hip and he mumbled my name like he was dreaming of me. Dreaming of fucking me, maybe?

Well shit, that thought woke me up, and my stomach fluttered with excitement. We'd been sleeping in the same bed for the better part of a week, but this was new. Or maybe just the first time I'd really woken up before Rhett.

Trying hard to behave myself—or trying a little—I rolled onto my side, snuggling back into his embrace.

Little spoon was the best. Rhett gave a small moan in his sleep, his hand gripping my hip and pulling me flush against his hard dick.

Whoops. I grinned into my pillow, rocking my hips slightly. Would he wake up? Or was he well immersed in his sex dream?

"Billie," he growled, voice thick with sleep as he ground against me. Well, that answered that. "Good morning, my beautiful Thorn."

My pussy heated as his lips found the back of my neck, sending shivers of arousal chasing through me. "Good morning, Zep," I replied in a husky whisper. "Were you having sweet dreams?"

He moaned the *sexiest* fucking sound, and his hand slipped beneath my t-shirt, cupping my bare breast. I'd taken my bra off before falling asleep on the bus, and I was *so* glad for that decision now.

"I was," he confirmed, toying with my nipple and making me squirm. Shit, that felt good, every tug and flick sparking the heat between my legs hotter still. "But being awake is looking a whole lot better now."

Sucking in a sharp breath, I tipped my head so that his lips could reach mine. He just teased me, though, brushing a light kiss across my lips before grinning.

"You have no idea how badly I've been wanting to

get you alone, Thorn," he admitted, his hand trailing down my body.

I gave a throaty chuckle. "Oh trust me, I can relate."

His fingers paused at the waistband of my panties. He must have taken my jeans off before tucking me into bed. Such a gentleman. "Oh yeah? Have you been thinking about fucking me, Billie Bellerose?" He toyed with the elastic but didn't go any further. Fuck. I groaned, rocking my butt against his diamond-hard cock. "Am I going to find you already soaked, babe?"

I swallowed hard, trying to catch my breath, but my whole damn body was tingling with anticipation. "Better check," I suggested. Then, because I was all kinds of impatient, I placed my hand over his, pushing it further inside my panties with a crystal-clear demand.

Rhett's breathing stuttered as his fingers dipped inside, confirming the fact that I was more than ready to take things further. "Fuck, Thorn, it's taking every single ounce of my willpower not to just rip those panties off and slam my dick into you right now."

I rocked my hips, pushing against his hand and taking his fingers deeper. "No one asked for slow and gentle, Zep. I thought you were a rock star, not a country singer."

His fingers stilled, and he gave a small gasp of

disbelief. Then all of a sudden, I was flat on my back with Rhett yanking my panties away and tossing them clear across the room.

"Oh, baby, those were fighting words," he informed me with a wicked grin. Then his face was buried between my legs, his tongue lashing my clit far better than my own fingers had *ever* managed to. Words caught in my throat as intense waves of pleasure filled my skin, my thighs tightening around his head on reflex.

Rhett was in charge, though, pinning my legs back down to the bed and spreading me wide so he could do as he pleased.

"Fuck, *fuck, Rhett...*" My moans were all just curses as he alternated between tongue-fucking me and sucking my clit. When he released one of my thighs to slide two fingers into my pussy, I died. The orgasm built up fast, and his fingers went to work in time with his tongue, pushing me over the edge without even a moment's hesitation. He didn't stop, even as I thrashed and gasped through the climax, then when I was done, he made a point of cleaning things up... with his tongue.

Holy shit.

"Rhett, I swear, if you don't have any condoms around here somewhere..." Not that I was unprotected, but it didn't hurt to be careful when fucking a rock star, right?

His smirk was all confidence as he sat up, though. "Don't move," he ordered, patting my inner thigh, then leaning across to the bedside table. Oh, smart boy was definitely on the same page as I was. There was a brand new box of condoms sitting there, and it only took him a few seconds to rip the plastic packaging off.

My limbs were all heavy and jellylike, so I just lay there and watched as he tucked a foil packet between his teeth and dragged his t-shirt off. Fuck Rhett was *ripped*. Not as broad as Jace or Angelo, but what he lacked in size, he made up for in sheer muscle definition. He had abs where I didn't even know abs existed, all gorgeously decorated with ink. He grinned at me as he sat back on his heels between my still spread legs.

"I want to ask you something, Thorn," he murmured, locking eyes with me as he tugged his boxers down to free his erection. I broke his gaze, needing to look. His dick was so pretty, and... *were those piercings along the underside of his shaft?* I'd had his cock in my hand before, but it hadn't gone far enough for me to explore. But here and now, with the room lit by morning sun creeping around curtains and Rhett kneeling before me, I saw everything.

And now all I could think about was what those piercings would feel like inside me.

Holy shit. I was practically drooling.

"Are you listening, baby?" His question made me realize that I was just *staring* at his cock. Could he blame me? The way his fingers wrapped around the thick shaft, his index finger stroking the metal rungs below his skin like it was an extension of his guitar...

"Totally listening," I lied.

He huffed a laugh, tearing open the condom packet and deftly rolling it over his weapon. A small part of me was tempted to tell him to take it off again so I could feel every piece of metal. But a bigger part was too sensible and didn't want to catch an STD, so I bit my tongue to keep quiet.

"I want you to stay," he told me, stroking himself to ensure the rubber was all in place. "Will you stay?"

Huh?

"Billie, will you? It's not safe for you to leave us now." He leaned forward, bracing his hands on the bed to either side of me and holding himself in some kind of kama-sutric push-up. That impressive cock pointed right between my legs like a homing beacon, but he didn't push forward. "So, will you?"

I gave myself a mental slap, bringing my eyes back to his. "Will I...?" What had he asked me again?

He smiled. "Stay. With me."

His gaze was so soft and full of affection, reminding me of that soul deep connection we seemed to share. It was like we'd known each other for years, not just days. Being with Rhett was just as natural as breathing, and I nodded without really processing the question.

Relief and elation crossed his face, and his breath rushed out. "Thank *fuck*," he groaned, then kissed me so hard I saw stars. His position shifted, the hot tip of his cock pressing gently to my still throbbing core. Only then did I really comprehend what I'd agreed to. And what the *consequences* of me staying on tour might be. Then the guilt that flooded through me nearly made me gasp.

"Wait," I said with a grimace. "I have to tell you something."

Rhett froze, the head of his dick already notched at my pussy. "Um, now?"

I nodded. "Yes, otherwise the guilt will totally ruin this..." *Spit it out, Billie. Rip off the Band-Aid.* "I kissed Grayson."

Rhett's brows hitched in an expression of shock. But he didn't move away, so that was something. Holy shit, talk about bad timing on my part. This was damn near torture having him just a half inch inside me when I wanted more. So much more. But I respected him too much to keep secrets, especially if we weren't parting ways tomorrow.

He licked his lips, his teeth tugging on his lip piercing as his eyes studied my face. "You kissed Grayson?"

I swallowed, then heard the big man's voice in my head, so I cringed. "He kissed me. But I wanted it, so... same thing."

Rhett was silent another moment, then shocked the ever-loving shit out of me when he thrust his whole length into me with one swift motion. I cried out, my nails sinking into his muscular back as my whole body quaked with pleasure. He was thick enough that it hurt a little, but in a good kind of way. The kind of way that reminded me it'd been way too long since I'd had any half-decent sex, and Rhett was about to blow my mind.

"Rhett," I panted, rocking my hips as my body begged for more.

"Let's discuss it later," he told me, dropping kisses on my parted lips. "If you can still remember his name when we're done."

Oh, *damn*. Rhett wasn't hurt or angry, he was *jealous*... and had clearly just decided I was worth fighting for. Why was that such a turn on?

"I'm okay with that plan," I whispered, stretching up to kiss him back.

His response was to pull out a little, then slam back in even harder. It made me squeak a little but also encouraged me to wrap my legs around him so I could take him deeper.

"You good, Thorn?" he asked with a husky chuckle.

I nodded so hard I probably looked like a bobblehead. "Yes, fuck yes, Rhett… fuck me like a rock star." Oh man, I could cheese it up like a pro. Rhett must have agreed because he barked a laugh before crushing his mouth to mine once more.

No more words were exchanged, our bodies doing all the communication we needed. Our tongues danced together as Rhett started to move, fucking me with slow, hard thrusts until I was a whimpering, slippery mess on the bed. I got the feeling he was holding back a little, though.

"Rhett," I gasped in his ear as my nails raked his back. "Harder. Please, I won't break. Fuck me *harder*."

He gave a pained groan, his eyes searching mine. Then his lips curled in one of those sinful smirks, and he sat back. His dick slipped free of my cunt, making me protest, but he just grabbed one of the pillows and slid it under my ass to boost me up higher. Then when he thrust back in, it was at a whole different angle.

Words failed me, and I gave incoherent noises of encouragement as he started to pump while raising my knees up to my chest and spreading them wide. Luckily, I was so fucking flexible because the harder he fucked, the wider my legs spread until my knees touched the mattress and my back arched.

I was helpless to do anything but pant and moan, crying out as I climaxed from penetration alone and shocked the hell out of myself. Rhett acknowledged my orgasm with kisses and a slower pace, but as my whole-body trembles subsided, he went hard and fast again.

"Are you gonna come for me again, Thorn?" he asked as he pounded me into the mattress. Holy shit, I'd said I wanted it hard, but this was beyond expectation. Rhett was doing his damnedest to totally ruin me for other men, that was for sure. Were the piercings increasing my stimulation, despite the condom, or was this all just Rhett? Both? It was definitely both.

I shook my head. "No," I moaned. "I can't." Hell, he'd made me come twice; that was as good as it got. Wasn't it? Maybe I could. Shit, I didn't know.

Rhett groaned. "You *can*, but I'm not going to last... God damn, Thorn, this pussy is like heaven. I knew it'd be good because it's *you*. But holy shit."

I licked my lips, my mouth all dry and fuzzy from my last orgasm and all the panting I was doing. "Do it. Fuck, Rhett, I need you to come. We have all day for repeats, don't we?"

That idea must have done it for him because a moment later he was thrusting deep, grunting his own release as his cock swelled and twitched inside my walls. A filthy part of my mind wanted to know what it'd feel like without the condom... what it'd be like to have Rhett come inside me for real. To feel the cold slide of metal until it turned hotter from our arousal.

He whispered something I couldn't quite make out, feathering kisses over my face as he released my legs. Then he slipped free of my pulsing core and didn't even bother to pull the condom off before sinking his face between my thighs once more.

"Rhett!" I shrieked as his tongue found my clit again.

"Hush, Thorn," he mumbled into my pussy. "Let me prove my point."

Well, shit. Who was I to argue with logic like that? Besides, I was curious... so my fingers threaded into his turquoise hair, holding him close as he leisurely tongue-fucked me once more. He wasn't rushing things or forcing the issue, he was content to just take his time like he was coaxing the third orgasm out of my body like a scared animal.

When it hit, I was so shocked I nearly blacked out. It was a slower release, but almost more intense for the difference. My toes curled against the mattress and my spine curved, while scalding hot bubbles of euphoria fizzed through me, leaving me dazed and confused.

"See?" Rhett grinned, kissing my inner thigh. I could barely hear him with how my ears were ringing. "You *can*. Now... what were we talking about?"

I blinked, drawing a blank. "Huh?"

His grin spread wide, and he gave a sexy chuckle. "Perfect."

thirty

RHETT

My phone rang from across the room where I'd dropped it in my exhausted state last night. It was too far to reach from the bed, and dragging myself from these soft depths was going to take a fuck load of will power. It wasn't exactly the bed, to be honest, but the warm body that occupied it. She was snuggled in close to me, her perfect tits pressed against my side, and my cock was fairly certain that we were just getting started with Billie Bellerose. Not just my cock, but every other part of me.

She groaned softly, the phone disturbing her, and that was what got my ass out of bed to snatch up the offending fucking piece. "What?" I whisper-snarled into the phone. "It's fucking dawn."

"It's after ten, dickhead." Grayson's tone was flat. "Get your ass into the gym."

The line went dead, and I sucked in a long breath . My gaze darted back to Billie for a second, and I was relieved to see that she was once again sleeping soundly. Pretty pink lips parted as she breathed deeply, and I swear to fuck my dick actually throbbed at the sight.

The sex we'd had was beyond my fantasies, and I'd had more than my share of those up to this morning. All I wanted to do was crawl back into that bed and bury my face between her legs, but Grayson had called me for a reason.

He was keeping a promise he'd made long ago. A promise that if he ever saw me falling off the rails of staying healthy and looking after myself, he would drag my ass to the gym and deliver food to my door...

Marching over, I opened up the hotel door, naked and not giving a single fuck. Sure enough, outside my door was a tray with protein and some fruit. There were also two large bottles of water. No note, but I didn't need one. This was how Grayson cared, and clearly, he knew I'd been more focused on Billie than myself recently. Which was all good—she needed the extra attention. But I was also a fucking idiot with myself at times, and I couldn't go back into the dark pit.

While Billie was great for me in some ways, she was also dangerous. I could lose myself in her; the obsession she created inside me was darker than I'd felt in a long time. How fucking odd that she made me feel both lighter than air and disturbingly obsessed.

I'd have to find a balance, and Grayson was reminding me how to do that.

Get my ass to the gym.

Ten minutes later, after I'd left a note for Billie and taken off with the protein mix in one hand and an apple in the other, I found my way into the hotel gym. It was empty, which was no surprise since Grayson would have either secured a private session or scared everyone the fuck away with his personality.

The clank of weights drew me across the room, and I breathed in the scent of sweat and disinfectant. This was a fancy hotel and they clearly kept it clean, but there was always an undertone of sweat in these places that could never be removed.

"About fucking time," Grayson said as he lifted his head from the Smith machine that he was using. His eyes traced across me, taking in the protein I was finishing up, and a small smile graced his lips before his perusal paused on my eyes.

Fuck.

No doubt my morning with Billie was written across my face, and I recalled that blast of hot jealousy I'd felt when she said she'd kissed Grayson. I really hoped I wasn't going to fight with my brother over his moment of weakness. Billie was both physically and mentally alluring, and I would have kissed the hell out of her too in his position, but it didn't mean I was cool with what'd happened.

"Things moving fast with Billie," Grayson said softly.

I swallowed hard before dropping the protein and apple core on the floor so I could set myself up with the free weights. Scrubbing a hand over my face, I let out a long breath. "I asked her to stay with us. I just... I'm not ready to let her go."

Would I ever be fucking ready? That was the question of the day.

"I like her."

There was a beat of silence after his words, and it wasn't that I was shocked. Far from it, especially after Billie's confession, but to hear Grayson say those words out loud... Grayson, who never stayed longer than a few hours with a chick and kicked them out faster than even Jace. Grayson, who made it no secret he gave zero fucks about anyone other than Bellerose members, suddenly had this air of vulnerability across his features, and I had no fucking idea how this was going to play out.

I didn't want to take Billie away from him, but on the other hand, *she was mine.*

"She told me you kissed," I said shortly, anger fizzling for a beat at the mental image of them together, before I remembered it was Grayson and I loved him like a brother. The need to beat the fuck out of him was only moderately strong after that.

"I kissed her," he shot back before he resumed his next set of shoulder presses. "It wasn't her fault."

Protecting her too. His feelings were maybe more serious than I expected.

"I'm not giving her up," I warned him, pumping the weights harder even though I'd barely warmed up. "So you're gonna have a fucking fight on your hands if you're not careful."

Grayson was silent for a moment. "I'm not asking you to give her up."

The weight almost slipped from my right hand, but I caught it at the last second. If he wasn't asking me to give her up, then what the hell was he asking me?

"You want to share? Like one of your fucking romance books?" The thought was instantly appealing and also abhorrent. Dueling emotions hit me so hard and fast that it was no wonder I almost lost the weight in my hand again.

"I don't share, you know that," Grayson said with a whole lot more bite in his tone.

I turned toward him, needing to see his expression, but he had himself tightly locked down. No sign of his true emotions could be seen on his physical form. When he wanted to be, Grayson was made of damn stone.

"So, it's a competition you're after?" He didn't answer immediately, and I was pretty sure I'd hit the fucking nail on the head. "You want us both to pursue her and see who Billie chooses?"

More silence. More confirmation.

Fuck's sake. "This is bullshit," I bit out. "I found her first."

"She's not a doll or missing piece of a puzzle," Grayson shot back at me. "You can't *find her first*. Billie's her own person, and she will ultimately decide. I just wanted to give you the head's up that I'm throwing my own interest into the mix."

A snort escaped me. "Arrogant of you to assume she's not a piece of our puzzle. But you know what? I never expected to be able to keep her without a fight."

I'd just thought the fight would come from Jace... because no way in hell was my best friend just going to let bygones be bygones with the *only* girl he'd ever loved.

Grayson let out a low sigh before he shot me a small smile. "It's not a fair fight, I know."

A snort of laughter escaped me. "No shit. She's naked in my bed right now, passed out from this morning when she came three fucking times on my dick and tongue."

Yeah, I was an asshole, but no one had said we had to play fair.

To my surprise, Grayson laughed too. "Three. Barely even seems like a challenge. Enjoy your opening round because I'm all in. Thanks for convincing her to stay, by the way. That makes things easier... for me."

A tinge of annoyance hit me. "This isn't just a game for you, right? Because she's *not* a toy. So if you hurt Billie, I will fucking kill you. Brother or not."

Grayson got to his feet and crossed to stand at my side. Giant bastard towered over me, and I somehow managed not to cringe when he dropped a heavy hand on my shoulder. "If I hurt her, I'll probably let you kill me."

He gave my shoulder one final squeeze, rendering me near broken-armed, and then he moved into personal trainer mode. For the next hour he kicked my ass from one side of the gym to the other, and by the time I was crawling my ass to the shower, I had to admit I felt better.

Calmer. More centered. And more ready than ever to show Billie Bellerose that I was the only fucking man she needed in her life.

Grayson was waiting for me in the hall when I emerged, and we walked silently toward our floor. No lie, my mind was already back in bed, anticipating what I'd find when I stepped inside my room. Would she still be asleep? Naked... those fucking tit—

A hand slammed into my chest, halting my steps, and I glared up at Grayson, about to snap at the heavy-handed fucker. Second time today he'd almost broken me. Only I realized a moment later why he'd stopped me in my tracks.

Florence.

Florence and Tom, to be more accurate, arguing in the hall.

"It's going too fucking far," she hissed at our scumbag temporary manager. "We just need to be done and worry about the rest later."

My gaze shifted to Grayson, who held a finger to his lips. I agreed with him that if this was a breakup fight, we definitely shouldn't interrupt. Thankfully, they stood in a small alcove in the hall, slightly hidden from view, which also meant we were hidden from them too.

"We could lose everything, you stupid bitch," Tom hissed back, and I wanted to crack that motherfucker in the face for the way he spoke to Flo. We'd all expressed our annoyance about it, but she'd asked us to stay out of it. We had to respect her wishes, but the moment he went too far... the moment I saw a bruise or loss of spirit from her, Tom was dead.

Dead and buried without an ounce of remorse or regret.

"How do you know that?" Flo whined. "Maybe it'll all be fine. Nothing has happened so far."

Wait. *Was this a breakup fight?* Or was there something else going on?

"Just remember the plan. You signed up for this. For us. And I'm not letting you ruin everything because you've found a fucking heart. You were nothing before me, and if you fuck this up, you'll be nothing again."

This time I held Grayson back because that fucker really would kill Tom. And we just didn't have time for the paperwork. Not today.

Florence didn't respond to her piece-of-shit boyfriend, and we straightened when they popped out of the alcove and continued down the hallway. Neither of them bothered to look back to where we were half-crouched. It pissed me the hell off to see they were holding hands as they went, so clearly, no breakup.

"Does he have her fucking grandma tied up in the basement or some shit?" I said with a sad shake of my head. "Like, in what world does it make sense for someone as awesome as Flo to get caught in the web of someone as fucking pathetic as Tom."

"I know she asked us not to interfere," Grayson rumbled, his voice lower and more pissed than I'd heard in a while, "but something has to be done about him. And soon."

I nodded as I thought it over. "We should try the label again. Surely there are better-qualified managers that can fill in for the rest of this tour. By then Brenda will be back from maternity leave, won't she?"

"Florence asked us not to fire him," Grayson reminded me.

"Right. But maybe we just do what we think is best for her. An intervention of sorts where we kick his ass right out of Bellerose. I'm sick of having his slimy fingers in our music."

I wasn't one for taking people's rights or choices away. Florence was a grown woman, hence the reason Tom had been here for this long, but I'd about had enough.

I'd seen the way that bastard looked at Billie, with calculating disgust. He wanted her gone—without even a cent of her rightfully owed royalties—and I knew that he was going to cause issues the moment he found out I'd asked her to stay.

And if it came down to Billie versus Tom…

Yeah, not even a fucking comparison. One would be gone and it wasn't the one this band was named after.

BILLIE

Disappointment shot through me like a bullet when I woke up alone. Had Rhett just hit it and quit it? It sure as fuck wouldn't be the first time for me, but Rhett was *different*. Or so I'd thought...

I lay there for a long moment, feeling sorry for myself and shedding a quick tear. Part of me even wondered if Jace had put him up to it, then I just wallowed in guilt and self-pity for a while. Eventually, I pulled my shit together enough to get out of bed... then discovered the note Rhett had left.

"Oh shit," I whispered aloud as my eyes scanned the handwritten letter on hotel notepaper. "Billie, you pathetic pessimistic bitch." He hadn't hit it and quit it, he'd gone to the gym to work out with Grayson.

"Fuck," I groaned, remembering my mid-sex confession about kissing Grayson. Maybe I should go down there and... what? Make sure they weren't killing each other? Even if they were, what the fuck did I think I could do to stop them?

Cringing, I checked the time, then spotted a message on my new phone from Flo, asking me if I wanted to meet her for coffee. So... I had two choices. Storm down to the gym and make an already awkward situation even more awkward or meet up with Flo while praying to the gods of coffee that Rhett had just *forgotten*.

Unlikely. But there was a glimmer of hope, wasn't there?

"Fuck it," I muttered, throwing my hands up and heading for the shower.

In the time it took me to wash, shave, shampoo, and condition, I'd changed my mind seventy-six times about whether to check on Rhett or not. Because I had a gut feeling that if he confronted Grayson, it wasn't going to be Gray nursing a black eye.

My decision was made for me with a knock on the door while I was pulling on a pair of jeans. I checked the peephole—because I wasn't a *total* moron—then opened it to greet Florence.

"Hey girl, you get my message?" she asked with an overly bright smile.

I nodded, my mind made up. "Yeah, sorry I didn't reply. I'm up for coffee, absolutely. I just need to dry my hair."

"All good, I need to sort out our security detail, anyway." Flo rolled her eyes and huffed a laugh. "I'll meet you downstairs in like twenty minutes?"

I agreed, and Flo hurried back along the hall toward the elevators. It took me a little more than twenty minutes to meet her in the end, thanks to the crappy, low-powered hotel hairdryer.

If anything, Flo seemed even more tense and cagey when I finally hurried over to where she waited with a handful of security guards. Her eyes were red-rimmed, and her smile fake as fuck.

"Are you okay?" I asked with concern, reaching out to touch her arm. "Did something happen?"

"Huh? Yeah, of course, I'm fine," she lied. "Let's go before Rhett tries to drag you back into bed or something." She gave a pointed look at my neck, and I flushed with embarrassment. Who even got hickies at this age?

"Maybe we can pick up some concealer or something," I murmured with a wince as Flo looped her arm through mine. She chuckled, leading me out to the waiting SUV with security floating around us like a gas cloud.

We both slid into the backseat, and she sighed heavily as the door closed behind us.

"Are you sure you're okay?" I tried again. "You seem upset."

This time her smile was even less convincing. "Yeah, girl. All good. Just one of those days, you know? I need a break from all the testosterone."

"Understandable. You're surrounded by dudes twenty-four seven. It must get lonely sometimes." Maybe that's why she put up with Tom?

Flo just shot me a tight smile back, flipping her sunglasses down from where they'd been perched on her hair. "So, there's a cute coffee shop slash book shop place I want to take you to. They serve these amazing little mini-cupcakes with all their coffees. The boys hate it, but it's so cute."

I bit the inside of my cheek to keep from pushing her when she was making such an obvious attempt to change the subject. Instead, I chatted with her about their plans for the rest of the tour. Over and over in my head, I could hear Rhett asking me to *stay* and me agreeing.

Now, in the light of day without the overwhelming sexual chemistry clouding my head, I was feeling like shit. Sex with Rhett was un-fucking-believable. Mind-blowingly good. But when he'd asked me to stay, it hadn't been *only* him I'd agreed to stay for.

I wanted to stay with him. With *Rhett*, my shining knight. But I also wanted to stay because of Grayson... and if I was being totally honest with myself, a little bit for Jace. It might have been a decade, but whatever had drawn me to my oldest friend in the first place remained a strong part of my soul. A part I couldn't purge no matter how much of an asshole he was.

"We're here," Florence said, jerking me out of my guilt party.

We waited for security to spread out and open the car door for us, and I breathed a small sigh of relief that only one of the burly men actually entered with us. Flo was right; it was adorable, with old Alice in Wonderland style furniture and bookshelves overflowing with well-worn novels.

"I'm confused," I admitted after we had sat down and ordered our coffees. "Grayson is a book lover, isn't he? He loaned me one the other night."

Flo grinned, a genuine smile this time as she tucked her sunglasses back up onto her head. "He is. But look at the size of the chairs. Last time I brought him here, he broke the leg off one when he sat down and then knocked over a whole tray of teacups on his way out. He was a whole-ass bull in a china shop and was *mortified* about it."

I winced but bit back a laugh. Poor Grayson. "Let me guess, Rhett and Jace gave him shit about it, too?"

Flo laughed loudly. "They were merciless until Gray kicked their asses in the gym, and then they all shut up about it."

"Boys," I muttered, rolling my eyes.

Flo chuckled. "Right? Necessary evil. So... did you and Rhett take advantage of the privacy last night?" She smirked, and my cheeks heated.

"Is it that obvious?" I groaned, rubbing at my tired eyes. Worth it, though.

She grinned. "It's like a neon sign above your head flashing *freshly fucked*. To be honest, I'm shocked you guys didn't just go for it on the bus."

"Uh yeah, I wasn't super into the idea of my ex listening to me getting railed by his best friend," I admitted in a dry voice right as the waitress arrived with our order.

The woman hesitated a moment after putting down our coffees and cakes, peering at Flo with wide eyes. "I'm so sorry," she gushed, "but are you Florence Foster? From Bellerose?"

I sat back, watching as Flo graciously chatted with the waitress, who claimed to be a *huge* Bellerose fan. She only lingered a few minutes and left with an autograph on her notepad, but I was impressed at how professionally Flo handled it. She didn't once appear irritated by being recognized, and I told her as much when the waitress left us.

Flo just shrugged. "I like it. When I'm out with the whole band, no one wants *me*. They all want to take selfies with the guys or get their tits signed by them. Hardly anyone ever squeals or faints when they meet me. Must be my lack of fat dick spirit."

I choked on the sip of coffee I'd just taken. "Sorry, *what*?"

Flo chuckled. "You know, big dick energy. My grandma used to call it fat dick spirit because she wanted to be cool but couldn't remember the right phrase."

"Oh my god, I love that. But that kind of sucks that the boys are soaking up the limelight... You're an equal part of the band. You've been with them since the beginning, right?"

Flo nodded, then gave me a funny look. "Well, as long as Rhett and Gray, anyway. Jace already had the recording contract and the concept of *Bellerose,* but he needed a band because..." She trailed off with a wince.

I nodded my understanding. Jace's original drummer and bass player hadn't been *amazing* musicians, nor did they have any delusions that they had star quality. There hadn't been any hurt feelings when Jace's contract offer had been contingent on a new band arrangement.

Angelo had been the lead guitarist back then—back when they'd been called Snake Soup. In fairness, they'd named the band when they were twelve. Even if things between the three of us hadn't blown up in such spectacular fashion, Angelo never could have signed on with Jace and Big Noise Records. His father *never* would have let him leave the family business.

"Anyway, I didn't ask you to come out so we could talk about ancient history," she quickly amended. "That shit last night was *insane,* and I wanted to check that you're doing okay."

That rendered me speechless for a moment. Florence wasn't cold by any means, but she also wasn't overly *warm...* so I'd figured she wanted to get coffee to take a break from Tom rather than for my benefit.

"Oh," I said, sounding stupid as fuck. "Yeah, I'm fine."

Was I though? Last night was *intense.* Kissing Grayson, the chick with the gun, Angelo's visit, and then mind-blowing sex with Rhett... Without even thinking about what I was doing, I slipped a hand into the pocket of my jeans. They were the same jeans I'd been wearing last night, and sure enough, there was a little scrap of paper folded within.

Angelo's number.

Swallowing back the panic rising in my chest, I changed the subject to ask Flo about *her*. How she got the position in the band, where she was from, about her family, literally anything to avoid the heavy shit weighing down my mind.

Eventually our security told us we needed to get going back to the hotel, so we finished off our third plate of cakes and paid the bill. Or Flo did, since I was still relying on charity. Ugh, that needed to change sooner rather than later.

"Shit, hang on," she said as we left the cafe. "I need to pee. Back in a sec."

She disappeared back inside with a security guard following her, leaving me on the sidewalk with the rest of our entourage.

"Ma'am?" one of the suited men prompted, indicating toward where our SUV waited across the street.

I hesitated, though. "Shouldn't we wait for Flo? She's the celebrity here, not me." It didn't feel good leaving her with only one guard. Not after some crazed fan had pulled a gun on them last night.

The guy in charge, whose name I didn't know, gave me a long look. "So you'd prefer to stand out here on the street like sitting ducks while Ms. Foster uses the bathroom? I'm no expert, but I think *you* will be safer in the vehicle, Ms. Thorn."

Thorn. Huh. So even the security didn't know who I was.

Still, he had a good point, so I meekly nodded and started across the road. Just as the guard ahead reached the car, several loud pops cut through the air, deafening me for a moment as I flinched. When I opened my eyes again, the guard who'd been about to open the car door was slumped on the ground, a bright spray of blood decorating the passenger window where his head had just been.

I screamed, looking around in panic as someone grabbed my arm and started hauling me backwards. On instinct, I fought back, thrashing and fighting to free myself, and then all of a sudden I was released.

Oh shit, that had been one of *our* guards trying to get me to safety, and now he was dead too. He'd released me because he'd been shot by one of the three guys in dark suits striding towards us.

My next scream turned into a strangled gulp as a

car came hurtling around the corner, and the door flew open before it had even stopped. As embarrassing as it was to admit, even to myself, I froze. I fucking *froze.* My eyes screwed shut, my breath held, I just...*froze.*

Shots fired, lots of them, and I braced myself for death. My ears were ringing, but no blinding pain ripped through my body. How?

Someone jerked me clean off my feet, and I gasped as I was swiftly manhandled into a car, but it wasn't until the vehicle started speeding again that I realized what had happened.

"Grayson?" I squeaked, finally prying my eyes open.

His glare was pure fire.

"Flo!" I shouted in a panic. "We need to go back for Flo! She was in the bathroom!"

Grayson's jaw twitched, but he didn't turn around. He didn't even slow down. "She's fine. They weren't after her, Prickles. They came for *you.*"

Oh shit. *Fuck.* "Riccis?"

Grayson jerked a nod, and a wave of nausea rolled through me. Angelo had warned me. He'd said that blood would be shed, and I'd fucking ignored him. What the *hell* did his father think I knew?

Whatever it was, it was worth killing for. But it was also possibly the only thing keeping me alive. I was in way over my head, and now I was dragging Bellerose down with me. Regardless of my promise to Rhett, I couldn't stay. Not now. There was only one thing I could do, and it sure as shit wasn't staying on the Bellerose tour.

"Grayson, pull over," I demanded, my skin going clammy and cold.

He ignored me. Of course he did.

"Grayson, *pull over!*" I shouted, then followed up with, "I'm going to be sick."

His jaw ticked, but he obliged by turning down a narrow alleyway and stopping the car. I fumbled my door handle a couple of times, my fingers stiff and uncoordinated, but eventually got it open. Then I just... ran.

thirty-two

BILLIE

At no point would I claim I had any real plan. Hell, I hadn't even really thought things through when I took off. I just knew that the only way I could keep Bellerose safe was to call Angelo. Call him and beg for his protection... because, surely, he would keep me safe. Surely, he wouldn't actually kill me when his father discovered I *knew nothing*.

At minimum I could let him know I was no longer with Bellerose, which would effectively keep them safe. Which was my ultimate goal, after all.

Of course it was stupid. Of course Grayson caught

up with me before I even reached the end of the alleyway. And to be fair, I was glad he did.

"What the *fuck* are you doing?" he roared when he grabbed me by the back of my neck and spun me to slam my back against the brick wall. It was rough, but I didn't care. Tears were already streaming down my face, and when Grayson saw them, he softened instantly.

"Prickles," he breathed, "why did you just—"

My brain wasn't fucking working right, because the next thing I knew, I was kissing him like he was my salvation. Grayson had no qualms kissing me back, though. His huge frame crushed me into the wall, and his mouth devoured mine in a way that sent shockwaves right through me. He kissed me like he was starving, like he'd been holding himself back and I'd just given permission to let go.

I wanted more. My hands found his waist, tracing the line of his belt until I got to the buckle, then tugging the leather free.

"Billie," he growled against my lips, and it was one of the hottest fucking things on earth. Until he gently shoved my hand away before I could unzip his jeans.

"Gray," I complained, nipping his lower lip with my teeth. He was already hard, his dick throbbing hot through the denim, and I was desperate to feel him in my hand. And in other parts of me, too.

A deep groan rolled through his chest, then all of a sudden he had me flipped around, my face to the wall and his hardness pressed against my backside.

"You're in shock, Prickles," he informed me with that low, commanding growl, "and you're scared. So here's what's going to happen..."

I swallowed hard as his fingers flicked the button of my jeans undone and the zipper practically fell down all on its own. Shit. *Shit*... was this going to totally screw things up with Rhett? The guilt almost made me back down, but I couldn't make myself move. I wanted this too fucking much, and if I was dead tomorrow... well, no regrets, right?

"I'm going to make you come, Prickles," Grayson rumbled in my ear, his teeth nipping my earlobe as his huge hand pushed inside my panties. I gasped but shifted my legs wider. "And after you come, I'm tossing your infuriating ass back into that car, driving us both to the hotel, then you're going to explain what in the *fuck* you were just thinking." Two of his thick fingers pushed into me, and I moaned embarrassingly loud. "Am I clear?"

My response was a gasp and full body tremble as he pushed those fingers deeper, his thumb swirling my clit. It was rough, fast, and dirty up against the alleyway wall, but holy *hell,* I was into it.

"The correct response, Prickles, is *yes, sir,*" Grayson informed me with a husky laugh. "But I'll let it slide. And before you get all in your head, Rhett won't mind."

What?!

He didn't leave me to dwell on that information. His free hand gripped my hair, tugging my head back until his mouth could claim mine, and his fingers went to work on my throbbing cunt. For several minutes, he swallowed my moans and gasps, kissing me like he was also getting off. When my orgasm flared through me, *way* faster than I'd ever even managed to get myself there, he held me tight as I shuddered. My knees went weak, but he didn't let me fall as he dragged an intoxicating release out of me like he had all the time in the world.

By the time he withdrew his hand from my pants, I was panting hard and my pulse raced like I'd run a damn marathon. Gray kept his strong arm around my waist, holding me close as he brushed a kiss over my puffy lips.

"Feel better?" he murmured, carefully rebuttoning my jeans for me. Could he tell that my brain was misfiring? I doubt I could have made my fingers move if I'd tried.

I had to swallow several times before I could form words. "Better."

"Good." Shifting his grip suddenly, he threw me over his shoulder and strode back along the alleyway toward the car.

I gave an incoherent squawk of protest, but by the time I was able to form fully fledged curse words, he was tossing me none too gently into the back seat of the car and slamming the door shut.

"Grayson, what the fuck?" I snapped, reaching for the door handle. It was pointless, though. I was fucking child locked in, and Grayson was already climbing into the driver's seat. "This is kidnapping, Gray; you can't just—"

"I can, and I am," he growled back, throwing the car into reverse to back out of the alleyway. "Put your damn seat belt on."

"Screw you!" I snapped back like a petulant child. But seriously, who did he think he was?

The next corner he took so sharply that I smacked my head on the window, so I gritted my teeth as I buckled my safety belt. Prick. I had to hand it to him, though, the urge to run had ebbed. Now all I wanted to do was kick him in the balls for manhandling me.

"We good?" he grunted, glancing in the rearview mirror. I extended my middle finger in response, and his lush lips tilted into a smirk. Fucking hell, *this* version of Grayson was a surprise. Who'd have guessed he liked to tease so hard?

For a few moments we were silent, then a wave of potent guilt made my chest ache. "We need to find Flo," I told him from between clenched teeth. "She might be—"

"She's fine," he cut me off. "She's in huge trouble, but she's fine. They came for *you*, Prickles. Has that fact not sunk in yet?"

I screwed my face up, shaking my head. "How, though? No one knew we would be— *Oh.*" The waitress. I'd bet she'd posted on social media about meeting Flo, and if she'd taken a photo without us knowing...

"You need to be more careful," Grayson informed me, like I was somehow planning to be *less* careful. Okay, stupid desire to run aside. "These guys aren't fucking around."

"I know," I snapped, folding my arms defensively.

There was a beat of silence within which I could feel his eyes on me in the mirror. Then he sighed and ran his hand over his messy hair. "What was your plan just now? Where were you going to go?"

My throat tightened, and I bit the inside of my cheek. I couldn't tell him. Admitting I was going to call

Angelo and then get as far from Bellerose as possible... well, it'd mean telling him about Angelo's visit last night. It'd also make me sound like some kind of martyr, when in fact, I was just a scared little girl clinging to the hope that Angelo would somehow spare me. Or that I could run far enough and hide well enough to escape the Ricci net.

When the silence stretched, Grayson huffed a frustrated sigh and shook his head, accepting the fact that I wasn't going to reply.

I wet my lips and plucked up some courage to change the subject because I really needed some answers before we got back to the hotel.

"What did you mean?" I asked, my voice hoarse with... guilt? Fear? Something like that.

Grayson's eyes flicked up to the mirror, meeting mine for a second, then he gave a small nod. He wasn't fucking around with pretending he didn't understand.

"I meant Rhett and I spoke this morning. You told him that we'd kissed." I jerked a nod, not trusting my voice anymore. They'd *talked*? "So, there's nothing to hide."

I blinked a couple of times, processing that logic. Then I scowled. "No, no, you said he *won't mind*. That's a little different from *he knows*."

Grayson's smirk was pure evil, and I gasped out

loud. "It was what you needed, Prickles. Didn't it help to calm you down?"

Yes, but that wasn't the fucking point. Okay, so Rhett and Grayson knew I was... *attracted* to both of them and... ugh, my head hurt. "You two are *okay* with this?" I asked in a strangled voice.

Grayson swiped a hand over his stubbled chin. "Sometimes you just need to live in the moment, sweetheart, and deal with the consequences another day."

That wasn't a yes.

"You're handling the shock of seeing bodies strewn across the street surprisingly well," he commented, shifting the subject again. "Better than I'd have expected."

I didn't know if it was my imagination, but that statement felt loaded. Was there a *right* way to react after seeing two bodyguards shot dead in front of me? I frowned. "So are you. Does Bellerose often encounter so much violence?"

Grayson's lips tilted. "Bellerose? No, this is new."

New for Bellerose but not for Grayson? Consider my interest piqued. There was no time to push him for more information, though, because he was already driving back through the hotel parking gates. Anxiety tied my stomach all up in knots as he parked in one of the reserved places, then got out to open my door for me.

"Gray," I whispered, placing my hand on his chest as he pushed the car door shut behind me. "What happens now? Those guys... it was broad daylight. The middle of the street. This is *bad*. Isn't it?"

He glanced down at where my palm rested on his t-shirt, then he gently gripped my face and tilted my head back until our eyes met. "You'd be amazed how easily the Riccis can clean up a mess. We should get upstairs before Jace breaks more shit."

Confusion creased my brow, but Grayson made no attempt to actually release me. In fact, he crowded me closer against the side of the car, making me smile lightly.

"Gray... you gonna let me go?"

His response was to crush his lips to mine once more. His tongue demanded entry, and I opened for him all too willingly. My fingers twisted the fabric of his shirt, pulling him close as he kissed me breathless and dizzy, so much so that I nearly didn't hear what he said as he finally released me.

"Never," he breathed against my lips, smacking another hot peck there before taking a few steps backward. "Come on, Prickles. Let's make sure Florence is back safe." The hungry look on his face said he'd rather stay here and finish what he'd just started, but better sense prevailed.

"I thought you said she was fine," I exclaimed, hurrying to catch up as he strode toward the elevator bank. "Gray, she could be—"

"Rhett and Tom were *right* behind me; they'd have grabbed her." Oh. Thank fuck for that. "And do I need to remind you again...?"

I swallowed hard. "They were there for me," I whispered in a husky voice.

Flo was fine. She *had* to be fine.

thirty-three

GRAYSON

The sting of jealousy that hit me when Billie launched herself at Rhett was harsher than I'd been prepared for. I had to curl my hands into fists to keep from ripping her away from him and going all caveman on her ass. She'd had enough of that from me for one day.

In fairness, though, I hadn't planned to escalate things between us quite so fast. Christ, she'd wanted more too. She'd wanted to fuck in that alleyway, and if I'd had a condom, I wouldn't have been able to deny her.

She'd tried to run. She'd tried to *leave*. All I knew was that I'd do anything to stop her... and if that meant feeling her tight cunt pulse and clench around my fingers while those delicious moans imprinted across my brain, well, who was I to argue?

Rhett's furious glare met my gaze over Billie's head, and I smirked, taunting him. Then I raised my fingers to my mouth and sucked them. His face darkened with rage, and I licked my lips in satisfaction. Share her? Hell no. I'd be winning her, and he'd just have to suck it the fuck up.

Right now wasn't the time, though. Later.

"I'm fine," Billie was saying, her voice muffled by Rhett's bear hug, "Seriously, I'm fine. Gray saved me."

Oh man, straight to the heart.

Rhett glared daggers, but it was tempered by relief and gratitude. Jace, though, was officially losing his cool.

"How the *fuck* did this happen?" he roared, storming back into the penthouse suite with his phone to his ear. "Best in the business, you told me, Leonard. Better than the Secret Service, you said. If that's what you call *best in business,* then I'm seriously concerned about national security now!"

He listened to something, then spat some curses and threw his phone across the room. It smashed against the wall, taking a chunk of drywall with it as it clattered to the floor. Then Jace stalked over to where

Billie stood in Rhett's embrace like he wanted to rip her away just like I wanted to. Except I wasn't so sure he had the same intentions as I had, so I stepped between my friend and the happy couple, blocking his progress.

"Simmer down, Jace," I told him in a warning tone.

His eye twitched in fury as he looked up at me. I only had a couple of inches on him, but it was enough.

"The scene is already scrubbed," Tom interrupted, his eyes wide in shock as he read something on his phone. "Like it never fucking happened. Holy shit, these dudes don't fuck around."

Florence came out of the bathroom then, wiping her tearstained face. Billie gasped, peeling herself free of Rhett and running to hug our punk-girl bassist. She'd been genuinely concerned for Flo, even though she barely knew her.

Both girls were sobbing now, and Tom cringed in disgust before looking back down at his phone. Rhett and Jace just stood there like they'd never seen a girl cry before, so I heaved a sigh and raked my fingers through my hair.

"Prickles, why don't you and Flo go hang out in her room. We need to sort shit out with security." Fucking *everyone* shot me weird looks at that, but Flo gave me an appreciative nod. Taking Billie's hand in hers, she led the way to the bedroom she was sharing with Tom.

Once the door closed, I leveled a hard look at Rhett and Jace—but ignored Tom. "I need to run back down to the car to... get something. We can sort this out when I get back."

"Yes, Daddy," Tom smirked from the couch, and my fist tightened with the need to punch his smug face in.

I only made it two steps before Rhett stopped me dead with one question. "Did she see you do it?" he demanded, his voice tight with anger. "Did she see you kill those guys?"

I didn't turn around. He wanted a fight, and I wasn't going to give it to him. Not now. Billie was already struggling with her attraction toward us both; she didn't need to hear us scrapping over her like she was a piece of meat in a dog fight.

"No," I replied. Then I continued out of the penthouse. I wasn't *sure* Billie had missed it, but she would have said something if she had. Wouldn't she? She surely wouldn't have tried to fuck me in an alleyway if she'd just witnessed me kill three of the Ricci muscle. She was surprisingly good at compartmentalizing the darker side of life that had been stealing pieces of her later.

For now, I needed to get back to the car and retrieve my gun. I'd tossed it into the footwell when I'd thrown Billie in, and she hadn't noticed it there. But I wasn't an idiot and it wasn't fucking safe to leave loaded weapons lying around, so I'd secure it, *then* deal with my bandmates.

As I headed out, I took the usual path, keeping an eye on my surroundings. There was no way that the Ricci family hadn't noticed someone was taking out their men anytime they got close to Billie, and while they might assume it was Bellerose security, I wasn't going to just rest on that. Someone could have seen me. It only took one of those assholes to report back, and then I'd have a target on my back.

A fact that didn't worry me outside of the issue of putting my bandmates in danger. I might be very good at what I did, but I was still only one person against the Ricci army. The math didn't add up for a happy ending, and fuck if anyone stole that from me. I'd sacrificed too damn much to give up now and allow those assholes to steal the girl and my life.

The car was where I'd left it, security standing nearby to keep an eye on it, but they knew better than to touch the vehicle. Their eyes all averted when I walked closer, I opened the door and found my piece exactly where I'd left it. Slipping it into the waistband of my jeans, I slid my shirt over the top to hide it, and then I headed back into the hotel.

"You can return the car now," I told the closest guard. "We'll be heading out in the bus soon."

I got a solid nod and no comment. Not that I needed one.

Back in my room, I secured the gun in my portable safe and handed it off to some of the staff who were packing up our rooms and getting us ready to head out. We had to be in New York today so that we could get to our soundcheck tomorrow.

It wouldn't be the tightest schedule we'd been on, but we did need to get moving.

When I emerged from the room, I found Jace and Rhett standing in the hall waiting for me.

"We need to leave," Rhett said, his voice low and without much expression. If I had to guess, he was still half in shock and half pissed to the point he wasn't sure how to manage his emotions. I'd been there and done that many times over the years. My first girlfriend had her head blown off in front of me when I was sixteen. It was the life I was born into, and at some point, it had gotten easier to deal, but Rhett didn't have the same upbringing.

Billie was opening his eyes to all the depravity in the world, and it was going to knock him around until he grew numb to the fear and violence. I hated that for him, but there was no way to avoid it forever.

"Focus on Billie," I said to him. There was no need for me to expand on that. No one could miss the meaning. I found myself adding to it anyway. "It'll help you deal."

Rhett's fists were clenched, and I noticed the dried blood littering his knuckles. "No competition until this is dealt with," he spat out. "Someone is with Billie at all times. I don't even fucking care if you're fucking her while I'm in the room. She isn't alone, and we don't play games to try and get one up on each other. Not while she's in danger and these cunts are actively shooting at her."

Jace looked a lot like he wanted to throw up, his face pale even as his anger rose. "No one is fucking Billie while I'm in the room. If you two even think about throwing this shit around near me, we're going to have more murders to worry about."

Bastard might want to pretend it was disgust that stopped him from pursuing Billie. Disgust and hatred. But I knew the truth... I recognized the truth. It was pain and fear.

Two emotions he would have to learn to deal with because running from the truth had done him no favors.

"We need to get back to Billie, then," I said shortly.

"You don't want her left alone, but who the fuck is watching her now?"

"Florence, Tom, and about sixteen security guards," Rhett replied, his tone just as clipped. "I might be more relaxed about this shit than you, but I'm not a fucking idiot. Billie needed a minute away from us to pull herself together, but her minute is up. Now... now she's going to have one of us attached to her hip at all times."

Memories of her soft moans in that alley briefly filled my mind, and I wanted to tell Rhett it wouldn't be her hip I was attached to, but in the spirit of this brief truce, I didn't mention anything.

I also didn't mention that Billie needed no fucking minutes away from us. She needed to learn how to trust in us when her life went to shit. A trust that would come in time. Fiercely independent people learned to never rely on anyone other than themselves through many moments of being let down when they needed help. It was a defense mechanism that Billie had in spades. But one day very soon, she would look for me in a crisis, and she would find me standing exactly where I'd promised: in the way of every fucking bullet heading in her direction.

"She tried to run away," I told Jace and Rhett as we started to head back to the rooms where Billie and the others were. "She lied about being sick, and when I stopped the car, she took the fuck off."

I mean, she wasn't going to get far, but I'd seen the blind panic on her face. She was sacrificing herself for us, and I'd never been as pissed as I was the moment I caught her.

"Told you she would bail when shit got hard," Jace said, an angry sound emerging from the back of his throat. "It's her fucking MO. That bitch can never stick around for the hard stuff."

I moved fast, hand reaching out to wrap around the back of his neck as I spun the stupid bastard and slammed him against the wall. Familiar move, but not as interesting as the last time in the alley. "Talk about her like that again, and you will be singing through busted vocal cords for the next six months."

Jace fought back, using his strength to try and move me out of his personal space. Good fucking luck with that.

"She wanted to protect us," I told him slowly, since he was clearly a moron today. "She wanted to stop anyone else from being killed because of Ricci's obsession with her. Two of our security died today, and she saw it all at close range."

Jace wanted to snap back, I saw the fire in his eyes,

but he appeared beyond argument as he settled for glaring at me.

"She was going back to Angelo?" Rhett asked, voice shocked. "Seriously?"

I released Jace because I'd made my point. "I think so. If I hadn't been there, she would be either dead or in their custody right now."

Jace huffed as he straightened and ran a hand across his throat. In normal circumstances, he was tough enough to take on nearly anyone. But I wasn't a normal circumstance.

For the first time in my life, I was glad for my training though. It had kept Billie alive today, and hopefully, it would the next time too.

Because I knew there'd be a next time. I could feel the tension brewing in the air.

Whatever the Ricci family was starting here, it was only the beginning.

thirty-four

BILLIE

Florence was still shaking and crying, but in the half an hour since the attack, I'd managed to pull myself together. Well, sort of, since I was feeling rather numb again as I sat on a couch, more security than I'd ever seen filling the room around me. Plus Tom and Florence, who perched on the other end of the suede couch.

My only focus at this point was on the other members of the band. Where were they? Unease filled my chest and would remain until I saw them again, safe and sound and not in the hands of the murderous Ricci clan. I'd been living in fantasy land thinking that these guys were too famous for anyone to fuck with them.

Clearly, that wasn't the case. Grayson could have been shot today. He'd been right in the midst of the attack. Rhett too.

That was why I'd tried to run. If one of them got hurt… or worse because of me, I would never forgive myself. I couldn't live with the guilt. It used to just be Jace and Angelo who made me feel that way, but even in the short time I'd known them, Rhett and Grayson were now on the list too.

The list of people who impacted my life. Who made me *feel alive*. Who I probably couldn't live without and be happy. But I'd do my damn best to get away from them if it meant keeping them alive. Florence had thankfully been inside at the time, but she too was on the list of those I had to protect.

Putting my hope in Angelo wasn't the smartest decision I could make, but getting away from Bellerose was now my number one priority. I'd slip away after their concert, and once I was a decent distance from them, I'd call Angelo and let him know I was on my own.

The Riccis would forget about Bellerose then, and I could stop having mini panic attacks about who I was going to get killed next.

This was probably where my eerie calm and numbness came from. This new plan, which should ensure everyone's safety except my own, was exactly how it should be. This was my problem, and I'd dropped them all in my shi—

"Billie!"

I jerked my head up to find Flo was much closer, her wide eyes locked on me. "Are you okay? I called your name like ten times."

Forcing a smile on my face, I nodded probably way too vigorously, but my body wasn't exactly obeying my commands at the minute. "Fine. Fine. Just... where are the guys? Shouldn't they be back by now?"

Her smile was slower, wobbling a bit at the sides. "They're the reason I was calling your name. They're waiting at the door for us to head toward the bus. United front and all that."

My head whipped around, and I locked eyes with Rhett, who was standing silently while Jace discussed something with a few of the security guards filling the doorway. I couldn't see Grayson at first, but then he stepped into view, taking in the room in one sweep of his steely gaze. When our eyes met, he jerked his head as if to say *get your ass over here,* and no lie, my body tightened at the command in that one movement.

He'd been like that in the alley. In the car. Basically every interaction, he'd taken control and demanded what he wanted from me. I never expected I'd be into that, but despite the numbness I'd been feeling, heat was already sliding through my body to settle in my center.

And I was on my damn feet giving that big bastard exactly what he wanted.

"Stay close to me," he said the moment I dodged the security guards to reach his side. I'd taken off without a word to Flo, hadn't even looked at another person, determined to step into the safety of Grayson. Well, safety and complete destruction of my vagina, which reminded me with a fluttering pulse exactly what had happened in that alley.

It was only when Rhett turned away from Jace and pushed in toward my right side that I felt a balance that allowed me to breathe again. Something about the two of them, the vastly different personalities that drew me in, allowed me to find an equilibrium within myself.

"Are you ready to go?" Rhett asked, expression concerned as he ran his gaze over me as if checking I was still in one piece.

"Yes," I said, nodding hard. "More than ready."

Making it to New York was step one of my plan. I couldn't think about step two, or I'd break down.

Just one step at a time, and then I'd keep them safe.

Grayson reached for me, and I let him wrap an arm around my body, dragging me into his side. Rhett didn't complain or even make a comment, he just drew in closer to my other side, so I was practically sandwiched between the pair of them.

"Jace, take the back," Rhett snapped out, but none of us stopped to look if he had.

I didn't have to look; I could feel his presence behind me as Grayson started to move. Move and drag me along with him as I remained in his protective hold.

The three of them were different but the same—I could feel it in their energies as they wrapped around me. That presence that gave them an extra spice of charisma.

In my experience, rock stars lived up to their clichés, something I'd known from a very young age since I'd lost myself completely in Jace. I was still lost, if I was being truthful with myself, hence why I had never cared for anyone else until I'd stumbled into the midst of Bellerose. Except Angelo.

It was definitely best that I got out of here before my need for these three sexy, famous, and rightfully crowned *most desirable* men in the world got me into big trouble. Might make the Ricci family coming after me look like a walk in the park.

One more night. That was all I had left, and as much as it hurt, I had to follow through with my plan.

When we reached the bus, Grayson didn't trust

anyone else to check it over. He left me with Rhett and a very silent Jace while he entered. Within a few seconds, Flo, Tom, and the majority of our security surrounded us, and not a single person entered the bus until Grayson gave the okay.

Something told me it would be very helpful to know Grayson's backstory, even if another part of me was very aware that prying that information from him wouldn't be an easy job.

It wouldn't be achieved in the short time I had left with them, but maybe one day I'd find out.

I was all about the small slivers of hope that I couldn't purge, even as the rest of me drew inside myself and back to reality. This had been a dream, living the rock star life. But it was not my dream.

Not my future.

Not any longer.

Only Bellerose, Tom, Mark—our driver—and I ended up on the bus. The rest were sent to the other two vehicles, as per usual, and we got moving much faster than we had before. We were on the road to New York within a few minutes, and it was a tense moment as everyone remained silent and unmoving in the living area. "I might go lie down," I finally said, needing to escape the tension.

Before anyone could reply, I took off toward the

bedroom and the only space in this bus to hide. It would appear normal to fall apart, but I couldn't raise any suspicions about what my plans were. For that reason, it was best not to be around them as much as possible until we reached the city. From there they'd be busy with their concert, and I would solidify my plans to escape from the venue during the show. It was my best chance—to get lost in the crowds and know that Grayson and Rhett were on stage and unable to keep as close an eye on me.

That was the moment I would run and never look back.

Grayson would be pissed, no doubt. He clearly didn't like losing control of anything. Rhett would be *hurt*, and that was almost enough to make me reconsider. Ultimately, though, I'd rather Rhett's feelings get hurt than him be dead. No question about it.

With a deep sigh, I dug my fingers into my pocket, searching for the scrap of paper with Angelo's phone number on it.

"No!" I gasped as my fingers touched nothing but cloth. "No, no, no!" I sat bolt upright, turning my pocket inside out to find the paper, *convinced* it was just stuffed in the corner or something. But there was nothing but lint.

Nausea washed through me, and my breath came fast as I checked all my other pockets. The paper was nowhere to be found, though. When did I last have it? In the car... right before I ran. Right before Grayson had finger fucked me against an alleyway wall and made me see fucking stars as he kissed me.

Had I dropped it? Or did he have it? Either way, I was utterly sick with worry.

What would Grayson do, if he had it? Would he try to confront Angelo? One thing was for damn sure, he was no ordinary rock star... if such a thing even existed. Grayson was an enigma and no stranger to violence. It made me want to crack his head open and understand what had made him the way he was. And work out how the fuck he'd ended up in *Bellerose*.

I flopped back down on the bed, running my hands over my face in exhaustion. It didn't change anything, not having Angelo's number. Not really. I'd just have to figure out how to either get spotted by someone who could let the Ricci family know or figure out how to contact someone in their organization to advise them that I was out of Bellerose. Then they could focus their attention away from the famous musicians. Which would keep the band safe.

A shudder of fear ran through me at the idea of facing Giovanni Ricci. He'd hated me as a teenager when Angelo and I were in love, so I doubted things had changed much since then.

Someone knocked softly on the door, and I sucked in a deep breath before sitting back up. "Come in," I called out, like this was *my* room or some shit.

Rhett cautiously opened the door, giving me a hopeful smile as he hesitated in the doorway. Just seeing him eased some of my tension and dread, so I beckoned him closer.

"I wanted to check on you," he admitted softly as he closed the door behind himself. There wasn't a whole lot of room at the end of the bed, so I placed a hand on his waist to pull him closer.

He gave me what I wanted, climbing onto the bed and bracing his arms on either side my head as I lay back down. Then he brushed soft kisses across my lips, dissolving the remaining anxiety still curling inside me.

"Grayson told us you tried to run," he said in a low voice, and I groaned.

"Grayson talks too much for a man who barely talks."

Rhett kissed me deeper, making my whole body flush with heat. "He was worried, Thorn. And understandably so. Would you really have left?"

I badly didn't want to lie to Rhett; he'd been nothing but good to me from the moment I ran into him outside the club in Siena that night. He'd constantly gone out of his way to protect me, even after discovering my past with Jace. I couldn't repay him with lies. So I just danced the line instead.

"It'd probably kill me if I did," I whispered, then wrapped my hand around the back of his neck to pull his face back to mine. Our time together was ticking away so fucking fast; I wanted to make the most of every damn second. If Jace couldn't deal... tough. "Rhett, I need to feel you inside me."

He hesitated a moment, but *only* a moment.

This time, there was no hiding what we were doing. And a twisted part of me couldn't stop picturing Grayson sitting out there, listening to us. Did it turn him on? Or piss him off? Both options appealed to me more than I cared to admit.

thirty-five

BILLIE

The drive to New York was quick enough that we checked into another hotel, and I made the most of my privacy with Rhett, waking him up by exploring those dick piercings with my tongue the next day.

He groaned sleepily as I tongued his balls, his fingers threading through my hair to urge me on. I grinned, licking my way back up his ladder rungs, then sucked him in like a popsicle.

"Shit," he hissed, his hips jerking and making me choke slightly. "I think I died and went to heaven. Or am I still asleep?"

I would have answered, but my mouth was more

than full as I bobbed up and down his hard cock. Rhett seemed totally fine with my lack of response, his fingers flexing on the back of my head as he encouraged me to take him deeper and faster. Before long, his hips were bucking as he fucked my mouth, and I just held onto his tattooed thighs to ride it out.

"Shit, babe, I'm gonna come," he groaned as his dick thickened and jerked against my tongue. I didn't flinch or pull away, though, instead sealing my lips around him tighter and flicking my tongue over his slit.

Curses fell out of his mouth as his fingers tugged my hair, then his hot cum filled my mouth in several jets. His breath came harsh and fast as his grip slowly relaxed, and I swallowed his load before releasing him.

"Thorn..." he groaned, collapsing back onto the bed, panting for breath. "That's easily my favorite way to wake up. No question about it."

I grinned, licking my puffy lips as I settled in beside him. "Good to know you're not one of those musicians who, like... can't fuck before a show."

Rhett wrinkled his nose. "Is that a thing? Surely not."

"I dunno, you guys are the only musicians I know," I admitted with a laugh. "Maybe I'm thinking of athletes."

Rhett's phone beeped on the bedside table, and I realized that was what'd woken me up in the first place. Someone had been trying to call him. Rhett groaned again as he reached for it, squinting at the message on the screen.

"Crap," he muttered. "I'm late for soundcheck."

That didn't seem to faze him, though, because he tossed his phone aside and rolled me over onto my back, his knee spreading my legs.

"I thought you were late for soundcheck," I teased, even as I lifted my hips for him to pull my panties down. If he was up for some reciprocation, I wasn't saying no.

To my disappointment, though, he'd barely even gotten started when someone knocked loudly on the door.

"Ignore it," Rhett growled, flicking his tongue over my clit and making me squirm.

Whoever was at the door must have heard him, though, because they knocked even louder. Asshole.

"Go," I told him regretfully, pushing his shoulder with my toe. "I'll wait." I dragged the sheets back over me, just in case it was Tom or someone equally undesirable at the door.

He grumbled and pouted, crossing over to the door without even bothering to put anything more than his boxer shorts on. Jerking it open, he scowled at whoever was knocking.

"I hate you," he announced, telling me it was one of his bandmates. Then he gave a grunt of surprise and yelled a protest as he was yanked out into the corridor.

Quick as lightning, Grayson swapped places with Rhett, slamming the door shut in his face and flipping the lock.

"Good morning, Gray," I snickered as Rhett pounded on the door and demanded to be let back in.

The big man just smirked and jumped onto the bed, crushing me into the mattress as he kissed me stupid and left me breathless. "Good morning, Prickles," he rumbled in the *sexiest* fucking voice. Crap, as if I wasn't already turned on enough.

"I swear to fuck, Grayson, I'm going to..." Rhett's threats were muffled, but the intensity was clear as day.

Grayson rolled his eyes and climbed off the bed again, casting a lingering look at me before unlocking the door once more and throwing it open. "We're late for soundcheck, Silver. Move your ass."

Rhett threw a halfhearted fist at Grayson's torso as he passed, but Gray dodged it with ease, chuckling. Scowling, Rhett slammed the door shut again, shutting Grayson out, but the big guy shouted another reminder that they were late.

"You better go," I told him with a smile. "I think Grayson will wait there until you come out."

Rhett just shrugged and yanked the sheet off me once more. "Tough. He can fucking well wait. I'm not leaving my girl high and dry when I woke up to the best blow job of my life."

"Trust me, Rhett," I gasped as his mouth found my pussy once more, "there's nothing dry about it."

Knowing we were short on time, he didn't waste one second, his tongue firm and consistent as it flicked over my clit before he sucked my sensitive flesh into his mouth and rolled the small nub around, sending me half off the bed. My cry was loud, and once again, I imagined Grayson on the other side of the door, listening to his bandmate tongue-fucking me.

Just the thought was enough to send the spiraling pleasure that had been building over the top, and I cried out Rhett's name, my hands gripping in his hair as I thrust against his mouth. He was relentless, not easing up on devouring me until I was completely destroyed.

"Fuck me," I breathed.

Rhett lifted his head, his grin lopsided, before he dragged himself up the bed to give me a long, lingering kiss. I could taste myself, and goddamn, it made me want to disappear with him under the sheets and not leave for five hours. "If I had the time," he murmured, pulling his head back, "I'd fuck you until you couldn't remember his name."

I blinked. "My name, right?"

Rhett's grin grew larger. "Both."

My gaze darted to the door then, and Rhett laughed before he rolled off the bed and, with a wink, ducked into the bathroom. He emerged ten minutes later, looking refreshed. He was still naked, and I tried not to drool as he strolled into the dressing room. He was a work of art, from the tatts to the piercings, and I tried not to mourn the fact that this morning might be the last time I'd ever run my hands... and tongue over all of that delicious man.

His life was worth more than my pleasure—more than the future I could see here because if I got these guys killed, then I'd die as well.

I just had to make sure he didn't see the goodbye in my eyes.

"Okay, Thorn. I've got to get to soundcheck, but I'll check on all the security outside before I leave."

He kissed me once more, and the minty flavor was nice, but it wasn't quite as good as before. "I promise to just stay here in the hotel," I told him. "Unless you want me at soundcheck?"

Pulling himself away, he shook his head. "Stay here.

You'll be at the concert tonight because we'll need the extra security there. For now, order some room service, relax, and I'll see you in a few hours."

"Have fun," I said before I snuggled back into the bed. Rhett hesitated for a beat, and it almost looked as if he wasn't going to leave before he shook his head and all but sprinted to the door.

"See you in a few hours," he called back.

When the door closed behind him, I was fairly sure I caught a glimpse of Grayson and Jace, but it might have also been my imagination. An imagination that would explode at the thought of both of them listening at the door as Rhett ate my pussy like it was his last damn meal.

Was there something wrong with me that I could imagine myself with all three men? I mean, Jace fucking hated me, and I wasn't too fond of his stubborn ass these days, but our attraction had been explosive when we were younger. To the point that we'd almost been expelled from school many times after getting caught in compromising situations. If Jace's family hadn't been friends with our principal, we definitely would have.

Or maybe that'd been the Ricci family, since Angelo always protected us too. Probably why I was falling back into old habits of thinking he would continue to protect me now. We'd been kids back then, and now we were all very different adults. Escaping into the past was no longer an option, and with an uncertain future, I wondered when my next moment of happiness even would be.

Feeling rather depressed, I dragged my ass out of bed and headed into the bathroom. Steam still filled the air from Rhett's quick shower before, and I wished he was here. It was easier that he wasn't, though, because if anyone could convince me not to run and take my chances on the streets, it was that clever-tongued guitarist. Knowing I was going to hurt him was killing me.

I felt marginally better after a shower and some room service, but then I was faced with hours alone in the hotel waiting for the band to return. If I'd been able to bail at this moment, I would have, but there were literally twenty or more security guards outside my door in the hallway—helpful security who had procured my food for me. No way could I get past them, and I wasn't quite at the stage of shimmying out the twenty-story window to try and escape.

The television held zero interest, even as I flicked through random channels for over thirty minutes until, eventually, I decided to just have a nap. It would be a long time before I had a chance to enjoy a mattress and thousand thread count sheets again, so I might as well take advantage while I had it.

Just as I was settling in to sleep, there was a knock at the door, and I'd been on my own for enough hours that it actually startled me. I'd kinda forgotten there were other people in the world.

Stumbling up, I dragged the edges of my dressing gown together before I strolled over and peered through the peephole. I mean, twenty security was nice, but I would never underestimate the Ricci family, even if the chances of them politely knocking was slim to none.

On the other side, Flo's gorgeous face peered back at me. Feeling a surge of relief that I was going to have some company, I yanked the chain off the security hook and pulled the door open in a huge rush.

Flo took a second to peruse my bed hair, white gown, and complete lack of makeup before she shook her head. "Girl, we have some work to do before tonight."

She stepped into the room then, and I finally noticed she had a garment bag in her right hand.

"Tonight?" I echoed softly before I checked the hall and saw the same security at the ready. With a nod, I closed the door and locked it again. "I thought you guys aren't supposed to leave the venue after soundcheck?"

Flo dropped the bag on the messy bed and spun around. "Fuck that, rules are made to be broken. As for that confused face, girl... This is our New York concert. You are getting super hot for your guy, hanging in the VIP section for a change, and taking in the entire experience. It's a once-in-a-lifetime. I promise, you don't want to miss this."

She dropped into the chair near the office table and grinned all proud-like.

My first instinct was to refuse, but then I thought about it.

This was my last night with the guys. I would have to take off before the concert ended, but that didn't mean I couldn't take in their incredible talent one last time.

One last time before it was a true goodbye.

"I'm in," I said.

Florence's squeal told me everything I needed to know about the rest of the day. It was time for a glam up.

thirty-six

BILLIE

Florence knew what she was doing, that was for damn sure. When she was done getting me glammed up for the concert, I barely recognized myself. The whole time she was buzzing with nervous energy, and I got the impression she was feeling some sort of guilt over the coffee shop mess yesterday.

I told her to cut it out after she apologized for the fifth time while doing my makeup. It wasn't her fault that she'd needed to pee right then, and it was *better* that she hadn't been in the line of fire. Fuck, I was relieved she had been inside, or maybe she wouldn't be here today.

Security surrounded us as we headed down to the parking garage and waiting limo—buses were too obvious and cumbersome in a city like this—with plenty of time to get back to the concert venue. The guys were all waiting for us. Apparently, Flo had *asked* to have time alone with me, and Rhett damn near fucked me against the side of the limo when he got his hands on me. Someone had been thinking about this morning. And he wasn't the only one.

"Cut it out," Jace snarled, curling his lip in disgust. "We've got a show to focus on. Reckon you can dilute the pheromones a bit, Rose?"

That question made me stiffen with shock. He was insulting, but... he'd also called me *Rose* again? What the shit? Guess it was a step up from *whore*, but also... it hurt to hear that name from him again.

He slid his cranky ass into the limo before I could come up with a snappy retort, so I just shrugged it off. At least *he* would be glad to see me gone. Selfishly, though, I didn't want to leave until after their show tonight... I wanted to actually *watch* this time and ignore the hateful lyrics about how I'd betrayed Jace back when I was sixteen. The idea of watching both Rhett *and* Grayson perform was appealing enough that I could get over myself.

"Come on, Thorn," Rhett whispered in my ear, then

kissed my throat. "I want to get this concert over with." Linking our fingers together, he led me into the car behind Jace and Grayson, with Flo and Tom behind us.

Rhett sat down in one of the bench seats, and I slipped into the gap between him and Grayson. Yes, I knew I had to leave them soon… my very presence was painting a target on Bellerose's back and I couldn't keep letting them take on that risk for me. But just for right now, just for the short drive to the concert venue, I wanted to feel both my sexy rock stars on either side of me.

Pity it had to include clothes, though.

Grayson casually looped his arm around my waist, tugging me closer, and Jace glared daggers. Oh well, he couldn't exactly hate me *more* could he? He could write another bestselling album about how I fucked his best friend. Again.

Just thinking of Angelo had my pulse racing in fear. He'd broken into the bus with a dozen security outside—did I seriously think I could outrun him forever? I had to, though. There was no other option. It'd be a fine line between calling a tip on myself to draw him away from Bellerose, and *not actually getting caught*.

"Are you okay?" Rhett asked softly as the limo carried us toward the concert venue. Everyone else was chatting about the set list and security detail, and I'd just been sitting quietly, lost in my own head. Grayson's hand still rested on my hip, his fingers stroking my skin above the band of my jeans, and Rhett's hand was on my knee. I loved it. I badly didn't want to lose it.

"Yeah, fine," I lied, offering a weak smile. "Just thinking."

Rhett's brow creased with concern as he brushed his fingers over my cheek. "Can I help?"

A warmer smile tugged my lips and my heart. "Help me think? I wish you could."

"If you're feeling guilty about yesterday," Tom interjected, his sneer permanently in place, "you'll be pleased to know the cops aren't coming to talk to anyone. The whole thing has been swept under the rug, which is kind of impressive considering there were five bodies to clean up in the middle of the day."

Flo jabbed Tom with her elbow and hissed at him to shut up, but he ignored her as he smirked in my direction.

"It's gotta make us wonder what's so fucking special about you, though," he continued, like this was an idea that'd been eating away at him. "They shot two security guards when they coulda just shot *you*. So why didn't they, huh? Why'd they want you alive, *Billie Bellerose*?"

I bristled at the accusation in his voice, my eyes narrowing. "What are you implying, Tucker?"

He gave an exaggerated shrug, still ignoring Flo's attempt to shut him up. "I'm not implying anything. I'm *saying* that you haven't been honest with us. You said you witnessed the Riccis kill some waitress bitch. So what? They just proved they can clean up murder in broad daylight. So why do they care *so much* about tracking *you* down?"

Ice formed in my belly, and Grayson stiffened beside me. Did he know? If he'd found Angelo's phone number in my pocket, then he *knew* I'd seen Angelo.

"Tom, leave it," Rhett snapped.

Tom was like a shark circling a wounded seal, though. "Nah, nah, this bitch is lying to us all. Aren't you? So what's the deal? Did you steal from them?"

My jaw dropped. "What? No! I didn't steal—"

"So it was a lovers thing, then? Lemme guess, you and Angelo have been bumping uglies this whole time and he caught you with another guy? Or... *guys*?" He gave an accusing look at the way both Grayson and Rhett were holding me. "You nearly got Flo killed yesterday, so you'd better start telling the truth."

"Tucker," Grayson rumbled, "shut your fucking trap. You sound pathetic."

Tom flicked a hurt look in Grayson's direction, then

refocused on me. "We're in New York now; shouldn't you be leaving us? Why are you still here, Billie? Trying to get knocked up with a rock star baby so you can bleed one of my friends for eighteen years of child support?"

Oh wow. It was totally untrue but still cut through me like a knife.

As if on reflex, my gaze shifted to Jace. He just stared back at me, though, a frown marring his brow as though he was also questioning my motives. He sure as shit didn't speak up in my defense, and quite frankly, it was *stupid* of me to think he would. The Jace Adams who'd once owned my heart was nothing but a distant memory. One I'd be better off without.

"How about the back pay of Bellerose royalties Billie is still owed?" Rhett argued back on my behalf. Always my dark knight. "How about the legal ramifications of Jace literally using her name for our band—and plastering it across all our platinum records—without ever asking her permission? Those seem like pretty good reasons for her to stay. Not to mention—"

"I asked her to stay," Grayson cut him off, taking the blame for my extended stay. "Because I like her. Is that a fucking problem for you, Tucker?"

Tom seemed momentarily stunned at that, then his sneer was right back in place as he practically oozed slut-shaming. "Both of them? What do you have, a fucking cocaine-laced pussy or something?"

"Tom, shut *up*," Flo shouted, rising out of her seat as she glared down at him. "You sound like a fucking pig right now." The limo slowed to a stop, and Flo peered out the window. "We're here. Let's go put on an epic show, alright?" Her hard gaze took in Jace, Rhett, and Grayson, then softened when she looked at me.

I'm sorry, she mouthed, and I offered a weak smile in return.

Somehow, Tom had gotten right under my skin. He'd left me flailing and without a comeback, so thank fuck for Rhett, Gray, and Flo.

Fuck Jace. He could go to hell.

Everyone started to climb out of the limo silently, but Tom gave me a glare, indicating that he'd be watching me, before wrapping his arm around Flo and dragging her off ahead of us.

"That bastard needs to take a short trip off a tall building," Grayson muttered, making Rhett snort a laugh.

"Maybe we can accidentally leave him behind when we head over to Europe," Rhett pondered out loud. "Sure would be a shame if he got caught with an ounce of coke in his bag while passing security."

"We should take a side trip into Thailand," Grayson

said with a slow smile. He didn't elaborate, and I had to assume that country had really terrible consequences for drug smuggling.

I tried not to let the warmth of their support fill me. Their protectiveness did things to me that I wasn't ready to examine. Not when I had to leave. Why would I hurt myself more than needed? But still, I'd never been the chick that thought I lost my feminist power by allowing others to care for me too. Balance worked for me.

Rhett and Grayson balanced me.

Fuck my life. Just fuck it.

"It's not fair."

The words slipped out before I could stop them, but thankfully, as I exited the limo, the guys were a few steps behind me and didn't appear to hear. Or at least they didn't question me.

Not even ten minutes into my charade for the evening I was already cracking at the edges. I had to get myself together, but it had been a long time since I'd had something to lose. It was throwing me into all kinds of turmoil.

Madison Square Garden—the venue for tonight's show—was utterly iconic, and it served as a decent distraction as we were ushered inside with a ton of security. Fans were screaming up and down the walkways but were a dozen or so yards from where we walked, so no one could reach out and touch the band. Much to the fans' disappointment.

I saw more than one dark expression leveled on me, and I tried not to think about how many ways I was going to have to change my appearance after this to truly disappear. Bellerose's fame had bled into me, and not in a good way. If the expressions I was seeing were any indication, these bitches would laugh as I got murdered by the Ricci family right in front of them.

Shaking my head, I turned away and did my best to ignore them. That was a future Billie problem, and I was determined that nothing would fuck with my last night. I was going to enjoy this concert. Music had been a huge part of my life, and seeing it live was a gift.

My last gift.

Rhett's arm slipped over my shoulder as we entered the side access to the venue. The doors closed behind us, and the lack of screaming fans was immediately noticeable. It wasn't quiet in here by any estimate, but it was much more relaxed than outside.

A roadie appeared a second later, clipboard in her arms. "You guys are needed now," she said in a rush. It wasn't a rude tone, but clearly the schedule was a concern, and she got that point across.

Rhett and Grayson nodded. The other band

members were already a few steps ahead, moving down a long hallway. This was similar to other venues we'd been in, and I knew that this would lead to the greenroom, dressing areas, and side of the stage.

The side of the stage and my last night with Bellerose. Was I ready for this?

Not a fucking chance.

BILLIE

We got there in another five minutes, and it was a hub of activity. The opening band had just finished and the stage was being reset, all the last minute checks happening, and the guys went into rock star mode. I'd noticed over my time with them, that each had their own pre-concert ritual, and without fail, they all followed through.

Jace went off on his own, heading for his dressing room where he'd change into one of the many ripped shirts and jeans he wore, showcasing his height and broad shoulders, his full right-arm sleeve tattoo always on display. I had no idea what he did in his dressing room alone, but as far as I could tell, no one ever entered during this preshow ritual.

A ritual I'd never know in more detail. Funny, when once upon a time, I knew every single part of that boy.

The others I had more of an idea about. Flo always did stretches and a light meditation. She preferred to do it in the chaos of setup though, just off to the side, and Tom watched her with a lecherous look on his face. Goddamn, I wanted to punch that fucking expression right off his face. I cared about Florence, and she could do so much better. It wasn't the rodent exterior; everyone had different attractions. Nope. It was the personality. Every inch of him was disgusting.

I hoped the band figured out a way to get rid of him.

If Rhett and Grayson were any indication, they were considering it. Speaking of, they were in the midst of their rituals too. I took a second to step back and really take them in. The glorious beauty of both was so captivating that my heart wasn't the only part of me aching.

Rhett liked to shadow box in the corner for a few minutes, psyching himself up, and he always checked the set list three times. As if he was scared to forget the order, even when he could do this in this sleep.

The green of his faux-hawk was extra bright

tonight. He'd had it colored today by the looks, and it brought out the green in his eyes, so they were near piercing. He also obsessively played with the ring in the corner of his lip, and all I could think about was kissing him. I didn't though, because interrupting their ritual was not in my schedule tonight. I'd get a kiss before he went on stage, just as I always did.

Then there was Grayson. Standing with his back against the wall, watching everything that went on. Only tonight, he was watching me. As our eyes met, I tried not to flinch at the steel in his. His observation was a worry, especially with my woeful acting skills. Had he seen the goodbye in my expression as I watched them all for the last time? Shit.

When I offered him a tentative smile, he lifted a hand and crooked a finger, indicating he wanted me to come toward him. Just like always, when this guy commanded me, my fucking legs moved.

He finally smiled. "Good girl," he rumbled when I reached his side, and fuck if my body didn't heat as my legs went a tiny bit weak.

"What's up?" I managed to choke out.

"Florence said that you're in the front VIP section tonight. Why?"

Blunt. No lifting of his gaze to give me a moment to breathe. My neck hurt as I had to crane it so far back to see his face, and still, I couldn't look away. "I want to see you properly tonight. A real concert experience. It's time for me to let go of my pain about the music and enjoy the talent of people I..." I swallowed roughly. "People I care about."

His huge palm wrapped around my face as he leaned down and gently pressed his lips to mine. "If you run, little hedgehog," he whispered as our lips parted, "I will find you."

He was gone then, leaving me absolutely breathless and broken. He'd seen right the fuck through me, and I wondered if even from on stage he would actually jump up from the drums to go right after me. That would destroy my plan in seconds. I just had to hope that there was a moment he wasn't watching me that I could escape. I needed minutes. Just minutes.

I'd find that somewhere.

Everything rushed by then, roadies and stage crew bustling around with their jobs, and then it was time for Bellerose to go on. At this point Flo hurried to my side. "The security will take you down the front," she said in a rush. "I told them you don't want them all surrounding you, and that it's a special VIP area. Is that alright? I just thought you'd want the full experience."

I was nodding before she'd even finished talking. It worked for me not to be surrounded. Not for the reason she suspected, but it was all the same. "Perfect. I want to experience the band in all your glory tonight. Tell them I'll check in with security before I go anywhere."

Leaning over, she pressed her lips to my cheek before she grimaced and quickly wiped off the mark she'd left. "Enjoy, friend," she told me, before her name was called with some urgency. "We'll play extra hard for you tonight."

"Break a leg," I called as she raced off.

Rhett took a second longer, giving me my kiss before he hit the stage, and I willed the burning in my eyes to subside. "Break a leg tonight," I whispered to him as he pulled away. "I'll be watching you from the front."

He didn't say anything, but his face was serious as he pressed his lips to mine once more. Then, "Stay close, Thorn. We play for you tonight."

Holy shit. This was going to kill us both, but I had to focus on the end goal: keeping them all safe.

When he left, two members of the security team came up to escort me down the small side entrance that would lead into the front section. As we emerged, the sounds of the audience screaming was near deafening, and I found excitement lifting inside me, even if it was mingled with sadness. In a different life, this could have been mine to keep.

When we reached the roped-off section, I noted that there was a lot of security stationed around, but most of them were circling the stage, clearly to stop crazed fans from jumping up there and body slamming into their favorite band.

Other than that, the VIP area had about thirty people in it, those who'd won or purchased these exclusive tickets. The security for our area was only on either end of the entrance, and I knew I'd be able to bail easily enough.

"We'll be off to the side," the guard who escorted me said. He pointed to the right, and I made my decision that left was my exit. "Find us if you need food, drink, or the bathroom."

"Absolutely," I lied. "I won't leave this area without finding one of you."

I got a succinct nod and no suspicion. Why would they be suspicious? They had to assume I wanted to remain alive, and with all the hits on me lately, only a fucking idiot would go off on their own.

Little did they know.

The lights dimmed then as the guards walked off, and I pushed into the crowd, wanting to be as close to the stage as I could. At least for the first few songs. I'd thought the screams before were loud, but the moment

Bellerose emerged on the stage, I was tempted to block my ears.

I didn't though. I absorbed the excitement, standing there, watching as they took their places. Rhett and Grayson both scanned the front area for me, but the stage lights were probably too bright for them to find me in the crowd. Which was fine with me. I wanted to be the silent observer, taking them in, and I didn't want them to notice when I crept away.

Jace moved to the front of the stage, the spotlight hitting him in a way that turned his hair platinum and his skin bronze. He looked otherworldly, and I wondered how I'd ever been in his life. It was like loving a Greek god—a perception that only deepened when his husky tones filled the air. "New York," he rumbled. "Are you fucking ready?"

They were ready. So *beyond* ready if the screams were an indication.

He strummed the first chords of their song "Broken and Bleeding," which wasn't their most popular tune but was probably in the top five. The crowd lost their minds, screaming until I wondered if I was about to suffer permanent hearing damage.

"Golden-haired angel, up the street from me."

The opening line always destroyed me because it was about the *before,* the way he saw me before everything went to shit. The rest of the song wasn't as happy, with the lyrics turning much darker.

"Broken and bleeding. Lost and alone. Betrayed and dismayed," he screamed into the mic, the others joining in, and I forced myself to pretend this wasn't about me. Instead, I just closed my eyes and found myself moving to the beat. Grayson's drums and Rhett's guitar. Florence's bass was perfectly mixed in there too.

They were so talented. Jace couldn't have found a better accompaniment to his angelic voice if he'd tried. Part of me was okay with this path for him; all of his hard work deserved the success he was seeing.

As I opened my eyes, I was drilled with a set of piercing blue eyes. Darker than usual and intense, Jace's gaze had managed what the others hadn't. He'd found me in the crowd, and he was singing right at me.

His anger bled into the words, and as his voice grew deeper, the intensity filling the air increased until I couldn't breathe. Fuck. I wasn't going to make it through any more than this first song if he kept this up.

Despite my best effort, the pain in my chest rose until a few tears leaked from the corners of my eyes, the emotions brought on from both the song and my lost love.

More than one lost love now since this was my last moment with them all.

My legs finally obeyed me as I started to back up, determined to disappear into the crowd. Jace was about to bring way too much attention my way if he kept this up.

Thankfully, the song ended a beat later, and he was forced to once again be a rock star, rather than a jilted lover.

Bellerose went straight into another one of their hits, a more upbeat number that I was fairly sure wasn't about me since it had lighter elements for most of the song. This allowed me a second to pull myself together, rubbing my hands over my arms to ward off a chill that was encapsulating me... despite the heat of the venue with the twenty thousand bodies inside.

I managed to last through another three songs, but my heart really wasn't in it.

"Ready to run, bitch?"

I spun at the snarky voice, finding Tom standing beside me. He was a rat for sure, creeping out of the darkness. He had to lean in closer for me to hear him, and I had to stop myself from actually clocking him in the nose.

"Run?" I bit out.

A derisive chuckle escaped him, and he was so close to my ear I shivered in disgust. "Come on, you know you're putting them in danger. I'll make it easy for you."

He clearly didn't realize I'd already been planning this and was trying to guilt me into making the choice I'd already made.

"You can't be so selfish to want them dead, right?" he pressed. "I'm happy to pay you off with a few hundred thousand. Give you a start in life. It appears you're owed money from the band anyway. We can call it even."

Fuck this fucker.

"I would never take money from you," I said, and I couldn't help but place my hands on his chest and shove him away. His next words were lost in the screams and music, and I could only be grateful for that.

Turning on my heel, I hurried toward the left side. With Tom here, it was time for me to bail. I had to leave this life behind once and for all and make sure Bellerose was safe.

When I reached security, I was stopped. "You aren't to leave without an escort," the big man said as he leaned in closer.

Dammit. Apparently, the orders regarding my safety had gone out to more than just Bellerose's personal security.

"I'm just going to get a drink and maybe use the bathroom," I shouted back.

He started to shake his head, only pausing when Tom appeared at my side. "She's authorized to go," the bastard told the security guard. "We have others watching her."

The big man shrugged then like he really didn't give a shit. He'd done his job, and everyone knew Tom, as interim manager or whatever the fuck he was, had authority here. More than he should have.

When the guard stepped aside, I wasted no time bailing out of the VIP area, making my way down a small walkway until I emerged into the general public. This was the standing-room-only area, with no seats, and as I turned back for one last look at the stage, I found Tom still standing at the VIP entrance smiling at me.

I didn't like that smile. It was the smile of a man who had won, and it went against every part of my being to let that happen. But what I was doing was not actually his plan. No matter what he thought, I knew the truth.

I'd done this for my boys, and I would get far away and alert Ricci to my newfound independence. Once they knew I wasn't with Bellerose anymore, it'd just be up to me to stay hidden. Alone, I would save them all.

As I had that thought and was about to turn back around to leave, a bag was slammed over my head. My scream was lost in the crowd, and a second later, when something heavy cracked into the side of my covered head, everything went fuzzy.

My last emotion before I passed out was an all-consuming rage.

Rage and fear.

thirty-eight

JACE

Flo had arranged for Billie to watch the concert from VIP, right in front of the damn stage. I hadn't said anything when she mentioned it to us, because I wanted her within line of sight while we were performing. So I'd much rather she be right there in front of us, instead of backstage somewhere where we had to rely on, frankly, incompetent security.

But shit, I was *not prepared* for how goddamn nervous it would make me. Especially on the song that meant the most to our story. At those opening notes of "Broken and Bleeding," my heart was torn open. All the pain and betrayal of that day eight years ago came slamming into me like a fresh wound. The whole thing grew infinitely worse as I pushed on, singing the signature track that'd scored Bellerose our first number one hit. My eyes flickered open, and there she was. Staring up at me with a gut-wrenching mixture of adoration and regret painted across her perfect face.

My voice hitched, and I gasped slightly while scrambling to get a grip. Rhett—that prick knew me better than anyone—caught it and smoothly shifted into an impromptu guitar solo while I pulled myself together with my back to the crowd. I made out like it was part of the show, but I was dying inside.

When I turned back, the lights had shifted. Or Billie had. Either way, I couldn't see her anymore, and it was equal parts relieving and distressing. For the rest of the concert, I searched for her in the VIP area. Sometimes I caught a glimpse of her beautiful face, but then I wondered if maybe I was imagining things.

This past week had been... torture. Seeing her with Rhett, watching how he looked at her with such unashamed affection, it was cutting me deeper than I ever could have imagined. I couldn't keep going like this. And Grayson announcing he'd asked her to stay? It was too much.

She couldn't stay. My heart couldn't take it. As soon as the show was finished, I would make plans. I'd transfer the entire contents of my savings to her, buy her a house, a car, whatever it took… but she couldn't stay on tour. I'd end up killing my best friends out of pure, poisonous jealousy.

For the first time in all my years of touring and concerts, I couldn't wait to get off stage. When the set *finally* ended, I all but ran off, needing air. Rhett was right behind me, though, shouting for Tom, who waited in the wings with a big shit-eating grin on his face.

"Where is she?" Rhett demanded, pushing me aside so he could grab Tom by the shirt and slam him against a wall. "Where's Billie?"

Panic rippled through me. "Whoa, bro, she was in VIP remember?" I pointed out, placing a hand on Rhett's arm. "She was just—"

"No, *she wasn't!*" Rhett snarled, still holding Tom by the shirt like he was about to kill him. "She disappeared halfway through 'Frozen in Time' and never came back. So *where the fuck is she, Tucker?*" He bellowed that question so hard that Tom flinched like the little bitch he was.

"Rhett, put him down!" Flo screamed, handing off her bass to one of the roadies. "This is insanity; Billie is literally tearing our band apart! Maybe it's better if she's gone."

Tom hit the floor in a pile as Rhett abruptly dropped him.

"What the fuck did you say?" Grayson asked in a low, dangerous voice, towering over Flo. "Why would she be gone?"

Tom coughed a nervous laugh, picking himself up off the ground. "It's true, though. She left, just like we knew she would. Jace, you said it yourself, when the going gets tough, Billie gets going, right? Why are you all so surprised? I clearly hit the nail on its head earlier, and she panicked."

Flo looked like she was going to be sick but pasted on a fake smile anyway. "Guys, we need to get back out there for the encore. We can sort this out later."

Rhett and Grayson were coiled so tight they were just one step short of murder, but they looked to me, nonetheless. No matter how much alpha male energy our band had, they still treated me as their leader.

"Fuck the encore," I snarled. "Tucker, answer Rhett. Where is she?"

Tom dusted off his t-shirt with indignation. "I told you. She took off the first chance she got. Don't believe me? Ask Little Jonny. He let her out of VIP; I saw him." He raised his arm, indicating for one of the huge security guards to join us, and repeated our question about where the fuck Billie had gone.

Jonny gave Tom a frown, then shrugged. "Dunno, boss. She said she wanted to use the crapper, and Tom said she had other security tailing her, so..." He shrugged again. "Then she didn't come back."

"Thank you, you can go." Tom dismissed him, then turned back to me with a smug expression.

Rhett wasn't in the fucking mood, though, and his fist cracked across Tom's face in a vicious punch. It sent the skinny man flying back into the wall, but he was lucky Rhett didn't kill him.

"You *said to let her go?*" my best friend bellowed. "Why?"

"Because it's better this way!" Tom shouted back, tears in his eyes as he nursed his face. "She wanted to go; I wasn't fucking stopping her! Look what she's done to us in just one week."

He pushed up from the floor and gave Rhett an accusing glare like *he* was the victim.

"Tom, that wasn't your fucking place," I said, feeling like my stomach was lined with lead. "You don't get to make decisions about—"

"Yes, I do!" he cut me off. "You were holding her captive, against her will. Bellerose doesn't need that PR nightmare, so *yeah*, I let her go. As a test. And what a shock, she didn't come back. Face it, Silver, she *used* you." He reached out for Flo, dragging her over to him as he shot Rhett another hate-filled glare, then stormed off.

For a moment, the three of us just stood there. Stunned silent. Then Rhett screamed a curse and snatched his guitar from his back.

"Rhett, don't—" I started to shout, but it was too late. His guitar smashed into the concrete floor with enough force to damage the instrument irreparably.

"Shit," Grayson breathed at my back.

Rhett *loved* that guitar; it was the first thing he'd ever spent "real" money on when we got our first paycheck. It was his lucky charm. And now it was little more than trash as he tossed it aside and turned to us in despair.

His eyes were huge and pleading as he shook his head. "She wouldn't," he croaked, seeking validation. "She wouldn't just *leave*."

I wet my lips. I wanted to reassure him, but all I could think of was that day she'd broken up with me eight years ago. I'd just signed my contract with Big Noise Records—Angelo had declined his—and I'd gone over to Billie's house to celebrate.

She'd answered the door with red-rimmed eyes, like she'd been crying all day, and wouldn't let me come inside. Instead, she sat out on the front steps of her house with me and systematically dismantled everything I thought I knew about love. She told me that she didn't love me anymore, and that her and Angelo wanted to be *exclusive*.

I'd been so gutted I barely even heard half the bullshit excuses she spat out at me. All that mattered was that she was *leaving* me. I had a fucking ring in my pocket. It was her sixteenth birthday, and I was going to give it to her as a promise. A commitment to *us* that we'd get married one day. And she was sitting there telling me she was in love with my best friend and that we were *over*.

So when Rhett turned to me with that utterly crushed expression, I didn't have it in me to lie to him. Not when I'd been in his shoes.

"It's just what she does," I heard myself say, my own voice echoing like I was in a tunnel. "Just be glad she didn't stay longer. Then it'd really break your heart."

Grayson muttered something under his breath, shoving past me with a shoulder check. "You're a fucking asshole sometimes, Adams," he told me in a low voice. "And you're wrong."

I swallowed hard, choking back old bitterness. "I hope I am," I replied, raw and honest. "But in that case, where is she?"

No one had an answer to that, and I soon found

myself standing there alone. Flo was gone with Tucker —we really had to kill that fucker—and Rhett had left with Grayson. The crowd was still going batshit out in the stands, screaming for an encore, but my band was gone. It was just me.

Driven by some kind of all-consuming guilt, self-hatred, and despair, I picked up my microphone and went back out onto the stage. The roadies gave me confused looks, but at my signal, they turned the lights back up.

The screams were deafening, but I ignored them all.

"This... is something new," I admitted into my microphone, gesturing for a roadie to bring me a guitar. "It's unfinished, but I'd like to play it for you, anyway."

Screams encouraged me on, and I sighed heavily as I attached my microphone to the stand and centered my focus inward. I needed to purge myself of Billie Bellerose, and this was the only way I knew how. My band had started with just me, so maybe that's how it'd end.

Eyes still closed, I strummed the guitar and let the music pour out of me.

The song had no name, but it'd been burning a hole in my mind since the first night Billie had reentered my life. So under the blinding lights of Madison Square Garden, I let it all out once more.

When I was done, the silence was so thick I wondered if the arena had magically emptied out. My cheeks were damp and my throat tight, and I didn't stick around for the Bellerose fan reaction.

"Thanks for listening," I said in a rough voice, then immediately exited stage left.

Behind me, the crowd went *crazy*, but my focus was all on one girl standing in the wings with tear-streaked makeup staining her face. One small girl, sobbing her heart out, her arms wrapped around herself as she looked up at me with pure regret all over her face.

"Jace," Florence whispered, shaking her head. "I'm so sorry. I fucked up. I fucked up big time. Please forgive me."

thirty-nine

BILLIE

Everything hurt. Everything. My pleas for mercy fell on deaf ears as another solid punch landed on my body. A sickening crack told me another rib had just broken, and I sobbed hysterically. They wanted to know *things,* and I didn't have the answers they wanted.

The moment they realized I was useless, though, I'd be dead. My only hope for survival was to bullshit them just enough to keep myself breathing, and meanwhile... fuck, I didn't know. I had no plan. No skills. Nothing useful. But I clung desperately to two thin threads of hope.

Grayson and Angelo.

If just one of them found me, I was *sure* I could be spared. I pleaded over and over to speak with Angelo, knowing these were Ricci goons who held me captive. So far, though, it was falling on deaf ears.

I lost track of time. They'd started out small, just smacking me around a bit. But as I'd dangled my fake information just out of their reach, they'd escalated. The water torture was the worst. I'd never been afraid of drowning before, but I was now. No question about it.

The one small mercy was that they were pacing themselves. Or preserving my ability to stay alive. Either way, the "questioning" only lasted a certain amount of time before I was tossed back into my cage —a literal cage that prevented me from standing or fully straightening out—and given some seriously stale bread and water.

As I lay there, curled up on my side, holding my broken body and sobbing quietly, the main door burst open with a loud bang. The goons had been keeping me in an old, closed-down night club, my cage on the dirty carpet while they played a hand of poker on the stripper stage.

"What the fuck is going on in here?" a man roared. There was something hauntingly familiar about that voice, but maybe it was pain making me imagine shit. It wouldn't be the first time.

The goons scrambled to their feet, their poker cards scattering. "Sir, uh, we didn't know you were in town," one of them babbled.

"I was told you're trying to meet with the boss," the newcomer barked. "He doesn't take meetings with the likes of you. That's *my* job, so why in the fuck are you bypassing the chain of command?" Why did he sound so much like...?

"Angelo, come on," the other goon said with a greasy voice. "It's not like that. He *asked* us to get—"

Greasy goon's excuse was cut short with the deafening crack of a gunshot. Must not have been a kill shot, though, because a high-pitched scream filled the room a second later. Damn.

Wait. *Angelo?*

"Talk," he snarled to the other goon. Fat goon, I called him. "Now."

"Th-the girl," fat goon babbled. "Giovanni wanted the girl. Said she had vital information."

A deathly silence filled the space. Not even greasy goon continued his wailing.

"And?" Angelo asked, somehow conveying death into that one word.

Fat goon babbled something more, pointing in the

direction of my cage. A split second later, a pair of shiny leather shoes appeared in front of my face, and the unmistakable smell of the expensive aftershave he wore, and the cinnamon of his favorite gum, wafted into my nose. It was worse than any of the goons' torture because it struck me in the heart.

Angel.

Two gunshots rang out, one after another, and my grasp on consciousness started to fade away. The cage shook, and I moaned out loud in pain, but then I was being lifted out. Strong arms cradled my broken body even as the sharp tang of fresh blood and gunpowder flooded my senses. I gave a weak protest, but Angelo shushed me.

"Stop it, Bella," he breathed, his heart racing in his chest where my bruised cheek was pressed. "Calm down, I have you. Just sleep, baby girl. Sleep. I'll keep you safe."

Despite my panic and dread, I couldn't fight it. The heady sense of safety that his voice brought me was all-consuming, wrapping around me like a blanket and lulling me into sleep. Car doors slammed, an engine revved, but Angelo never let me go.

Whatever happened next, it was all a blur. Fragments of medical staff checking me over, of Angelo pulling a gun on a doctor, and then the blissful fizz of medication filling my veins. As the painkillers swept through me, Angelo held my hand tight, his head bowed and his husky voice silent.

I wasn't in a hospital when I woke, and that really should have been my first clue.

Instead, the sheets I lay between were a thick, luxurious gray and the pillows far superior to those in an ICU ward. I should know, having spent so long there after the fire that'd nearly killed me eight years ago. Angelo had stayed with me then, too.

Drugs must still have been pumping through my system because nothing hurt. It should, but instead, I could barely even feel my body. When I lifted my arm, squinting at the IV lines taped down to my skin, it felt like it wasn't even connected to my shoulder.

Blinking slowly, I tried to orient myself. A low voice murmured in conversation somewhere nearby, and it took a frustratingly long time for me to pinpoint the speaker. Which was stupid because he was right beside the bed, sitting in a huge wingback armchair.

"Angel," I whispered, my voice coming out barely louder than a breath. "You saved me." Again.

Tears pricked at my eyes as I remembered how he'd carried me out of the house fire that'd killed my parents and left me scarred. He was always saving me, my Angel.

He reached out, gently taking my hand in his, even though his phone remained against his ear.

"I understand that, sir," he said tersely. He was speaking to his father. "But like I said, circumstances have changed. Whatever Billie knows, I will uncover myself, but she is not to be harmed again. She's not to even be touched. Not while she's carrying your grandson inside her."

What?!

Angelo didn't flinch away from my startled gaze, his frown deepening as he listened to his father's response. Then his jaw ticked as he ground his teeth together.

"Understood, sir. She won't be a problem anymore. I promise you I have this under control." He dropped my hand, and it felt like a vacuum of space had just opened between us. "I'll send you the image now."

He ended the call, and I released a heavy breath, shaking my head. "Angel, you lied to him," I croaked, full of fear for what Giovanni would do when he found out. "He will never believe this."

Angelo swallowed visibly, pulling something from his jacket pocket. "Yes, Bella, he will." He took a photo of whatever was on the paper and, I presume, sent the image to his father. "After all, it wouldn't be the first time for us. Right?"

Dread washed over me, and panic clawed at the

edges of my mind. I wet my lips, reaching for the paper in his hand. "What is that?" I whispered in horror.

He handed it over, and my soul dropped clean out of my ass. A sharp sob wracked through my chest as I stared down at the eight-year-old sonogram image. The date had been doctored, but the rest of the details were authentic.

"How?" I gasped, my head spinning and my vision sparkling with darkness. "You kept this? Why?"

Angelo's expression was harder than ice as he took the image back out of my hand and tucked it into his pocket. "Does it matter? It just saved your life, Bella. Say thank you, and let it the fuck go."

He pushed to his feet and stormed out of the room without giving me a chance to ask anything more. Gut deep sobs shook my body as my brain processed what the fuck had just happened. Angelo had just used my old sonogram image to lie to his father, to keep me alive. An image of the baby I'd lost the same night I'd lost my parents. When my whole world came crashing down even harder than the day I'd lost Jace.

I wasn't strong enough to face that reality again. But as I lay there in Angelo's bed, crying my heart out, it became painfully clear I didn't have a choice in the matter.

The night I'd run into both Jace and Angelo, I'd thought things couldn't possibly get worse.

I'd been wrong.

To be continued in

Dirty Truths

Boys of Bellerose #2

also by tate james

Madison Kate

#1 HATE

#2 LIAR

#3 FAKE

#4 KATE

#4.5 VAULT (to be read after Hades series)

Hades

#1 7th Circle

#2 Anarchy

#3 Club 22

#4 Timber

The Guild

#1 Honey Trap

#2 Dead Drop

#3 Kill Order

Valenshek Legacy

#1 Heist

Dark Legacy

#1 Broken Wings

#2 Broken Trust

#3 Broken Legacy

#4 Dylan (standalone)

Royals of Arbon Academy

#1 Princess Ballot

#2 Playboy Princes

#3 Poison Throne

Hijinx Harem

#1 Elements of Mischief

#2 Elements of Ruin

#3 Elements of Desire

The Wild Hunt Motorcycle Club

#1 Dark Glitter

#2 Cruel Glamour (TBC)

#3 Torn Gossamer (TBC)

Foxfire Burning

#1 The Nine

#2 The Tail Game (TBC)

#3 TBC (TBC)

Undercover Sinners

#1 Altered By Fire

#2 Altered by Lead

#3 Altered by Pain (TBC)

Book One: Dragon Marked

Book Two: Dragon Mystics

Book Three: Dragon Mated

Book Four: Broken Compass

Book Five: Magical Compass

Book Six: Louis

Book Seven: Elemental Compass

Supernatural Academy (Complete Urban Fantasy/PNR 18+)

Year One

Year Two

Year Three

Royals of Arbon Academy (Complete Dark Contemporary Romance 18+)

Book One: Princess Ballot

Book Two: Playboy Princes

Book Three: Poison Throne

Titan's Saga (Complete PNR/UF. Sexy and humorous 18+)

Book One: Releasing the Gods

Book Two: Wrath of the Gods

Book Three: Revenge of the Gods

Dark Legacy (Complete Dark Contemporary high school romance 18+)

Book One: Broken Wings

Book Two: Broken Trust

Book Three: Broken Legacy

Secret Keepers Series (Complete PNR/Urban Fantasy)

Book One: House of Darken

Book Two: House of Imperial

Book Three: House of Leights

Book Four: House of Royale

Storm Princess Saga (Complete High Fantasy)

Book One: The Princess Must Die

Book Two: The Princess Must Strike

Book Three: The Princess Must Reign

Curse of the Gods Series (Complete Reverse Harem Fantasy 18+)

Book One: Trickery

Book Two: Persuasion

Book Three: Seduction

Book Four: Strength

Novella: Neutral

Book Five: Pain

NYC Mecca Series (Complete - UF series)

Book One: Queen Heir

Book Two: Queen Alpha

Book Three: Queen Fae

Book Four: Queen Mecca

A Walker Saga (Complete - YA Fantasy)

Book One: First World

Book Two: Spurn

Book Three: Crais

Book Four: Regali

Book Five: Nephilius

Book Six: Dronish

Book Seven: Earth

Hive Trilogy (Complete UF/PNR series)

Book One: Ash

Book Two: Anarchy

Book Three: Annihilate

Sinclair Stories (Standalone Contemporary Romance)

Songbird